The Moon
AND Sixpence

BY W. SOMERSET MAUGHAM

PAUL GAUGUIN   A SELF-PORTRAIT

ILLUSTRATED BY FREDERIC DORR STEELE
AND PAUL GAUGUIN

BY W. SOMERSET MAUGHAM

The Moon
AND Sixpence

THE HERITAGE PRESS, NEW YORK: *Publisher*

In Explanation

EXCERPTS FROM A BRIEF CORRESPONDENCE BETWEEN THE PUBLISHER OF THIS EDITION AND THE AUTHOR OF THE NOVEL

October 20, 1939; to W. SOMERSET MAUGHAM, VILLA MAURESQUE, CAP FERRAT, ALPES MARITIMES: "I have for several years been told by those who like illustrated books that there should be a fine edition of *The Moon and Sixpence*. I think that an edition illustrated with reproductions of some of the paintings by Paul Gauguin would become a happy possession of admirers of the book. Since the reproduction of these paintings, as illustrations for the novel, would prove an expensive undertaking, such an edition would be beyond the reach or desire of the ordinary 'trade' publisher. I write you now to ask whether *we* could have your permission to issue such an edition upon payment of a proper royalty?" GEORGE MACY.

November 5, 1939; to GEORGE MACY, THE HERITAGE PRESS, NEW YORK: "Forgive this casual way of writing, but I am busy with war work, rushed to death, and with no secretary at the moment. Yes, I should be very glad; but you must also arrange with Doubleday Doran." W. SOMERSET MAUGHAM.

December 9, 1939; to W. SOMERSET MAUGHAM, CAP FERRAT: "I now report this to you, that Doubleday Doran have given us permission to proceed with an edition of *The Moon and Sixpence*. I have a special idea for the illustrations. I plan to ask a living illustrator to make a series of pen drawings, as much in the fashion of the illustrative drawings of the late nineteenth century as possible, to illustrate the narrative of the first section of the book: the time which Strickland spends in London and Paris. At the time when Strickland exhibits a painting of his for the first time, it is my idea that an apposite painting by Gauguin, reproduced in full color, should be shown resting on the easel. Then the remainder of the narrative, covering the time spent by Strickland in Tahiti, should be illustrated with reproductions in color of paintings by Gauguin. I am afraid that I think this a clever idea; but I do not like to proceed with it without asking whether you object to it." GEORGE MACY.

December 22, 1939; to GEORGE MACY, THE HERITAGE PRESS: "I think your idea for the illustrations of *The Moon and Sixpence* is a very good one. I should be very foolish to object to it." W. SOMERSET MAUGHAM.

January 24, 1941; to GEORGE MACY, THE HERITAGE PRESS: "I think your edition of *The Moon and Sixpence* is grand and your method of illustration very interesting and ingenious. I should like to congratulate every one concerned on this fine piece of work." W. SOMERSET MAUGHAM.

How This Book Came To Be

BY JOHN T. WINTERICH

"I AM A WRITER AS I MIGHT HAVE BEEN A DOCTOR OR A lawyer," wrote William Somerset Maugham in *The Summing Up,* that pellucid autobiography of a craftsman, almost of a craft. "It is so pleasant a profession that it is not surprising if a vast number of persons adopt it who have no qualifications for it."

Maugham not only might have been a doctor—he was. Born in Paris in 1874, he first saw England at the age of ten, following the deaths of his mother and father. French was so dominantly his language that he won inevitable guffaws from his island schoolfellows by pronouncing unstable as if it rhymed with Dunstable. He studied medicine at St. Thomas's Hospital, London, for several years, and never practised it.

Just as easily, he might have been a lawyer. The profession had the sanctity of tradition behind it among the Maughams. Grandfather Maugham had been a founder of the Incorporated Law Society, the British equivalent of the American Bar Association, and Father Maugham a counsellor of the British Embassy in Paris.

Out of his training at St. Thomas's came, at twenty-three, Maugham's first book, *Liza of Lambeth.* He had sent the manuscript of two short stories to T. Fisher Unwin, who was bringing out the Pseudonym Series—an old publishing device designed to exploit fresh talent and to set people talking. Un-

7

win returned the stories and asked if the author did not have a novel to submit. Maugham had no novel handy, but Unwin's encouragement was so flattering that he immediately sat down and wrote one. It was accepted and went so well that a second edition was called for within a month. Maugham, prepared now to rest on his laurels and his royalties, took a trip abroad. A year later he received his first check from Unwin. It was for twenty pounds.

Maugham was not the first to sense the literary potentialities of Lambeth. That distinction belongs to George Gissing (though I am not forgetting that William Blake found God and all his angels there). Read Gissing's *Thyrza*—its poignancy wears well. It was an early reading of *Thyrza* that on my first visit to London made me more eager to explore Lambeth than the Abbey or the Strand. I crossed Westminster Bridge (there, early on the morning of September 3, 1802, stood William Wordsworth and composed the sonnet that begins "Earth has not anything to show more fair"—his back was toward Lambeth), leaving the Houses of Parliament behind me on my right, the Victoria Embankment and New Scotland Yard on my left. Ahead, on my right, squarely across from the Houses of Parliament, stood the red-brick facade of St. Thomas's Hospital, which, I now learn from Findlay Muirhead's *London and Its Environs*, contains 652 beds, and where "over 8000 in-patients and 60,000 out-patients are treated yearly." Lambeth Palace, London residence of the Archbishops of Canterbury, is hard by—its library shelters many magnificent medieval manuscripts and early printed books, including Caxtons and a Gutenberg Bible on vellum (our own Library of Congress has one of the other extant five). Not far away is the world's oldest surviving mental hospital, antedating the Gutenberg Bible—Bethlem, whence the good dictionary word bedlam. Muirhead, I note, refers to it as "now a charitable institution for the better-class insane."

May there not be a point in the social scheme where class distinctions no longer exist?

Nothing in Muirhead, though, about the meanness and squalor of the Lambeth that lies behind the impressive and historic river front. I did not find as much of meanness and squalor there as I had expected, but any slum is likely to be picturesque if it is in an alien city and if one does not have to live in it.

Liza of Lambeth did not profit Maugham greatly in the things of this world, but it set his feet definitely and unequivocally in the path of letters. *The Making of a Saint, Orientations*, and *The Hero* quickly followed. *The Making of a Saint* is especially noteworthy in that it was the first of Maugham's books to be published in America; eleven more years were to elapse before another Maugham title was to be available on this side of the Atlantic. *Mrs. Craddock* (1903) was his first real fictional success, and *Lady Frederick* the first of his plays to win public acclaim, though two others had preceded it. Maugham's career attained its creative climax in 1915 with *Of Human Bondage*, which in the ensuing quarter-century has convincingly proved its capacity for permanence. Basically the story is autobiographical—a dangerous and tricky word about which there will be more to say presently.

Toward the end of the World War, in which he served with distinction in the Intelligence Department of the British Army, Maugham journeyed to the South Seas. His mother and her only sister had died of tuberculosis; Maugham had good reason to be aware of his own susceptibility to the disease, and his work in the war had added to his awareness. But he was seeking something more than the beneficent air of Polynesia. He was contemplating a novel based on the life of Paul Gauguin.

Up to the time of the appearance of *The Summing Up* in 1938 Maugham had never, I believe, declared openly that

The Moon and Sixpence owed its genesis to Gauguin. Additional confirmation is now available in the form of a letter which he wrote me in response to a query on this point, and which I have Mr. Maugham's permission to quote in this introduction. The letter, incidentally, had for a time a melancholy importance beyond its subject matter. When the German *panzer* divisions swept down from the Belgian frontier in the spring of 1940, concern was felt for Maugham's safety. He was then at his home in southern France—Villa Mauresque, at Cap Ferrat, Alpes Maritimes. Dispatches from what was left of France declared that Maugham had not been heard from in "several weeks." We know now that he returned to England safely, and after just such harrowing experiences as must be expected in a war that makes no distinction between combatant and civilian. For a time, therefore, the following letter was the last word that had been received from Maugham before the fog of invasion cut him off from what remained of civilization:

"I spent a year in Paris on Montparnasse when I was just thirty and lived with a number of painters who greatly admired Gauguin and one of whom, Roderick O'Connor, had painted with him in Pont Aven. I was told a great deal about Gauguin and it occurred to me that there was in his life and character the idea for a novel. I kept the idea in mind and when I had occasion to go to Tahiti heard a good deal more about him. This was in 1917. I wrote the book during the summer of 1919 when I was recovering from tuberculosis which I contracted during the war."

The Moon and Sixpence, therefore, was fifteen years in gestation. Once completed, it was quickly put in type. The original London edition of 1919 was an unadorned and unprepossessing book. The paper was a thick clayey pulp, frog-belly white in hue, unpleasant to eye and hand alike. That, of course, was the fault of the war, not of Mr. Maugham or of his publisher, William Heinemann.

Heinemann died the following year; it must therefore have been while *The Moon and Sixpence* was in process of publication that the following incident occurred, which Maugham related to Frederick Whyte when the latter was preparing his memoir of Heinemann. "I was in Heinemann's office," said Maugham, "and happened to see a book in Braille. I made some reference to it, and he said quite casually: 'Oh, yes, I'm studying it; you know, the oculists tell me I'm going blind and I want to learn it while I have the chance.' It seemed to me to show a very fine and courageous spirit." Death claimed Heinemann before this last infirmity could assail him.

The Moon and Sixpence, obviously, is not a mere fictionalized life of Gauguin. This question of the autobiographical or biographical content of a novel is one which must cause any novelist extreme annoyance. All writing is one or the other or both to the extent that no author can ever reach outside the orbit of his own imagination, and his imagination is as much a part of his "biography" as his comings out and his goings in. Be he a Maugham or a Dickens or a Shakespeare, that unbreakable tether chains him. The greater the genius, the longer the tether and the more extensive the pasturage, but it is forever with him, a more intimate possession than his trousers or his eyebrows. Maugham himself, in *The Summing Up*, discusses this "biographical" factor with eloquence and finality:

"I have been blamed because I have drawn my characters from living persons, and from criticisms that I have read one might suppose that nobody had ever done this before. That is nonsense. It is the universal custom. From the beginning of literature authors have had originals for their creations. . . . I suspect that the writers who deny that they use actual persons deceive themselves (which is not impossible, since you can be a very good novelist without being very intelligent) or deceive us. When they tell the truth and have in fact had no particular person in mind it will be found, I think, that they owe their characters rather to their memory than to their creative instinct. How many times have we met d'Artagnan, Mrs. Proudie, Archdeacon Grantley, Jane Eyre and Jérôme Coignard with other names and in other dress! I should say that the practice of drawing characters from actual models is not only universal but necessary. I do not see why any writer should be ashamed to acknowledge it. As Turgenev said, it is only if you have a definite person in your mind that you can give vitality and idiosyncrasy to your own creation.

"I insist that it is a creation. We know very little even of the persons we know most intimately; we do know them enough to transfer them to the pages of a book and make human beings of them. People are too elusive, too shadowy, to be copied; and they are also too incoherent and contradictory. The writer does not copy his originals; he takes what he wants from them, a few traits that have caught his attention, a turn of mind that has fired his imagination, and therefrom constructs his character. He is not concerned whether it is a truthful likeness; he is concerned only to create a plausible harmony convenient for his own purposes."

This theory of "plausible harmony" is illustrated in *The Moon and Sixpence* with admirable effectiveness. While Charles Strickland would never have been created if Paul Gauguin had never been born, Charles Strickland is no more Paul Gauguin than he is Paul Revere. There is the primary obvious fact that Gauguin was a Frenchman, the son of a partly Peruvian mother, and that Strickland is an all-out Englishman. Unlike Strickland, Gauguin did not keep from his wife the fact that he was studying painting; he had, in fact, already exhibited at the Salon de Paris before his "liberation". Strickland does not retire to Brittany; he does not write his memoirs; he does not attempt suicide; he is not unhappy in the South Seas; he does not return to Paris and then go back to Tahiti, all of which Gauguin did. Maugham simply saw in Gauguin's career an exemplification of the dramatic but explicable thesis of a business man throwing everything overboard for art's sake. Maugham's Tahiti sojourn made it convenient for him to put Strickland where Gauguin had been— saved him, let us say, a little imaginative labor.

Richard Aldington, in an appreciative note on Maugham, has expressed some astonishment at the popular success of *The Moon and Sixpence*, since, he says, "it would be difficult to imagine a more 'unpleasant' and 'unpopular' character than Strickland." Yet, he continues, "by sheer mastery of his art Maugham compelled multitudes of readers to find matter for entertainment in the impossible Strickland."

This, in my view, is unmitigated bosh. Unpleasant characters make unpleasant reading—was there ever a less tenable critical thesis? On that basis, much of Shakespeare and most of Hardy could go out of print, and the production of detective stories (now, I believe, on something like a one-a-day basis) could be summarily discontinued.

There is a paragraph near the beginning of Chapter XLI of *The Moon and Sixpence* which provides the best possible rebuttal to Mr. Aldington's argument:

"Until long habit has blunted the sensibility, there is something disconcerting to the writer in the instinct which causes him to take an interest in the singularities of human nature so absorbing that his moral sense is powerless against it. He recognizes in himself an artistic satisfaction in the contemplation of evil which a little startles him; but sincerity forces him to confess that the disapproval he feels for certain actions is not nearly so strong as his curiosity in their reasons. The character of a scoundrel, logical and complete, has a fascination for his creator which is an outrage to law and order. I expect that Shakespeare devised Iago with a gusto which he never knew when, weaving moonbeams with his fancy, he imagined Desdemona. It may be that in his rogues the writer gratifies instincts deep-rooted in him, which the manners and customs of a civilized world have forced back to the mysterious recesses of the subconscious. In giving to the character of his invention flesh and bones he is giving life to that part of himself which finds no other means of expression. His satisfaction is a sense of liberation.''

Does the above not hold equally true if, for ''writer'' and ''creator'', one substitutes ''reader''?

Maugham was by no means the first author to relish the presentation of ''unpleasant'' characters and to be man enough to admit it. Robert Louis Stevenson conceded, nay boasted, that he had an overpowering affection for Long John Silver. (*Treasure Island*, by the way, seems to be holding up fairly well for a book dominated by an unpleasant personality.)

It is possible, of course, for a rogue to be dull. But not when Somerset Maugham has the fashioning of him.

List of Illustrations

Part One

ILLUSTRATED BY FREDERIC DORR STEELE

Part Two

ILLUSTRATED BY PAUL GAUGUIN

The Moon
AND Sixpence

I

1

I confess that when first I made acquaintance with Charles Strickland I never for a moment discerned that there was in him anything out of the ordinary. Yet now few will be found to deny his greatness. I do not speak of that greatness which is achieved by the fortunate politician or the successful soldier; that is a quality which belongs to the place he occupies rather than to the man; and a change of circumstances reduces it to very discreet proportions. The Prime Minister out of office is seen, too often, to have been but a pompous rhetorician, and the General without an army is but the tame hero of a market town. The greatness of Charles Strickland was authentic. It may be that you do not like his art, but at all events you can hardly refuse it the tribute of your interest. He disturbs and arrests. The time has passed when he was an object of ridicule, and it is no longer a mark of eccentricity to defend or of perversity to extol him. His faults are accepted as the necessary complement to his merits. It is still possible to discuss his place in art, and the adulation of his admirers is perhaps no less capricious than the disparagement of his detractors; but one thing can never be doubtful, and that is that he had genius. To my mind the most interesting thing in art is the personality of the artist; and if that is singular, I am willing to excuse a thousand faults. I suppose Velasquez was a better painter than El Greco, but custom stales one's admiration for him: the Cretan, sensual and tragic, proffers the mystery of his soul like a standing sacrifice. The artist, painter, poet, or musician, by his decoration, sublime or beautiful, satisfies the æsthetic sense; but that is akin to the sexual instinct, and shares its barbarity: he lays before you also the greater gift of himself. To pursue his secret has something of the fascination of a detective story. It is a riddle which shares with the universe the merit of having no answer. The most insignificant of Strickland's works suggests a personality which is strange, tormented, and complex; and it is this surely which prevents even those who do not like his pictures from being indifferent to them; it is this which has excited so curious an interest in his life and character.

It was not till four years after Strickland's death that Maurice Huret wrote that article in the *Mercure de France* which rescued the unknown painter from oblivion and blazed the trail which succeeding writers, with more or less docility, have followed. For a long time no critic has enjoyed in France a more incontestable authority, and it was impossible not to be impressed by the claims he made; they seemed extravagant; but later judgments have confirmed his estimate, and the reputation of Charles Strickland is now firmly established on the lines which he laid down. The rise of this reputation is one of the most romantic incidents in the history of art. But I do not propose to deal with Charles Strickland's work except in so far as it touches upon his character. I cannot agree with the painters who claim superciliously that the layman can understand nothing of painting, and that he can best show his appreciation of their works by silence and a cheque-book. It is a grotesque misapprehension which sees in art no more than a craft comprehensible perfectly only to the craftsman: art is a manifestation of emotion, and emotion speaks a language that all may understand. But I will allow that the critic who has not a practical knowledge of technique is seldom able to say anything on the subject of real value, and my ignorance of painting is extreme. Fortunately, there is no need for me to risk the adventure, since my friend, Mr. Edward Leggatt, an able writer as well as an admirable painter, has exhaustively discussed Charles Strickland's work in a little book * which is a charming example of a style, for the most part, less happily cultivated in England than in France.

Maurice Huret in his famous article gave an outline of Charles Strickland's life which was well calculated to whet the appetites of the inquiring. With his disinterested passion for art, he had a real desire to call the attention of the wise to a talent which was in the highest degree original; but he was too good a journalist to be unaware that the "human interest" would enable him more easily to effect his purpose. And when such as had come in contact with Strickland in the past, writers who had known him in London, painters who had met him in the cafés of Montmartre, discovered to their amazement that where they had seen but an unsuccessful artist, like another, authentic genius had rubbed shoulders with them, there began to appear in the magazines of France and America a succession of articles, the reminiscences of one, the appreciation of another, which added to Strickland's notoriety, and fed without satisfying the curiosity of the public. The subject was grateful, and the industrious Weitbrecht-Rotholz in his imposing monograph † has been able to give a remarkable list of authorities.

The faculty for myth is innate in the human race. It seizes with avidity upon any incidents, surprising or mysterious, in the career of those who have at all distinguished them-

---

* "A Modern Artist: Notes on the Work of Charles Strickland," by Edward Leggatt, A.R.H.A. Martin Secker, 1917.

† "Karl Strickland: sein Leben und seine Kunst," by Hugo Weitbrecht-Rotholz, Ph.D. Schwingel und Hanisch. Leipzig, 1914.

selves from their fellows, and invents a legend to which it
then attaches a fanatical belief. It is the protest of romance
against the commonplace of life. The incidents of the legend
become the hero's surest passport to immortality. The ironic
philosopher reflects with a smile that Sir Walter Raleigh
is more safely inshrined in the memory of mankind because
he set his cloak for the Virgin Queen to walk on than
because he carried the English name to undiscovered countries. Charles Strickland lived obscurely. He made enemies
rather than friends. It is not strange, then, that those who
wrote of him should have eked out their scanty recollections
with a lively fancy, and it is evident that there was enough
in the little that was known of him to give opportunity to
the romantic scribe; there was much in his life which was
strange and terrible, in his character something outrageous,
and in his fate not a little that was pathetic. In due course
a legend arose of such circumstantiality that the wise historian would hesitate to attack it.

But a wise historian is precisely what the Rev. Robert
Strickland is not. He wrote his biography * avowedly to
"remove certain misconceptions which had gained cur-
rency" in regard to the later part of his father's life, and
which had "caused considerable pain to persons still living." It is obvious that there was much in the commonly
received account of Strickland's life to embarrass a respectable family. I have read this work with a good deal of amusement, and upon this I congratulate myself, since it is colour-
less and dull. Mr. Strickland has drawn the portrait of an
excellent husband and father, a man of kindly temper,
industrious habits, and moral disposition. The modern
clergyman has acquired in his study of the science which

---

* "Strickland: The Man and His Work," by his son, Robert Strickland.
Wm. Heinemann, 1913.

I believe is called exegesis an astonishing facility for explaining things away, but the subtlety with which the Rev. Robert Strickland has "interpreted" all the facts in his father's life which a dutiful son might find it inconvenient to remember must surely lead him in the fullness of time to the highest dignities of the Church. I see already his muscular calves encased in the gaiters episcopal. It was a hazardous, though maybe a gallant thing to do, since it is probable that the legend commonly received has had no small share in the growth of Strickland's reputation; for there are many who have been attracted to his art by the detestation in which they held his character or the compassion with which they regarded his death; and the son's well-meaning efforts threw a singular chill upon the father's admirers. It is due to no accident that when one of his most important works, *The Woman of Samaria,** was sold at Christie's shortly after the discussion which followed the publication of Mr. Strickland's biography, it fetched £235 less than it had done nine months before when it was bought by the distinguished collector whose sudden death had brought it once more under the hammer. Perhaps Charles Strickland's power and originality would scarcely have sufficed to turn the scale if the remarkable mythopœic faculty of mankind had not brushed aside with impatience a story which disappointed all its craving for the extraordinary. And presently Dr. Weitbrecht-Rotholz produced the work which finally set at rest the misgivings of all lovers of art.

Dr. Weitbrecht-Rotholz belongs to that school of historians which believes that human nature is not only about as bad as it can be, but a great deal worse; and certainly the

---

* This was described in Christie's catalogue as follows: "A nude woman, a native of the Society Islands, is lying on the ground beside a brook. Behind is a tropical landscape with palm-trees, bananas, etc. 60 in. x 48 in."

reader is safer of entertainment in their hands than in those of the writers who take a malicious pleasure in representing the great figures of romance as patterns of the domestic virtues. For my part, I should be sorry to think that there was nothing between Anthony and Cleopatra but an economic situation; and it will require a great deal more evidence than is ever likely to be available, thank God, to persuade me that Tiberius was as blameless a monarch as King George V. Dr. Weitbrecht-Rotholz has dealt in such terms with the Rev. Robert Strickland's innocent biography that it is difficult to avoid feeling a certain sympathy for the unlucky parson. His decent reticence is branded as hypocrisy, his circumlocutions are roundly called lies, and his silence is vilified as treachery. And on the strength of peccadillos, reprehensible in an author, but excusable in a son, the Anglo-Saxon race is accused of prudishness, humbug, pretentiousness, deceit, cunning, and bad cooking. Personally I think it was rash of Mr. Strickland, in refuting the account which had gained belief of a certain "unpleasantness" between his father and mother, to state that Charles Strickland in a letter written from Paris had described her as "an excellent woman," since Dr. Weitbrecht-Rotholz was able to print the letter in facsimile, and it appears that the passage referred to ran in fact as follows: *God damn my wife. She is an excellent woman. I wish she was in hell.* It is not thus that the Church in its great days dealt with evidence that was unwelcome.

Dr. Weitbrecht-Rotholz was an enthusiastic admirer of Charles Strickland, and there was no danger that he would whitewash him. He had an unerring eye for the despicable motive in actions that had all the appearance of innocence. He was a psycho-pathologist, as well as a student of art, and the subconscious had few secrets from him. No mystic ever saw deeper meaning in common things. The mystic sees the ineffable, and the psycho-pathologist the unspeakable. There is a singular fascination in watching the eagerness with which the learned author ferrets out every circumstance which may throw discredit on his hero. His heart warms to him when he can bring forward some example of cruelty or meanness, and he exults like an inquisitor at the *auto da fé* of an heretic when with some forgotten story he can confound the filial piety of the Rev. Robert Strickland. His industry has been amazing. Nothing has been too small to escape him, and you may be sure that if Charles Strickland left a laundry bill unpaid it will be given you *in extenso,* and if he forebore to return a borrowed half-crown no detail of the transaction will be omitted.

When so much has been written about Charles Strickland, it may seem unnecessary that I should write more. A painter's monument is his work. It is true I knew him more intimately than most: I met him first before ever he became a painter, and I saw him not infrequently during the difficult years he spent in Paris; but I do not suppose I should ever have set down my recollections if the hazards of the war had not taken me to Tahiti. There, as is notorious, he spent the last years of his life; and there I came across persons who were familiar with him. I find myself in a position to throw light on just that part of his tragic career which has remained most obscure. If they who believe in Strickland's greatness are right, the personal narratives of such as knew him in the flesh can hardly be superfluous. What would we not give for the reminiscences of someone who had been as intimately acquainted with El Greco as I was with Strickland?

But I seek refuge in no such excuses. I forget who it was that recommended men for their soul's good to do each day two things they disliked: it was a wise man, and it is a precept that I have followed scrupulously; for every day I have got up and I have gone to bed. But there is in my nature a strain of asceticism, and I have subjected my flesh each week to a more severe mortification. I have never failed to read the Literary Supplement of *The Times*. It is a salutary discipline to consider the vast number of books that are written, the fair hopes with which their authors see them published, and the fate which awaits them. What chance is there that any book will make its way among that multitude? And the successful books are but the successes of a season. Heaven knows what pains the author has been at, what bitter experiences he has endured and what heartache suffered, to give some chance reader a few hours' relaxation or to while away the tedium of a journey. And if I may judge from the reviews, many of these books are well and carefully written; much thought has gone to their composition; to some even has been given the anxious labour of a lifetime. The moral I draw is that the writer should seek his reward in the pleasure of his work and in release from the burden of his thought; and, indifferent to aught else, care nothing for praise or censure, failure or success.

Now the war has come, bringing with it a new attitude. Youth has turned to gods we of an earlier day knew not, and it is possible to see already the direction in which those who come after us will move. The younger generation, conscious of strength and tumultuous, have done with knocking at the door; they have burst in and seated themselves in our seats. The air is noisy with their shouts. Of their elders some, by imitating the antics of youth, strive to persuade themselves that their day is not yet over; they shout with the lustiest, but the war cry sounds hollow in their mouths; they are like poor wantons attempting with pencil, paint and powder, with shrill gaiety, to recover the illusion of their spring. The wiser go their way with a decent grace. In their chastened smile is an indulgent mockery. They remember that they too trod down a sated generation, with just such clamor and with just such scorn, and they foresee that these brave torch-bearers will presently yield their place also. There is no last word. The new evangel was old when Nineveh reared her greatness to the sky. These gallant words which seem so novel to those that speak them were said in accents scarcely changed a hundred times before. The pendulum swings backwards and forwards. The circle is ever travelled anew.

Sometimes a man survives a considerable time from an era in which he had his place into one which is strange to him, and then the curious are offered one of the most singular spectacles in the human comedy. Who now, for example, thinks of George Crabbe? He was a famous poet in his day, and the world recognised his genius with a unanimity which the greater complexity of modern life has rendered infrequent. He had learnt his craft at the school of Alexander Pope, and he wrote moral stories in rhymed couplets. Then came the French Revolution and the Napoleonic Wars, and the poets sang new songs. Mr. Crabbe continued to write moral stories in rhymed couplets. I think he must have read the verse of these young men who were making so great a stir in the world, and I fancy he found it poor stuff. Of course, much of it was. But the odes of Keats and of Wordsworth, a poem or two by Coleridge, a few more by Shelley, discovered vast realms of the spirit that none had explored before. Mr. Crabbe was as dead as mutton, but Mr. Crabbe continued to write moral stories in rhymed couplets. I have read desultorily the writings of the younger generation. It may be that among them a more fervid Keats, a more ethereal Shelley, has already published numbers the world will willingly remember. I cannot tell. I admire their polish —their youth is already so accomplished that it seems absurd to speak of promise—I marvel at the felicity of their style; but with all their copiousness (their vocabulary suggests that they fingered Roget's *Thesaurus* in their cradles) they say nothing to me: to my mind they know too much and feel too obviously; I cannot stomach the heartiness with which they slap me on the back or the emotion with which they hurl themselves on my bosom; their passion seems to me a little anæmic and their dreams a trifle dull. I do not like them. I am on the shelf. I will continue to write moral stories in rhymed couplets. But I should be thrice a fool if I did it for aught but my own entertainment.

But all this is by the way.

I was very young when I wrote my first book.

By a lucky chance it excited attention, and various persons sought my acquaintance.

It is not without melancholy that I wander among my recollections of the world of letters in London when first, bashful but eager, I was introduced to it. It is long since I frequented it, and if the novels that describe its present singularities are accurate much in it is now changed. The venue is different. Chelsea and Bloomsbury have taken the place of Hampstead, Notting Hill Gate, and High Street, Kensington. Then it was a distinction to be under forty, but now to be more than twenty-five is absurd. I think in those days we were a little shy of our emotions, and the fear of ridicule tempered the more obvious forms of pretentiousness. I do not believe that there was in that genteel Bohemia an intensive culture of chastity, but I do not remember so crude a promiscuity as seems to be practised in the present day. We did not think it hypocritical to draw over our vagaries the curtain of a decent silence. The spade was not invariably called a bloody shovel. Woman had not yet altogether come into her own.

I lived near Victoria Station, and I recall long excursions by bus to the hospitable houses of the literary. In my timidity I wandered up and down the street while I screwed up my courage to ring the bell; and then, sick with apprehension, was ushered into an airless room full of people. I was introduced to this celebrated person after that one, and the kind words they said about my book made me excessively uncomfortable. I felt they expected me to say clever things, and I never could think of any till after the party was over. I tried to conceal my embarrassment by handing round cups of tea and rather ill-cut bread-and-butter. I wanted no one to take notice of me, so that I could observe these famous creatures at my ease and listen to the clever things they said.

I have a recollection of large, unbending women with great noses and rapacious eyes, who wore their clothes as though they were armour; and of little, mouse-like spinsters, with soft voices and a shrewd glance. I never ceased to be fascinated by their persistence in eating buttered toast with their gloves on, and I observed with admiration the unconcern with which they wiped their fingers on their chair when they thought no one was looking. It must have been bad for the furniture, but I suppose the hostess took her revenge on the furniture of her friends when, in turn, she visited them. Some of them were dressed fashionably, and they said they couldn't for the life of them see why you should be dowdy just because you had written a novel; if you had a neat figure you might as well make the most of it, and a smart shoe on a small foot had never prevented an editor from taking your "stuff." But others thought this frivolous, and they wore "art fabrics" and barbaric jewelry. The men were seldom eccentric in appearance. They tried to look as little like authors as possible. They wished to be taken for men of the world, and could have passed anywhere for the managing clerks of a city firm. They always seemed a little tired. I had never known writers before, and I found them very strange, but I do not think they ever seemed to me quite real.

I remember that I thought their conversation brilliant, and I used to listen with astonishment to the stinging humour with which they would tear a brother-author to pieces the moment that his back was turned. The artist has this advantage over the rest of the world, that his friends offer not only their appearance and their character to his satire, but also their work. I despaired of ever expressing myself with such aptness or with such fluency. In those days conversation was still cultivated as an art; a neat repartee was more highly valued than the crackling of thorns under a pot; and the epigram, not yet a mechanical appliance by which the dull may achieve a semblance of wit, gave sprightliness to the small talk of the urbane. It is sad that I can remember nothing of all this scintillation. But I think the conversation never settled down so comfortably as when it turned to the details of the trade which was the other side of the art we practised. When we had done discussing the merits of the latest book, it was natural to wonder how many copies had been sold, what advance the author had received, and how much he was likely to make out of it. Then we would speak of this publisher and of that, comparing the generosity of one with the meanness of another; we would argue whether it was better to go to one who gave handsome royalties or to another who "pushed" a book for all it was worth. Some advertised badly and some well. Some were modern and some were old-fashioned. Then we would talk of agents and the offers they had obtained for us; of editors and the sort of contributions they welcomed, how much they paid a thousand, and whether they paid promptly or otherwise. To me it was all very romantic. It gave me an intimate sense of being a member of some mystic brotherhood.

No one was kinder to me at that time than Rose Waterford. She combined a masculine intelligence with a feminine perversity, and the novels she wrote were original and disconcerting. It was at her house one day that I met Charles Strickland's wife. Miss Waterford was giving a tea-party, and her small room was more than usually full. Everyone seemed to be talking, and I, sitting in silence, felt awkward; but I was too shy to break into any of the groups that

"I was led up to Mrs. Strickland"

seemed absorbed in their own affairs. Miss Waterford was a good hostess, and seeing my embarrassment came up to me.

"I want you to talk to Mrs. Strickland," she said. "She's raving about your book."

"What does she do?" I asked.

I was conscious of my ignorance, and if Mrs. Strickland

was a well-known writer I thought it as well to ascertain the fact before I spoke to her.

Rose Waterford cast down her eyes demurely to give greater effect to her reply.

"She gives luncheon-parties. You've only got to roar a little, and she'll ask you."

Rose Waterford was a cynic. She looked upon life as an opportunity for writing novels and the public as her raw material. Now and then she invited members of it to her house if they showed an appreciation of her talent and entertained with proper lavishness. She held their weakness for lions in good-humoured contempt, but played to them her part of the distinguished woman of letters with decorum.

I was led up to Mrs. Strickland, and for ten minutes we talked together. I noticed nothing about her except that she had a pleasant voice. She had a flat in Westminster, over-looking the unfinished cathedral, and because we lived in the same neighbourhood we felt friendly disposed to one another. The Army and Navy Stores are a bond of union between all who dwell between the river and St. James's Park. Mrs. Strickland asked me for my address, and a few days later I received an invitation to luncheon.

My engagements were few, and I was glad to accept. When I arrived, a little late, because in my fear of being too early I had walked three times round the cathedral, I found the party already complete. Miss Waterford was there and Mrs. Jay, Richard Twining and George Road. We were all writers. It was a fine day, early in spring, and we were in a good humour. We talked about a hundred things. Miss Waterford, torn between the æstheticism of her early youth, when she used to go to parties in sage green, holding a daffodil, and the flippancy of her maturer

years, which tended to high heels and Paris frocks, wore a
new hat. It put her in high spirits. I had never heard her
more malicious about our common friends. Mrs. Jay, aware
that impropriety is the soul of wit, made observations in
tones hardly above a whisper that might well have tinged
the snowy tablecloth with a rosy hue. Richard Twining bub-
bled over with quaint absurdities, and George Road,
conscious that he need not exhibit a brilliancy which was
almost a by-word, opened his mouth only to put food into it.
Mrs. Strickland did not talk much, but she had a pleasant
gift for keeping the conversation general; and when there
was a pause she threw in just the right remark to set it
going once more. She was a woman of thirty-seven, rather
tall and plump, without being fat; she was not pretty, but
her face was pleasing, chiefly, perhaps, on account of her
kind brown eyes. Her skin was rather sallow. Her dark hair
was elaborately dressed. She was the only woman of the
three whose face was free of make-up, and by contrast with
the others she seemed simple and unaffected.

The dining-room was in the good taste of the period. It
was very severe. There was a high dado of white wood and
a green paper on which were etchings by Whistler in neat
black frames. The green curtains with their peacock design,
hung in straight lines, and the green carpet, in the pattern
of which pale rabbits frolicked among leafy trees, suggested
the influence of William Morris. There was blue delft on
the chimneypiece. At that time there must have been five
hundred dining-rooms in London decorated in exactly the
same manner. It was chaste, artistic, and dull.

When we left I walked away with Miss Waterford, and
the fine day and her new hat persuaded us to saunter
through the Park.

"That was a very nice party," I said.

"Did you think the food was good? I told her that if she wanted writers she must feed them well."

"Admirable advice," I answered. "But why does she want them?"

Miss Waterford shrugged her shoulders.

"She finds them amusing. She wants to be in the movement. I fancy she's rather simple, poor dear, and she thinks we're all wonderful. After all, it pleases her to ask us to luncheon, and it doesn't hurt us. I like her for it."

Looking back, I think that Mrs. Strickland was the most harmless of all the lion-hunters that pursue their quarry from the rarefied heights of Hampstead to the nethermost studios of Cheyne Walk. She had led a very quiet youth in the country, and the books that came down from Mudie's Library brought with them not only their own romance, but the romance of London. She had a real passion for reading (rare in her kind, who for the most part are more interested in the author than in his book, in the painter than in his pictures), and she invented a world of the imagination in which she lived with a freedom she never acquired in the world of every day. When she came to know writers it was like adventuring upon a stage which till then she had known only from the other side of the footlights. She saw them dramatically, and really seemed herself to live a larger life because she entertained them and visited them in their fastnesses. She accepted the rules with which they played the game of life as valid for them, but never for a moment thought of regulating her own conduct in accordance with them. Their moral eccentricities, like their oddities of dress, their wild theories and paradoxes, were an entertainment which amused her, but had not the slightest influence on her convictions.

"Is there a Mr. Strickland?" I asked.

"Oh yes; he's something in the city. I believe he's a stock-broker. He's very dull."

"Are they good friends?"

"They adore one another. You'll meet him if you dine there. But she doesn't often have people to dinner. He's very quiet. He's not in the least interested in literature or the arts."

"Why do nice women marry dull men?"

"Because intelligent men won't marry nice women."

I could not think of any retort to this, so I asked if Mrs. Strickland had children.

"Yes; she has a boy and a girl. They're both at school."

The subject was exhausted, and we began to talk of other things.

During the summer I met Mrs. Strickland not infrequently. I went now and then to pleasant little luncheons at her flat, and to rather more formidable tea-parties. We took a fancy to one another. I was very young, and perhaps she liked the idea of guiding my virgin steps on the hard road of letters; while for me it was pleasant to have someone I could go to with my small troubles, certain of an attentive ear and reasonable counsel. Mrs. Strickland had the gift of sympathy. It is a charming faculty, but one often abused by those who are conscious of its possession: for there is something ghoulish in the avidity with which they will pounce upon the misfortune of their friends so that they may exercise their dexterity. It gushes forth like an oil-well, and the

sympathetic pour out their sympathy with an abandon that
is sometimes embarrassing to their victims. There are
bosoms on which so many tears have been shed that I cannot bedew them with mine. Mrs. Strickland used her advantage with tact. You felt that you obliged her by accepting
her sympathy. When, in the enthusiasm of my youth, I
remarked on this to Rose Waterford, she said:

"Milk is very nice, especially with a drop of brandy in it,
but the domestic cow is only too glad to be rid of it. A
swollen udder is very uncomfortable."

Rose Waterford had a blistering tongue. No one could say
such bitter things; on the other hand, no one could do more
charming ones.

There was another thing I liked in Mrs. Strickland. She
managed her surroundings with elegance. Her flat was
always neat and cheerful, gay with flowers, and the chintzes
in the drawing-room, notwithstanding their severe design,
were bright and pretty. The meals in the artistic little dining-room were pleasant; the table looked nice, the two maids
were trim and comely; the food was well cooked. It was
impossible not to see that Mrs. Strickland was an excellent
housekeeper. And you felt sure that she was an admirable
mother. There were photographs in the drawing-room of
her son and daughter. The son—his name was Robert—
was a boy of sixteen at Rugby; and you saw him in flannels
and a cricket cap, and again in a tail-coat and a stand-up
collar. He had his mother's candid brow and fine, reflective
eyes. He looked clean, healthy, and normal.

"I don't know that he's very clever," she said one day,
when I was looking at the photograph, "but I know he's
good. He has a charming character."

The daughter was fourteen. Her hair, thick and dark like
her mother's, fell over her shoulders in fine profusion, and

she had the same kindly expression and sedate, untroubled eyes.

"They're both of them the image of you," I said.

"Yes; I think they are more like me than their father."

"Why have you never let me meet him?" I asked.

"Would you like to?"

She smiled, her smile was really very sweet, and she blushed a little; it was singular that a woman of that age should flush so readily. Perhas her naïveté was her greatest charm.

"You know, he's not at all literary," she said. "He's a perfect philistine."

She said this not disparagingly, but affectionately rather, as though, by acknowledging the worst about him, she wished to protect him from the aspersions of her friends.

"He's on the Stock Exchange, and he's a typical broker. I think he'd bore you to death."

"Does he bore you?" I asked.

"You see, I happen to be his wife. I'm very fond of him."

She smiled to cover her shyness, and I fancied she had a fear that I would make the sort of gibe that such a confession could hardly have failed to elicit from Rose Waterford. She hesitated a little. Her eyes grew tender.

"He doesn't pretend to be a genius. He doesn't even make much money on the Stock Exchange. But he's awfully good and kind."

"I think I should like him very much."

"I'll ask you to dine with us quietly some time, but mind, you come at your own risk; don't blame me if you have a very dull evening."

But when at last I met Charles Strickland, it was under circumstances which allowed me to do no more than just make his acquaintance. One morning Mrs. Strickland sent me round a note to say that she was giving a dinner-party that evening, and one of her guests had failed her. She asked me to stop the gap. She wrote:

"It's only decent to warn you that you will be bored to extinction. It was a thoroughly dull party from the beginning, but if you will come I shall be uncommonly grateful. And you and I can have a little chat by ourselves."

It was only neighbourly to accept.

When Mrs. Strickland introduced me to her husband, he gave me a rather indifferent hand to shake. Turning to him gaily, she attempted a small jest.

"I asked him to show him that I really had a husband. I think he was beginning to doubt it."

Strickland gave the polite little laugh with which people acknowledge a facetiousness in which they see nothing funny, but did not speak. New arrivals claimed my host's attention, and I was left to myself. When at last we were all assembled, waiting for dinner to be announced, I reflected, while I chatted with the woman I had been asked to "take in," that civilised man practises a strange ingenuity in wasting on tedious exercises the brief span of his life. It was the kind of party which makes you wonder why the hostess has troubled to bid her guests, and why the guests have troubled to come. There were ten people. They

met with indifference, and would part with relief. It was,
of course, a purely social function. The Stricklands "owed"
dinners to a number of persons, whom they took no interest
in, and so had asked them; these persons had accepted.

*"When at last I met
Charles Strickland . . ."*

Why? To avoid the tedium of dining *tête-à-tête*, to give their
servants a rest, because there was no reason to refuse,
because they were "owed" a dinner.

The dining-room was inconveniently crowded. There was

a K.C. and his wife, a Government official and his wife, Mrs. Strickland's sister and her husband, Colonel MacAndrew, and the wife of a Member of Parliament. It was because the Member of Parliament found that he could not leave the House that I had been invited. The respectability of the party was portentous. The women were too nice to be well dressed, and too sure of their position to be amusing. The men were solid. There was about all of them an air of well-satisfied prosperity.

Everyone talked a little louder than natural in an instinctive desire to make the party go, and there was a great deal of noise in the room. But there was no general conversation. Each one talked to his neighbour; to his neighbour on the right during the soup, fish, and entrée; to his neighbour on the left during the roast, sweet, and savoury. They talked of the political situation and of golf, of their children and the latest play, of the pictures at the Royal Academy, of the weather and their plans for the holidays. There was never a pause, and the noise grew louder. Mrs. Strickland might congratulate herself that her party was a success. Her husband played his part with decorum. Perhaps he did not talk very much, and I fancied there was towards the end a look of fatigue in the faces of the women on either side of him. They were finding him heavy. Once or twice Mrs. Strickland's eyes rested on him somewhat anxiously.

At last she rose and shepherded the ladies out of the room. Strickland shut the door behind her, and, moving to the other end of the table, took his place between the K.C. and the Government official. He passed round the port again and handed us cigars. The K.C. remarked on the excellence of the wine, and Strickland told us where he got it. We began to chat about vintages and tobacco. The K.C. told us of a case he was engaged in, and the Colonel talked about polo. I had nothing to say and so sat silent, trying politely to show interest in the conversation; and because I thought no one was in the least concerned with me, examined Strickland at my ease. He was bigger than I expected: I do not know why I had imagined him slender and of insignificant appearance; in point of fact he was broad and heavy, with large hands and feet, and he wore his evening clothes clumsily. He gave you somewhat the idea of a coachman dressed up for the occasion. He was a man of forty, not good-looking, and yet not ugly, for his features were rather good; but they were all a little larger than life-size, and the effect was ungainly. He was clean shaven, and his large face looked uncomfortably naked. His hair was reddish, cut very short, and his eyes were small, blue or grey. He looked commonplace. I no longer wondered that Mrs. Strickland felt a certain embarrassment about him; he was scarcely a credit to a woman who wanted to make herself a position in the world of art and letters. It was obvious that he had no social gifts, but these a man can do without; he had no eccentricity even, to take him out of the common run; he was just a good, dull, honest, plain man. One would admire his excellent qualities, but avoid his company. He was null. He was probably a worthy member of society, a good husband and father, an honest broker; but there was no reason to waste one's time over him.

The season was drawing to its dusty end, and everyone I knew was arranging to go away. Mrs. Strickland was tak-

ing her family to the coast of Norfolk, so that the children
might have the sea and her husband golf. We said good-
bye to one another, and arranged to meet in the autumn.
But on my last day in town, coming out of the Stores, I met
her with her son and daughter; like myself, she had been
making her final purchases before leaving London, and we
were both hot and tired. I proposed that we should all go
and eat ices in the park.

I think Mrs. Strickland was glad to show me her children,
and she accepted my invitation with alacrity. They were
even more attractive than their photographs had suggested,
and she was right to be proud of them. I was young enough
for them not to feel shy, and they chattered merrily about
one thing and another. They were extraordinarily nice,
healthy young children. It was very agreeable under the
trees.

When in an hour they crowded into a cab to go home, I
strolled idly to my club. I was perhaps a little lonely, and it
was with a touch of envy that I thought of the pleasant
family life of which I had had a glimpse. They seemed
devoted to one another. They had little private jokes of
their own which, unintelligible to the outsider, amused them
enormously. Perhaps Charles Strickland was dull judged
by a standard that demanded above all things verbal
scintillation; but his intelligence was adequate to his surroundings, and that is a passport, not only to reasonable
success, but still more to happiness. Mrs. Strickland was a
charming woman, and she loved him. I pictured their lives,
troubled by no untoward adventure, honest, decent, and, by
reason of those two upstanding, pleasant children, so obviously destined to carry on the normal traditions of their
race and station, not without significance. They would grow
old insensibly; they would see their son and daughter come

to years of reason, marry in due course—the one a pretty
girl, future mother of healthy children; the other a handsome, manly fellow, obviously a soldier; and at last, prosperous in their dignified retirement, beloved by their
descendants, after a happy, not unuseful life, in the fullness
of their age they would sink into the grave.

That must be the story of innumerable couples, and the
pattern of life it offers has a homely grace. It reminds you
of a placid rivulet, meandering smoothly through green
pastures and shaded by pleasant trees, till at last it falls
into the vasty sea; but the sea is so calm, so silent, so indifferent, that you are troubled suddenly by a vague uneasiness. Perhaps it is only by a kink in my nature, strong in me
even in those days, that I felt in such an existence, the share
of the great majority, something amiss. I recognised its
social values, I saw its ordered happiness, but a fever in my
blood asked for a wilder course. There seemed to me something alarming in such easy delights. In my heart was a
desire to live more dangerously. I was not unprepared for
jagged rocks and treacherous shoals if I could only have
change—change and the excitement of the unforeseen.

On reading over what I have written of the Stricklands, I
am conscious that they must seem shadowy. I have been able
to invest them with none of those characteristics which
make the persons of a book exist with a real life of their
own; and, wondering if the fault is mine, I rack my brains
to remember idiosyncrasies which might lend them vivid-
ness. I feel that by dwelling on some trick of speech or some

queer habit I should be able to give them a significance peculiar to themselves. As they stand they are like the figures in an old tapestry; they do not separate themselves from the background, and at a distance seem to lose their pattern, so that you have little but a pleasing piece of colour. My only excuse is that the impression they made on me was no other. There was just that shadowiness about them which you find in people whose lives are part of the social organism, so that they exist in it and by it only. They are like cells in the body, essential, but, so long as they remain healthy, engulfed in the momentous whole. The Stricklands were an average family in the middle class. A pleasant, hospitable woman, with a harmless craze for the small lions of literary society; a rather dull man, doing his duty in that state of life in which a merciful Providence had placed him; two nice-looking, healthy children. Nothing could be more ordinary. I do not know that there was anything about them to excite the attention of the curious.

When I reflect on all that happened later, I ask myself if I was thick-witted not to see that there was in Charles Strickland at least something out of the common. Perhaps. I think that I have gathered in the years that intervene between then and now a fair knowledge of mankind, but even if when I first met the Stricklands I had the experience which I have now, I do not believe that I should have judged them differently. But because I have learnt that man is incalculable, I should not at this time of day be so surprised by the news that reached me when in the early autumn I returned to London.

I had not been back twenty-four hours before I ran across Rose Waterford in Jermyn Street.

"You look very gay and sprightly," I said. "What's the matter with you?"

She smiled, and her eyes shone with a malice I knew already. It meant that she had heard some scandal about one of her friends, and the instinct of the literary woman was all alert.

"You did meet Charles Strickland, didn't you?"

Not only her face, but her whole body, gave a sense of alacrity. I nodded. I wondered if the poor devil had been hammered on the Stock Exchange or run over by an omnibus.

"Isn't it dreadful? He's run away from his wife."

Miss Waterford certainly felt that she could not do her subject justice on the curb of Jermyn Street, and so, like an artist, flung the bare fact at me and declared that she knew no details. I could not do her the injustice of supposing that so trifling a circumstance would have prevented her from giving them, but she was obstinate.

"I tell you I know nothing," she said, in reply to my agitated questions, and then, with an airy shrug of the shoulders: "I believe that a young person in a city tea-shop has left her situation."

She flashed a smile at me, and, protesting an engagement with her dentist, jauntily walked on. I was more interested than distressed. In those days my experience of life at first hand was small, and it excited me to come upon an incident among people I knew of the same sort as I had read in books. I confess that time has now accustomed me to incidents of this character among my acquaintance. But I was a little shocked. Strickland was certainly forty, and I thought it disgusting that a man of his age should concern himself with affairs of the heart. With the superciliousness of extreme youth, I put thirty-five as the utmost limit at which a man might fall in love without making a fool of himself. And this news was slightly disconcerting to me personally, because I had written from the country to Mrs. Strickland, announcing my return, and had added that unless I heard from her to the contrary, I would come on a certain day to drink a dish of tea with her. This was the very day, and I had received no word from Mrs. Strickland. Did she want to see me or did she not? It was likely enough that in the agitation of the moment my note had escaped her memory. Perhaps I should be wiser not to go. On the other hand, she might wish to keep the affair quiet, and it might be highly indiscreet on my part to give any sign that this strange news had reached me. I was torn between the fear of hurting a nice woman's feelings and the fear of being in the way. I felt she must be suffering, and I did not want to see a pain which I could not help; but in my heart was a desire, that I felt a little ashamed of, to see how she was taking it. I did not know what to do.

Finally it occurred to me that I would call as though nothing had happened, and send a message in by the maid asking Mrs. Strickland if it was convenient for her to see me. This would give her the opportunity to send me away. But I was overwhelmed with embarrassment when I said to the maid the phrase I had prepared, and while I waited for the answer in a dark passage I had to call up all my strength of mind not to bolt. The maid came back. Her manner suggested to my excited fancy a complete knowledge of the domestic calamity.

"Will you come this way, sir?" she said.

I followed her into the drawing-room. The blinds were partly drawn to darken the room, and Mrs. Strickland was sitting with her back to the light. Her brother-in-law, Colonel MacAndrew, stood in front of the fireplace, warming his back at an unlit fire. To myself my entrance seemed excessively awkward. I imagined that my arrival had taken them by surprise, and Mrs. Strickland had let me come in only because she had forgotten to put me off. I fancied that the Colonel resented the interruption.

"I wasn't quite sure if you expected me," I said, trying to seem unconcerned.

"Of course I did. Anne will bring the tea in a minute."

Even in the darkened room, I could not help seeing that Mrs. Strickland's face was all swollen with tears. Her skin, never very good, was earthy.

"You remember my brother-in-law, don't you? You met at dinner, just before the holidays."

We shook hands. I felt so shy that I could think of nothing to say, but Mrs. Strickland came to my rescue. She asked me what I had been doing with myself during the summer, and with this help I managed to make some conversation till tea was brought in. The Colonel asked for a whisky-and-soda.

"You'd better have one too, Amy," he said.

"No; I prefer tea."

This was the first suggestion that anything untoward had happened. I took no notice, and did my best to engage Mrs. Strickland in talk. The Colonel, still standing in front of the fireplace, uttered no word. I wondered how soon I could decently take my leave, and I asked myself why on earth Mrs. Strickland had allowed me to come. There were no flowers, and various knick-knacks, put away during the summer, had not been replaced; there was something cheerless and stiff about the room which had always seemed so friendly; it gave you an odd feeling, as though someone were lying dead on the other side of the wall. I finished tea.

"Will you have a cigarette?" asked Mrs. Strickland.

She looked about for the box, but it was not to be seen.

"I'm afraid there are none."

Suddenly she burst into tears, and hurried from the room.

I was startled. I suppose now that the lack of cigarettes, brought as a rule by her husband, forced him back upon her recollection, and the new feeling that the small comforts she was used to were missing gave her a sudden pang. She realised that the old life was gone and done with. It was impossible to keep up our social pretences any longer.

"I dare say you'd like me to go," I said to the Colonel, getting up.

"I suppose you've heard that blackguard has deserted her," he cried explosively.

I hesitated.

"You know how people gossip," I answered. "I was vaguely told that something was wrong."

"He's bolted. He's gone off to Paris with a woman. He's left Amy without a penny."

"I'm awfully sorry," I said, not knowing what else to say.

The Colonel gulped down his whisky. He was a tall, lean man of fifty, with a drooping moustache and grey hair. He had pale blue eyes and a weak mouth. I remembered from my previous meeting with him that he had a foolish face, and was proud of the fact that for the ten years before he left the army he had played polo three days a week.

"I don't suppose Mrs. Strickland wants to be bothered with me just now," I said. "Will you tell her how sorry I am? If there's anything I can do, I shall be delighted to do it."

He took no notice of me.

"I don't know what's to become of her. And then there are the children. Are they going to live on air? Seventeen years."

"What about seventeen years?"

"They've been married," he snapped. "I never liked him. Of course he was my brother-in-law, and I made the best of it. Did you think him a gentleman? She ought never to have married him."

"Is it absolutely final?"

"There's only one thing for her to do, and that's to divorce him. That's what I was telling her when you came in. 'Fire in with your petition, my dear Amy,' I said. 'You owe it to yourself and you owe it to the children.' He'd better not let me catch sight of him. I'd thrash him within an inch of his life."

I could not help thinking that Colonel MacAndrew might have some difficulty in doing this, since Strickland had struck me as a hefty fellow, but I did not say anything. It is always distressing when outraged morality does not possess the strength of arm to administer direct chastisement on the sinner. I was making up my mind to another attempt at going when Mrs. Strickland came back. She had dried her eyes and powdered her nose.

"I'm sorry I broke down," she said. "I'm glad you didn't go away."

She sat down. I did not at all know what to say. I felt a certain shyness at referring to matters which were no concern of mine. I did not then know the besetting sin of woman, the passion to discuss her private affairs with anyone who is willing to listen. Mrs. Strickland seemed to make an effort over herself.

"Are people talking about it?" she asked.

I was taken aback by her assumption that I knew all about her domestic misfortune.

"I've only just come back. The only person I've seen is Rose Waterford."

Mrs. Strickland clasped her hands.

"Tell me exactly what she said." And when I hesitated, she insisted. "I particularly want to know."

"You know the way people talk. She's not very reliable, is she? She said your husband had left you."

"Is that all?"

I did not choose to repeat Rose Waterford's parting reference to a girl from a tea-shop. I lied.

" 'Are people talking
about it?' she asked"

"She didn't say anything about his going with anyone?"

"No."

"That's all I wanted to know."

I was a little puzzled, but at all events I understood that I might now take my leave. When I shook hands with Mrs. Strickland I told her that if I could be of any use to her I should be very glad. She smiled wanly.

"Thank you so much. I don't know that anybody can do anything for me."

Too shy to express my sympathy, I turned to say good-bye to the Colonel. He did not take my hand.

"I'm just coming. If you're walking up Victoria Street, I'll come along with you."

"All right," I said. "Come on."

"This is a terrible thing," he said, the moment we got out into the street.

I realised that he had come away with me in order to discuss once more what he had been already discussing for hours with his sister-in-law.

"We don't know who the woman is, you know," he said. "All we know is that the blackguard's gone to Paris."

"I thought they got on so well."

"So they did. Why, just before you came in Amy said they'd never had a quarrel in the whole of their married life. You know Amy. There never was a better woman in the world."

Since these confidences were thrust on me, I saw no harm in asking a few questions.

"But do you mean to say she suspected nothing?"

"Nothing. He spent August with her and the children in Norfolk. He was just the same as he'd always been. We went down for two or three days, my wife and I, and I played golf with him. He came back to town in September to let his partner go away, and Amy stayed on in the country. They'd taken a house for six weeks, and at the end of her tenancy she wrote to tell him on which day she was arriving in London. He answered from Paris. He said he'd made up his mind not to live with her any more."

"What explanation did he give?"

"My dear fellow, he gave no explanation. I've seen the letter. It wasn't more than ten lines."

"But that's extraordinary."

We happened then to cross the street, and the traffic prevented us from speaking. What Colonel MacAndrew had told me seemed very improbable, and I suspected that Mrs. Strickland, for reasons of her own, had concealed from him some part of the facts. It was clear that a man after seventeen years of wedlock did not leave his wife without certain occurrences which must have led her to suspect that all was not well with their married life. The Colonel caught me up.

"Of course, there was no explanation he could give except that he'd gone off with a woman. I suppose he thought she could find that out for herself. That's the sort of chap he was."

"What is Mrs. Strickland going to do?"

"Well, the first thing is to get our proofs. I'm going over to Paris myself."

"And what about his business?"

"That's where he's been so artful. He's been drawing in his horns for the last year."

"Did he tell his partner he was leaving?"

"Not a word."

Colonel MacAndrew had a very sketchy knowledge of business matters, and I had none at all, so I did not quite understand under what conditions Strickland had left his affairs. I gathered that the deserted partner was very angry and threatened proceedings. It appeared that when everything was settled he would be four or five hundred pounds out of pocket.

"It's lucky the furniture in the flat is in Amy's name. She'll have that at all events."

"Did you mean it when you said she wouldn't have a bob?"

"Of course I did. She's got two or three hundred pounds and the furniture."

"But how is she going to live?"

"God knows."

The affair seemed to grow more complicated, and the Colonel, with his expletives and his indignation, confused rather than informed me. I was glad that, catching sight of the clock at the Army and Navy Stores, he remembered an engagement to play cards at his club, and so left me to cut across St. James's Park.

A day or two later Mrs. Strickland sent me round a note asking if I could go and see her that evening after dinner. I found her alone. Her black dress, simple to austerity, suggested her bereaved condition, and I was innocently astonished that notwithstanding a real emotion she was able to dress the part she had to play.

"You said that if I wanted you to do anything you wouldn't mind doing it," she remarked.

"It was quite true."

"Will you go over to Paris and see Charlie?"

"I?"

I was taken aback. I reflected that I had only seen him once. I did not know what she wanted me to do.

"Fred is set on going." Fred was Colonel MacAndrew. "But I'm sure he's not the man to go. He'll only make things worse. I don't know who else to ask."

Her voice trembled a little, and I felt a brute even to hesitate.

"But I've not spoken ten words to your husband. He doesn't know me. He'll probably just tell me to go to the devil."

"That wouldn't hurt you," said Mrs. Strickland, smiling.

"What is it exactly you want me to do?"

She did not answer directly.

"I think it's rather an advantage that he doesn't know you. You see, he never really liked Fred; he thought him a fool; he didn't understand soldiers. Fred would fly into a passion, and there'd be a quarrel, and things would be worse instead of better. If you said you came on my behalf, he couldn't refuse to listen to you."

"I haven't known you very long," I answered. "I don't see how anyone can be expected to tackle a case like this unless he knows all the details. I don't want to pry into what doesn't concern me. Why don't you go and see him yourself?"

"You forget he isn't alone."

I held my tongue. I saw myself calling on Charles Strickland and sending in my card; I saw him come into the room, holding it between finger and thumb:

"To what do I owe this honour?"

"I've come to see you about your wife."

"Really. When you are a little older you will doubtless learn the advantage of minding your own business. If you will be so good as to turn your head slightly to the left, you will see the door. I wish you good-afternoon."

I foresaw that it would be difficult to make my exit with dignity, and I wished to goodness that I had not returned to London till Mrs. Strickland had composed her difficulties. I stole a glance at her. She was immersed in thought. Presently she looked up at me, sighed deeply, and smiled.

"It was all so unexpected," she said. "We'd been married seventeen years. I never dreamed that Charlie was the sort of man to get infatuated with anyone. We always got on very well together. Of course, I had a great many interests that he didn't share."

"Have you found out who"—I did not quite know how to express myself—"who the person, who it is he's gone away with?"

"No. No one seems to have an idea. It's so strange. Generally when a man falls in love with someone people see them about together, lunching or something, and her friends always come and tell the wife. I had no warning—nothing. His letter came like a thunderbolt. I thought he was perfectly happy."

She began to cry, poor thing, and I felt very sorry for her. But in a little while she grew calmer.

"It's no good making a fool of myself," she said, drying her eyes. "The only thing is to decide what is the best thing to do."

She went on, talking somewhat at random, now of the recent past, then of their first meeting and their marriage; but presently I began to form a fairly coherent picture of their lives; and it seemed to me that my surmises had not been incorrect. Mrs. Strickland was the daughter of an Indian civilian, who on his retirement had settled in the depths of the country, but it was his habit every August to take his family to Eastbourne for change of air; and it was here, when she was twenty, that she met Charles Strickland. He was twenty-three. They played together, walked on the front together, listened together to the nigger minstrels; and she had made up her mind to accept him a week before he proposed to her. They lived in London, first in Hampstead, and then, as he grew more prosperous, in town. Two children were born to them.

"He always seemed very fond of them. Even if he was tired of me, I wonder that he had the heart to leave them. It's all so incredible. Even now I can hardly believe it's true."

At last she showed me the letter he had written. I was curious to see it, but had not ventured to ask for it.

"MY DEAR AMY,

"I think you will find everything all right in the flat. I have given Anne your instructions, and dinner will be ready for you and the children when you come. I shall not be there to meet you. I have made up my mind to live apart from you, and I am going to Paris in the morning. I shall post this letter on my arrival. I shall not come back. My decision is irrevocable.

"Yours always,

"CHARLES STRICKLAND."

"Not a word of explanation or regret. Don't you think it's inhuman?"

"It's a very strange letter under the circumstances," I replied.

"There's only one explanation, and that is that he's not

himself. I don't know who this woman is who's got hold of
him, but she's made him into another man. It's evidently
been going on a long time.''

''What makes you think that?''

''Fred found that out. My husband said he went to the
club three or four nights a week to play bridge. Fred knows
one of the members, and said something about Charles
being a great bridge-player. The man was surprised. He
said he'd never even seen Charles in the card-room. It's
quite clear now that when I thought Charles was at his
club he was with her.''

I was silent for a moment. Then I thought of the children.

''It must have been difficult to explain to Robert,'' I
said.

''Oh, I never said a word to either of them. You see, we
only came up to town the day before they had to go back to
school. I had the presence of mind to say that their father
had been called away on business.''

It could not have been very easy to be bright and careless
with that sudden secret in her heart, nor to give her attention to all the things that needed doing to get her children
comfortably packed off. Mrs. Strickland's voice broke
again.

''And what is to happen to them, poor darlings? How
are we going to live?''

She struggled for self-control, and I saw her hands clench
and unclench spasmodically. It was dreadfully painful.

''Of course I'll go over to Paris if you think I can do
any good, but you must tell me exactly what you want me
to do.''

''I want him to come back.''

''I understood from Colonel MacAndrew that you'd made
up your mind to divorce him.''

"I'll never divorce him," she answered with a sudden violence. "Tell him that from me. He'll never be able to marry that woman. I'm as obstinate as he is, and I'll never divorce him. I have to think of my children."

I think she added this to explain her attitude to me, but I thought it was due to a very natural jealousy rather than to maternal solicitude.

"Are you in love with him still?"

"I don't know. I want him to come back. If he'll do that we'll let bygones be bygones. After all, we've been married for seventeen years. I'm a broadminded woman. I wouldn't have minded what he did as long as I knew nothing about it. He must know that his infatuation won't last. If he'll come back now everything can be smoothed over, and no one will know anything about it."

It chilled me a little that Mrs. Strickland should be concerned with gossip, for I did not know then how great a part is played in women's life by the opinion of others. It throws a shadow of insincerity over their most deeply felt emotions.

It was known where Strickland was staying. His partner, in a violent letter, sent to his bank, had taunted him with hiding his whereabouts: and Strickland, in a cynical and humourous reply, had told his partner exactly where to find him. He was apparently living in an hotel.

"I've never heard of it," said Mrs. Strickland. "But Fred knows it well. He says it's very expensive."

She flushed darkly. I imagined that she saw her husband installed in a luxurious suite of rooms, dining at one smart restaurant after another, and she pictured his days spent at race-meetings and his evenings at the play.

"It can't go on at his age," she said. "After all, he's forty. I could understand it in a young man, but I think it's horrible in a man of his years, with children who are nearly grown up. His health will never stand it.''

Anger struggled in her breast with misery.

''Tell him that our home cries out for him. Everything is just the same, and yet everything is different. I can't live without him. I'd sooner kill myself. Talk to him about the past, and all we've gone through together. What am I to say to the children when they ask for him? His room is exactly as it was when he left it. It's waiting for him. We're all waiting for him.''

Now she told me exactly what I should say. She gave me elaborate answers to every possible observation of his.

''You will do everything you can for me?'' she said pitifully. ''Tell him what a state I'm in.''

I saw that she wished me to appeal to his sympathies by every means in my power. She was weeping freely. I was extraordinarily touched. I felt indignant at Strickland's cold cruelty, and I promised to do all I could to bring him back. I agreed to go over on the next day but one, and to stay in Paris till I had achieved something. Then, as it was growing late and we were both exhausted by so much emotion, I left her.

During the journey I thought over my errand with misgiving. Now that I was free from the spectacle of Mrs. Strickland's distress I could consider the matter more calmly. I was puzzled by the contradictions that I saw in her behaviour. She was very unhappy, but to excite my sympathy she was able to make a show of her unhappiness. It was evident that she had been prepared to weep, for she had provided herself with a sufficiency of handkerchiefs; I admired her forethought, but in retrospect it made her tears perhaps less moving. I could not decide whether she desired the return of her husband because she loved him, or because she dreaded the tongue of scandal; and I was perturbed by the suspicion that the anguish of love contemned was alloyed in her broken heart with the pangs, sordid to my young mind, of wounded vanity. I had not yet learnt how contradictory is human nature; I did not know how much pose there is in the sincere, how much baseness in the noble, nor how much goodness in the reprobate.

But there was something of an adventure in my trip, and my spirits rose as I approached Paris. I saw myself, too, from the dramatic standpoint, and I was pleased with my rôle of the trusted friend bringing back the errant husband to his forgiving wife. I made up my mind to see Strickland the following evening, for I felt instinctively that the hour must be chosen with delicacy. An appeal to the emotions is little likely to be effectual before luncheon. My own thoughts were then constantly occupied with love, but I never could imagine connubial bliss till after tea.

I enquired at my hotel for that in which Charles Strickland was living. It was called the Hôtel des Belges. But the concierge, somewhat to my surprise, had never heard of it. I had understood from Mrs. Strickland that it was a large and sumptuous place at the back of the Rue de Rivoli. We looked it out in the directory. The only hotel of that name was in the Rue des Moines. The quarter was not fashionable; it was not even respectable. I shook my head.

"I'm sure that's not it," I said.

The concierge shrugged his shoulders. There was no

other hotel of that name in Paris. It occurred to me that Strickland had concealed his address, after all. In giving his partner the one I knew he was perhaps playing a trick on him. I do not know why I had an inkling that it would appeal to Strickland's sense of humour to bring a furious stockbroker over to Paris on a fool's errand to an ill-famed house in a mean street. Still, I thought I had better go and see. Next day about six o'clock I took a cab to the Rue des Moines, but dismissed it at the corner, since I preferred to walk to the hotel and look at it before I went in. It was a street of small shops subservient to the needs of poor people, and about the middle of it, on the left as I walked down, was the Hôtel des Belges. My own hotel was modest enough, but it was magnificent in comparison with this. It was a tall, shabby building, that cannot have been painted for years, and it had so bedraggled an air that the houses on each side of it looked neat and clean. The dirty windows were all shut. It was not here that Charles Strickland lived in guilty splendour with the unknown charmer for whose sake he had abandoned honour and duty. I was vexed, for I felt that I had been made a fool of, and I nearly turned away without making an enquiry. I went in only to be able to tell Mrs. Strickland that I had done my best.

The door was at the side of a shop. It stood open, and just within was a sign: *Bureau au premier*. I walked up narrow stairs, and on the landing found a sort of box, glassed in, within which were a desk and a couple of chairs. There was a bench outside, on which it might be presumed the night porter passed uneasy nights. There was no one about, but under an electric bell was written *Garçon*. I rang, and presently a waiter appeared. He was a young man with furtive eyes and a sullen look. He was in shirt-sleeves and carpet slippers.

I do not know why I made my enquiry as casual as possible.

"Does Mr. Strickland live here by any chance?" I asked.

"Number thirty-two. On the sixth floor."

I was so surprised that for a moment I did not answer.

"Is he in?"

The waiter looked at a board in the *bureau*.

"He hasn't left his key. Go up and you'll see."

I thought it as well to put one more question.

"Madame est là?"

"Monsieur est seul."

The waiter looked at me suspiciously as I made my way upstairs. They were dark and airless. There was a foul and musty smell. Three flights up a woman in a dressing-gown, with touzled hair, opened a door and looked at me silently as I passed. At length I reached the sixth floor, and knocked at the door numbered thirty-two. There was a sound within, and the door was partly opened. Charles Strickland stood before me. He uttered not a word. He evidently did not know me.

I told him my name. I tried my best to assume an airy manner.

"You don't remember me. I had the pleasure of dining with you last July."

"Come in," he said cheerily. "I'm delighted to see you. Take a pew."

I entered. It was a very small room, overcrowded with furniture of the style which the French know as Louis Philippe. There was a large wooden bedstead on which was a billowing red eiderdown, and there was a large wardrobe, a round table, a very small washstand, and two stuffed chairs covered with red rep. Everything was dirty and shabby. There was no sign of the abandoned luxury that

Colonel MacAndrew had so confidently described. Strickland threw on the floor the clothes that burdened one of the chairs, and I sat down on it.

"What can I do for you?" he asked.

In that small room he seemed even bigger than I remembered him. He wore an old Norfolk jacket, and he had not shaved for several days. When last I saw him he was spruce enough, but he looked ill at ease: now, untidy and ill-kempt, he looked perfectly at home. I did not know how he would take the remark I had prepared.

"I've come to see you on behalf of your wife."

"I was just going out to have a drink before dinner. You'd better come too. Do you like absinthe?"

"I can drink it."

"Come on, then."

He put on a bowler hat much in need of brushing.

"We might dine together. You owe me a dinner, you know."

"Certainly. Are you alone?"

I flattered myself that I had got in that important question very naturally.

"Oh yes. In point of fact I've not spoken to a soul for three days. My French isn't exactly brilliant."

I wondered as I preceded him downstairs what had happened to the little lady in the tea-shop. Had they quarrelled already, or was his infatuation passed? It seemed hardly likely if, as appeared, he had been taking steps for a year to make his desperate plunge. We walked to the Avenue de Clichy, and sat down at one of the tables on the pavement of a large café.

The Avenue de Clichy was crowded at that hour, and a lively fancy might see in the passers-by the personages of many a sordid romance. There were clerks and shopgirls; old fellows who might have stepped out of the pages of Honoré de Balzac; members, male and female, of the professions which make their profit of the frailties of mankind. There is in the streets of the poorer quarters of Paris a thronging vitality which excites the blood and prepares the soul for the unexpected.

"Do you know Paris well?" I asked.

"No. We came on our honeymoon. I haven't been since."

"How on earth did you find out your hotel?"

"It was recommended to me. I wanted something cheap."

The absinthe came, and with due solemnity we dropped water over the melting sugar.

"I thought I'd better tell you at once why I had come to see you," I said, not without embarrassment.

His eyes twinkled.

"I thought somebody would come along sooner or later. I've had a lot of letters from Amy."

"Then you know pretty well what I've got to say."

"I've not read them."

I lit a cigarette to give myself a moment's time. I did not quite know now how to set about my mission. The eloquent phrases I had arranged, pathetic or indignant, seemed out of place on the Avenue de Clichy. Suddenly he gave a chuckle.

"Beastly job for you this, isn't it?"

"Oh, I don't know," I answered.

"Well, look here, you get it over, and then we'll have a jolly evening."

I hesitated.

"Has it occurred to you that your wife is frightfully unhappy?"

"She'll get over it."

I cannot describe the extraordinary callousness with which he made this reply. It disconcerted me, but I did my best not to show it. I adopted the tone used by my Uncle Henry, a clergyman, when he was asking one of his relatives for a subscription to the Additional Curates Society.

"You don't mind my talking to you frankly?"

He shook his head, smiling.

"Has she deserved that you should treat her like this?"

"No."

"Have you any complaint to make against her?"

"None."

"Then, isn't it monstrous to leave her in this fashion, after seventeen years of married life, without a fault to find with her?"

"Monstrous."

I glanced at him with surprise. His cordial agreement with all I said cut the ground from under my feet. It made my position complicated, not to say ludicrous. I was prepared to be persuasive, touching, and hortatory, admonitory and expostulating, if need be vituperative even, indignant and sarcastic; but what the devil does a mentor do when the sinner makes no bones about confessing his sin? I had no experience, since my own practice has always been to deny everything.

"What, then?" asked Strickland.

I tried to curl my lip.

"Well, if you acknowledge that, there doesn't seem much more to be said."

"I don't think there is."

I felt that I was not carrying out my embassy with any great skill. I was distinctly nettled.

"Hang it all, one can't leave a woman without a bob."

"Why not?"

"How is she going to live?"

"I've supported her for seventeen years. Why shouldn't she support herself for a change?"

"She can't."

"Let her try."

Of course there were many things I might have answered to this. I might have spoken of the economic position of woman, of the contract, tacit and overt, which a man accepts by his marriage, and of much else; but I felt that there was only one point which really signified.

"Don't you care for her any more?"

"Not a bit," he replied.

The matter was immensely serious for all the parties concerned, but there was in the manner of his answers such a cheerful effrontery that I had to bite my lips in order not to laugh. I reminded myself that his behaviour was abominable. I worked myself up into a state of moral indignation.

"Damn it all, there are your children to think of. They've never done you any harm. They didn't ask to be brought into the world. If you chuck everything like this, they'll be thrown on the streets."

"They've had a good many years of comfort. It's much more than the majority of children have. Besides, somebody will look after them. When it comes to the point, the Mac-Andrews will pay for their schooling."

"But aren't you fond of them? They're such awfully nice kids. Do you mean to say you don't want to have anything more to do with them?"

"I liked them all right when they were kids, but now they're growing up I haven't got any particular feeling for them."

"It's just inhuman."

"I dare say."

"You don't seem in the least ashamed."

"I'm not."

I tried another tack.

"Everyone will think you a perfect swine."

"Let them."

"Won't it mean anything to you to know that people loathe and despise you?"

"No."

His brief answer was so scornful that it made my question, natural though it was, seem absurd. I reflected for a minute or two.

"I wonder if one can live quite comfortably when one's conscious of the disapproval of one's fellows? Are you sure it won't begin to worry you? Everyone has some sort of a conscience, and sooner or later it will find you out. Supposing your wife died, wouldn't you be tortured by remorse?"

He did not answer, and I waited for some time for him to speak. At last I had to break the silence myself.

"What have you to say to that?"

"Only that you're a damned fool."

"At all events, you can be forced to support your wife and children," I retorted, somewhat piqued. "I suppose the law has some protection to offer them."

"Can the law get blood out of a stone? I haven't any money. I've got about a hundred pounds."

I began to be more puzzled than before. It was true that his hotel pointed to the most straitened circumstances.

"What are you going to do when you've spent that?"

"Earn some."

He was perfectly cool, and his eyes kept that mocking smile which made all I said seem rather foolish. I paused for a little while to consider what I had better say next. But it was he who spoke first.

"Why doesn't Amy marry again? She's comparatively young, and she's not unattractive. I can recommend her as an excellent wife. If she wants to divorce me I don't mind giving her the necessary grounds."

Now it was my turn to smile. He was very cunning, but it was evidently this that he was aiming at. He had some reason to conceal the fact that he had run away with a woman, and he was using every precaution to hide her whereabouts. I answered with decision.

"Your wife says that nothing you can do will ever induce her to divorce you. She's quite made up her mind. You can put any possibility of that definitely out of your head."

He looked at me with an astonishment that was certainly not feigned. The smile abandoned his lips, and he spoke quite seriously.

"But, my dear fellow, I don't care. It doesn't matter a twopenny damn to me one way or the other."

I laughed.

"Oh, come now; you mustn't think us such fools as all that. We happen to know that you came away with a woman."

He gave a little start, and then suddenly burst into a shout of laughter. He laughed so uproariously that people sitting near us looked round, and some of them began to laugh too.

"I don't see anything very amusing in that."

"Poor Amy," he grinned.

Then his face grew bitterly scornful.

"What poor minds women have got! Love. It's always love. They think a man leaves only because he wants others. Do you think I should be such a fool as to do what I've done for a woman?"

"Do you mean to say you didn't leave your wife for another woman?"

"Of course not."

"On your word of honour?"

I don't know why I asked for that. It was very ingenuous of me.

"On my word of honour."

"Then, what in God's name have you left her for?"

"I want to paint."

I looked at him for quite a long time. I did not understand. I thought he was mad. It must be remembered that I was very young, and I looked upon him as a middle-aged man. I forgot everything but my own amazement.

"But you're forty."

"That's what made me think it was high time to begin."

"Have you ever painted?"

"I rather wanted to be a painter when I was a boy, but my father made me go into business because he said there was no money in art. I began to paint a bit a year ago. For the last year I've been going to some classes at night."

"Was that where you went when Mrs. Strickland thought you were playing bridge at your club?"

"That's it."

"Why didn't you tell her?"

"I preferred to keep it to myself."

"Can you paint?"

"Not yet. But I shall. That's why I've come over here. I couldn't get what I wanted in London. Perhaps I can here."

"Do you think it's likely that a man will do any good when he starts at your age? Most men begin painting at eighteen."

"I can learn quicker than I could when I was eighteen."

"What makes you think you have any talent?"

" 'I tell you I've got to paint. I can't help myself' "

He did not answer for a minute. His gaze rested on the passing throng, but I do not think he saw it. His answer was no answer.

"I've got to paint."

"Aren't you taking an awful chance?"

He looked at me. His eyes had something strange in them,

so that I felt rather uncomfortable.

"How old are you? Twenty-three?"

It seemed to me that the question was beside the point. It was natural that I should take chances; but he was a man whose youth was past, a stockbroker with a position of respectability, a wife and two children. A course that would have been natural for me was absurd for him. I wished to be quite fair.

"Of course a miracle may happen, and you may be a great painter, but you must confess the chances are a million to one against it. It'll be an awful sell if at the end you have to acknowledge you've made a hash of it."

"I've got to paint," he repeated.

"Supposing you're never anything more than third-rate, do you think it will have been worth while to give up everything? After all, in any other walk in life it doesn't matter if you're not very good; you can get along quite comfortably if you're just adequate; but it's different with an artist."

"You blasted fool," he said.

"I don't see why, unless it's folly to say the obvious."

"I tell you I've got to paint. I can't help myself. When a man falls into the water it doesn't matter how he swims, well or badly: he's got to get out or else he'll drown."

There was real passion in his voice, and in spite of myself I was impressed. I seemed to feel in him some vehement power that was struggling within him; it gave me the sensation of something very strong, overmastering, that held him, as it were, against his will. I could not understand. He seemed really to be possessed of a devil, and I felt that it might suddenly turn and rend him. Yet he looked ordinary enough. My eyes, resting on him curiously, caused him no embarrassment. I wondered what a stranger would have taken him to be, sitting there in his old Norfolk jacket and his unbrushed bowler; his trousers were baggy, his hands were not clean; and his face, with the red stubble of the unshaved chin, the little eyes, and the large, aggressive nose, was uncouth and coarse. His mouth was large, his lips were heavy and sensual. No; I could not have placed him.

"You won't go back to your wife?" I said at last.

"Never."

"She's willing to forget everything that's happened and start afresh. She'll never make you a single reproach."

"She can go to hell."

"You don't care if people think you an utter blackguard? You don't care if she and your children have to beg their bread?"

"Not a damn."

I was silent for a moment in order to give greater force to my next remark. I spoke as deliberately as I could.

"You are a most unmitigated cad."

"Now that you've got that off your chest, let's go and have dinner."

I dare say it would have been more seemly to decline this proposal. I think perhaps I should have made a show of the indignation I really felt, and I am sure that Colonel Mac-Andrew at least would have thought well of me if I had been able to report my stout refusal to sit at the same table with a man of such character. But the fear of not being able to carry it through effectively has always made me shy of assuming the moral attitude; and in this case the certainty that my sentiments would be lost on Strickland made it peculiarly embarrassing to utter them. Only the poet or the saint can water an asphalt pavement in the confident anticipation that lilies will reward his labour.

I paid for what we had drunk, and we made our way to a cheap restaurant, crowded and gay, where we dined with pleasure. I had the appetite of youth and he of a hardened conscience. Then we went to a tavern to have coffee and liqueurs.

I had said all I had to say on the subject that had brought me to Paris, and though I felt it in a manner treacherous to Mrs. Strickland not to pursue it, I could not struggle against his indifference. It requires the feminine temperament to repeat the same thing three times with unabated zest. I solaced myself by thinking that it would be useful for me to find out what I could about Strickland's state of mind. It also interested me much more. But this was not an easy thing to do, for Strickland was not a fluent talker. He seemed to express himself with difficulty, as though words were not the medium with which his mind worked; and you had to guess the intentions of his soul by hackneyed phrases, slang, and vague, unfinished gestures. But though he said nothing of any consequence, there was something in his personality which prevented him from being dull. Perhaps it was sincerity.

He did not seem to care much about the Paris he was now seeing for the first time (I did not count the visit with his wife), and he accepted sights which must have been strange to him without any sense of astonishment. I have been to Paris a hundred times, and it never fails to give me a thrill of excitement; I can never walk its streets without feeling myself on the verge of adventure. Strickland remained placid. Looking back, I think now that he was blind to everything but to some disturbing vision in his soul.

One rather absurd incident took place. There were a number of harlots in the tavern: some were sitting with men, others by themselves; and presently I noticed that one of these was looking at us. When she caught Strickland's eye she smiled. I do not think he saw her. In a little while she went out, but in a minute returned and, passing our table, very politely asked us to buy her something to drink. She sat down and I began to chat with her; but it was plain that her interest was in Strickland. I explained that he knew no more than two words of French. She tried to talk to him, partly by signs, partly in pidgin French, which, for some reason, she thought would be more comprehensible to him, and she had half a dozen phrases of English. She made me translate what she could only express in her own tongue, and eagerly asked for the meaning of his replies. He was quite good-tempered, a little amused, but his indifference was obvious.

"I think you've made a conquest," I laughed.

"I'm not flattered."

In his place I should have been more embarrassed and less calm. She had laughing eyes and a most charming mouth. She was young. I wondered what she found so attractive in Strickland. She made no secret of her desires, and I was bidden to translate.

"She wants you to go home with her."

"I'm not taking any," he replied.

I put his answer as pleasantly as I could. It seemed to me a little ungracious to decline an invitation of that sort, and I ascribed his refusal to lack of money.

"But I like him," she said. "Tell him it's for love."

When I translated this, Strickland shrugged his shoulders impatiently.

"Tell her to go to hell," he said.

His manner made his answer quite plain, and the girl threw back her head with a sudden gesture. Perhaps she reddened under her paint. She rose to her feet.

"*Monsieur n'est pas poli,*" she said.

She walked out of the inn. I was slightly vexed.

"There wasn't any need to insult her that I can see," I said. "After all, it was rather a compliment she was paying you."

"That sort of thing makes me sick," he said roughly.

I looked at him curiously. There was a real distaste in his face, and yet it was the face of a coarse and sensual man. I suppose the girl had been attracted by a certain brutality in it.

"I could have got all the women I wanted in London. I didn't come here for that."

During the journey back to England I thought much of Strickland. I tried to set in order what I had to tell his wife. It was unsatisfactory, and I could not imagine that she would be content with me; I was not content with myself. Strickland perplexed me. I could not understand his motives. When I had asked him what first gave him the idea of being a painter, he was unable or unwilling to tell me. I could make nothing of it. I tried to persuade myself than an obscure feeling of revolt had been gradually coming to a head in his slow mind, but to challenge this was the undoubted fact that he had never shown any impatience with the monotony of his life. If, seized by an intolerable boredom, he had determined to be a painter merely to break with irksome ties, it would have been comprehensible, and commonplace; but commonplace is precisely what I felt he was not. At last, because I was romantic, I devised an explanation which I acknowledged to be far-fetched, but which was the only one that in any way satisfied me. It was this: I asked myself whether there was not in his soul some deep-rooted instinct of creation, which the circumstances of his life had obscured, but which grew relentlessly, as a cancer may grow in the living tissues, till at last it took possession of his whole being and forced him irresistibly to action. The cuckoo lays its egg in the strange bird's nest, and when the young one is hatched it shoulders its foster-brothers out and breaks at last the nest that has sheltered it.

But how strange it was that the creative instinct should seize upon this dull stockbroker, to his own ruin, perhaps, and to the misfortune of such as were dependent on him; and yet no stranger than the way in which the spirit of God has seized men, powerful and rich, pursuing them with stubborn vigilance till at last, conquered, they have abandoned the joy of the world and the love of women for the painful austerities of the cloister. Conversion may come under many shapes, and it may be brought about in many ways. With some men it needs a cataclysm, as a stone may be broken to fragments by the fury of a torrent; but with some it comes gradually, as a stone may be worn away by the ceaseless fall of a drop of water. Strickland had the directness of the fanatic and the ferocity of the apostle.

But to my practical mind it remained to be seen whether the passion which obsessed him would be justified of its

works. When I asked him what his brother-students at the
night classes he had attended in London thought of his
painting, he answered with a grin:

"They thought it a joke."

"Have you begun to go to a studio here?"

"Yes. The blighter came round this morning—the master,
you know; when he saw my drawing he just raised his eyebrows and walked on."

Strickland chuckled. He did not seem discouraged. He was
independent of the opinion of his fellows.

And it was just that which had most disconcerted me in
my dealings with him. When people say they do not care
what others think of them, for the most part they deceive
themselves. Generally they mean only that they will do as
they choose, in the confidence that no one will know their
vagaries; and at the utmost only that they are willing to act
contrary to the opinion of the majority because they are
supported by the approval of their neighbours. It is not
difficult to be unconventional in the eyes of the world when
your unconventionality is but the convention of your set.
It affords you then an inordinate amount of self-esteem.
You have the self-satisfaction of courage without the incon-
venience of danger. But the desire for approbation is perhaps the most deeply seated instinct of civilised man. No
one runs so hurriedly to the cover of respectability as the
unconventional woman who has exposed herself to the
slings and arrows of outraged propriety. I do not believe
the people who tell me they do not care a row of pins for the
opinion of their fellows. It is the bravado of ignorance.
They mean only that they do not fear reproaches for peccadillos which they are convinced none will discover.

But here was a man who sincerely did not mind what people thought of him, and so convention had no hold on him;

he was like a wrestler whose body is oiled; you could not get
a grip on him; it gave him a freedom which was an outrage.
I remember saying to him:

"Look here, if everyone acted like you, the world couldn't
go on."

"That's a damned silly thing to say. Everyone doesn't
want to act like me. The great majority are perfectly content to do the ordinary thing."

And once I sought to be satirical.

"You evidently don't believe in the maxim: Act so that
every one of your actions is capable of being made into a
universal rule."

"I never heard it before, but it's rotten nonsense."

"Well, it was Kant who said it."

"I don't care; it's rotten nonsense."

Nor with such a man could you expect the appeal to
conscience to be effective. You might as well ask for a reflec-
tion without a mirror. I take it that conscience is the guard-
ian in the individual of the rules which the community has
evolved for its own preservation. It is the policeman in all
our hearts, set there to watch that we do not break its laws.
It is the spy seated in the central stronghold of the ego.
Man's desire for the approval of his fellows is so strong,
his dread of their censure so violent, that he himself has
brought his enemy within his gates; and it keeps watch
over him, vigilant always in the interests of its master to
crush any half-formed desire to break away from the herd.
It will force him to place the good of society before his own.
It is the very strong link that attaches the individual to the
whole. And man, subservient to interests he has persuaded
himself are greater than his own, makes himself a slave to
his taskmaster. He sits him in a seat of honour. At last, like
a courtier fawning on the royal stick that is laid about his

shoulders, he prides himself on the sensitiveness of his conscience. Then he has no words hard enough for the man who does not recognise its sway; for, a member of society now, he realises accurately enough that against him he is powerless. When I saw that Strickland was really indifferent to the blame his conduct must excite, I could only draw back in horror as from a monster of hardly human shape.

The last words he said to me when I bade him good-night were:

"Tell Amy it's no good coming after me. Anyhow, I shall change my hotel, so she wouldn't be able to find me."

"My own impression is that she's well rid of you," I said.

"My dear fellow, I only hope you'll be able to make her see it. But women are very unintelligent."

When I reached London I found waiting for me an urgent request that I should go to Mrs. Strickland's as soon after dinner as I could. I found her with Colonel MacAndrew and his wife. Mrs. Strickland's sister was older than she, not unlike her, but more faded; and she had the efficient air, as though she carried the British Empire in her pocket, which the wives of senior officers acquire from the consciousness of belonging to a superior caste. Her manner was brisk, and her good-breeding scarcely concealed her conviction that if you were not a soldier you might as well be a counter-jumper. She hated the Guards, whom she thought conceited, and she could not trust herself to speak of their ladies, who were so remiss in calling. Her gown was dowdy and expensive.

Mrs. Strickland was plainly nervous.

"Well, tell us your news," she said.

"I saw your husband. I'm afraid he's quite made up his mind not to return." I paused a little. "He wants to paint."

"What do you mean?" cried Mrs. Strickland, with the utmost astonishment.

"Did you never know that he was keen on that sort of thing."

"He must be as mad as a hatter," exclaimed the Colonel.

Mrs. Strickland frowned a little. She was searching among her recollections.

"I remember before we were married he used to potter about with a paint-box. But you never saw such daubs. We used to chaff him. He had absolutely no gift for anything like that."

"Of course it's only an excuse," said Mrs. MacAndrew.

Mrs. Strickland pondered deeply for some time. It was quite clear that she could not make head or tail of my announcement. She had put some order into the drawing-room by now, her housewifely instincts having got the better of her dismay; and it no longer bore that deserted look, like a furnished house long to let, which I had noticed on my first visit after the catastrophe. But now that I had seen Strickland in Paris it was difficult to imagine him in those surroundings. I thought it could hardly have failed to strike them that there was something incongruous in him.

"But if he wanted to be an artist, why didn't he say so?" asked Mrs. Strickland at last. "I should have thought I was the last person to be unsympathetic to—to aspirations of that kind."

Mrs. MacAndrew tightened her lips. I imagine that she had never looked with approval on her sister's leaning towards persons who cultivated the arts. She spoke of "culchaw" derisively.

Mrs. Strickland continued:

"After all, if he had any talent I should be the first to encourage it. I wouldn't have minded sacrifices. I'd much rather be married to a painter than to a stockbroker. If it weren't for the children, I wouldn't mind anything. I could be just as happy in a shabby studio in Chelsea as in this flat."

"My dear, I have no patience with you," cried Mrs. MacAndrew. "You don't mean to say you believe a word of this nonsense?"

"But I think it's true," I put in mildly.

She looked at me with good-humoured contempt.

"A man doesn't throw up his business and leave his wife and children at the age of forty to become a painter unless there's a woman in it. I suppose he met one of your—artistic friends, and she's turned his head."

A spot of colour rose suddenly to Mrs. Strickland's pale cheeks.

"What is she like?"

I hesitated a little. I knew that I had a bombshell.

"There isn't a woman."

Colonel MacAndrew and his wife uttered expressions of incredulity, and Mrs. Strickland sprang to her feet.

"Do you mean to say you never saw her?"

"There's no one to see. He's quite alone."

"That's preposterous," cried Mrs. MacAndrew.

"I knew I ought to have gone over myself," said the Colonel. "You can bet your boots I'd have routed her out fast enough."

"I wish you had gone over," I replied, somewhat tartly. "You'd have seen that every one of your suppositions was wrong. He's not at a smart hotel. He's living in one tiny room in the most squalid way. If he's left his home, it's not to live a gay life. He's got hardly any money."

"Do you think he's done something that we don't know about, and is lying doggo on account of the police?"

The suggestion sent a ray of hope in all their breasts, but I would have nothing to do with it.

"If that were so, he would hardly have been such a fool as to give his partner his address," I retorted acidly. "Anyhow, there's one thing I'm positive of, he didn't go away with anyone. He's not in love. Nothing is farther from his thoughts."

There was a pause while they reflected over my words.

"Well, if what you say is true," said Mrs. MacAndrew at last, "things aren't so bad as I thought."

Mrs. Strickland glanced at her, but said nothing. She was very pale now, and her fine brow was dark and lowering. I could not understand the expression of her face. Mrs. MacAndrew continued:

"If it's just a whim, he'll get over it."

"Why don't you go over to him, Amy?" hazarded the Colonel. "There's no reason why you shouldn't live with him in Paris for a year. We'll look after the children. I dare say he'd got stale. Sooner or later he'll be quite ready to come back to London, and no great harm will have been done."

"I wouldn't do that," said Mrs. MacAndrew. "I'd give him all the rope he wants. He'll come back with his tail between his legs and settle down again quite comfortably." Mrs. MacAndrew looked at her sister coolly. "Perhaps you weren't very wise with him sometimes. Men are queer creatures, and one has to know how to manage them."

Mrs. MacAndrew shared the common opinion of her sex

that a man is always a brute to leave a woman who is attached to him, but that a woman is much to blame if he does. *Le cœur a ses raisons que la raison ne connaît pas.*

Mrs. Strickland looked slowly from one to another of us.

"He'll never come back," she said.

"Oh, my dear, remember what we've just heard. He's been used to comfort and to having someone to look after him. How long do you think it'll be before he gets tired of a scrubby room in a scrubby hotel? Besides, he hasn't any money. He must come back."

"As long as I thought he'd run away with some woman I thought there was a chance. I don't believe that sort of thing ever answers. He'd have got sick to death of her in three months. But if he hasn't gone because he's in love, then it's finished."

"Oh, I think that's awfully subtle," said the Colonel, putting into the word all the contempt he felt for a quality so alien to the traditions of his calling. "Don't you believe it. He'll come back, and, as Dorothy says, I dare say he'll be none the worse for having had a bit of a fling."

"But I don't want him back," she said.

"Amy!"

It was anger that had seized Mrs. Strickland, and her pallor was the pallor of a cold and sudden rage. She spoke quickly now, with little gasps.

"I could have forgiven it if he'd fallen desperately in love with someone and gone off with her. I should have thought that natural. I shouldn't really have blamed him. I should have thought he was led away. Men are so weak, and women are so unscrupulous. But this is different. I hate him. I'll never forgive him now."

Colonel MacAndrew and his wife began to talk to her together. They were astonished. They told her she was mad.

They could not understand. Mrs. Strickland turned desperately to me.

"Don't *you* see?" she cried.

"I'm not sure. Do you mean that you could have forgiven him if he'd left you for a woman, but not if he's left you for an idea? You think you're a match for the one, but against the other you're helpless?"

Mrs. Strickland gave me a look in which I read no great friendliness, but did not answer. Perhaps I had struck home. She went on in a low and trembling voice:

"I never knew it was possible to hate anyone as much as I hate him. Do you know, I've been comforting myself by thinking that however long it lasted he'd want me at the end? I knew when he was dying he'd send for me, and I was ready to go; I'd have nursed him like a mother, and at the last I'd have told him that it didn't matter, I'd loved him always, and I forgave him everything."

I have always been a little disconcerted by the passion women have for behaving beautifully at the death-bed of those they love. Sometimes it seems as if they grudge the longevity which postpones their chance of an effective scene.

"But now—now it's finished. I'm as indifferent to him as if he were a stranger. I should like him to die miserable, poor, and starving, without a friend. I hope he'll rot with some loathsome disease. I've done with him."

I thought it as well then to say what Strickland had suggested.

"If you want to divorce him, he's quite willing to do whatever is necessary to make it possible."

"Why should I give him his freedom?"

"I don't think he wants it. He merely thought it might be more convenient to you."

Mrs. Strickland shrugged her shoulders impatiently. I think I was a little disappointed in her. I expected then people to be more of a piece than I do now, and I was distressed to find so much vindictiveness in so charming a creature. I did not realise how motley are the qualities that go to make up a human being. Now I am well aware that pettiness and grandeur, malice and charity, hatred and love, can find place side by side in the same human heart.

I wondered if there was anything I could say that would ease the sense of bitter humiliation which at present tormented Mrs. Strickland. I thought I would try.

"You know, I'm not sure that your husband is quite responsible for his actions. I do not think he is himself. He seems to me to be possessed by some power which is using him for its own ends, and in whose hold he is as helpless as a fly in a spider's web. It's as though someone had cast a spell over him. I'm reminded of those strange stories one sometimes hears of another personality entering into a man and driving out the old one. The soul lives unstably in the body, and is capable of mysterious transformations. In the old days they would say Charles Strickland had a devil."

Mrs. MacAndrew smoothed down the lap of her gown, and gold bangles fell over her wrists.

"All that seems to me very far-fetched," she said acidly. "I don't deny that perhaps Amy took her husband a little too much for granted. If she hadn't been so busy with her own affairs, I can't believe that she wouldn't have suspected something was the matter. I don't think that Alec could have something on his mind for a year or more without my having a pretty shrewd idea of it."

The Colonel stared into vacancy, and I wondered whether anyone could be quite so innocent of guile as he looked.

"But that doesn't prevent the fact that Charles Strickland is a heartless beast.'' She looked at me severely. ''I can tell you why he left his wife—from pure selfishness and nothing else whatever.''

''That is certainly the simplest explanation,'' I said. But I thought it explained nothing. When, saying I was tired, I rose to go, Mrs. Strickland made no attempt to detain me.

What followed showed that Mrs. Strickland was a woman of character. Whatever anguish she suffered she concealed. She saw shrewdly that the world is quickly bored by the recital of misfortune, and willingly avoids the sight of distress. Whenever she went out—and compassion for her misadventure made her friends eager to entertain her—she bore a demeanour that was perfect. She was brave, but not too obviously; cheerful, but not brazenly; and she seemed more anxious to listen to the troubles of others than to discuss her own. Whenever she spoke of her husband it was with pity. Her attitude towards him at first perplexed me. One day she said to me:

''You know, I'm convinced you were mistaken about Charles being alone. From what I've been able to gather from certain sources that I can't tell you, I know that he didn't leave England by himself.''

''In that case he has a positive genius for covering up his tracks.''

She looked away and slightly coloured.

''What I mean is, if anyone talks to you about it, please

don't contradict it if they say he eloped with somebody.''

''Of course not.''

She changed the conversation as though it were a matter to which she attached no importance. I discovered presently that a peculiar story was circulating among her friends. They said that Charles Strickland had become infatuated with a French dancer, whom he had first seen in the ballet at the Empire, and had accompanied her to Paris. I could not find out how this had arisen, but, singularly enough, it created much sympathy for Mrs. Strickland, and at the same time gave her not a little prestige. This was not without its use in the calling which she had decided to follow. Colonel MacAndrew had not exaggerated when he said she would be penniless, and it was necessary for her to earn her own living as quickly as she could. She made up her mind to profit by her acquaintance with so many writers, and without loss of time began to learn shorthand and type-writing. Her education made it likely that she would be a typist more efficient than the average, and her story made her claims appealing. Her friends promised to send her work, and took care to recommend her to all theirs.

The MacAndrews, who were childless and in easy circumstances, arranged to undertake the care of the children, and Mrs. Strickland had only herself to provide for. She let her flat and sold her furniture. She settled in two tiny rooms in Westminster, and faced the world anew. She was so efficient that it was certain she would make a success of the adventure.

It was about five years after this that I decided to live in Paris for a while. I was growing stale in London. I was tired of doing much the same thing every day. My friends pursued their course with uneventfulness; they had no longer any surprises for me, and when I met them I knew pretty well what they would say; even their love-affairs had a tedious banality. We were like tram-cars running on their lines from terminus to terminus, and it was possible to calculate within small limits the number of passengers they would carry. Life was ordered too pleasantly. I was seized with panic. I gave up my small apartment, sold my few belongings, and resolved to start afresh.

I called on Mrs. Strickland before I left. I had not seen her for some time, and I noticed changes in her: it was not only that she was older, thinner, and more lined; I think her character had altered. She had made a success of her business, and now had an office in Chancery Lane; she did little typing herself, but spent her time correcting the work of the four girls she employed. She had had the idea of giving it a certain daintiness, and she made much use of blue and red inks; she bound the copy in coarse paper, that looked vaguely like watered silk, in various pale colours; and she had acquired a reputation for neatness and accuracy. She was making money. But she could not get over the idea that to earn her living was somewhat undignified, and she was inclined to remind you that she was a lady by birth. She could not help bringing into her conversation the names of people she knew which would satisfy you that she had not sunk in the social scale. She was a little ashamed of her courage and business capacity, but delighted that she was going to dine the next night with a K.C. who lived in South Kensington. She was pleased to be able to tell you that her son was at Cambridge, and it was with a little laugh that she spoke of the rush of dances to which her daughter, just out, was invited. I suppose I said a very stupid thing.

"Is she going into your business?" I asked.

"Oh no; I wouldn't let her do that," Mrs. Strickland answered. "She's so pretty. I'm sure she'll marry well."

"I should have thought it would be a help to you."

"Several people have suggested that she should go on the stage, but of course I couldn't consent to that. I know all the chief dramatists, and I could get her a part to-morrow, but I shouldn't like her to mix with all sorts of people."

I was a little chilled by Mrs. Strickland's exclusiveness.

"Do you ever hear of your husband?"

"No; I haven't heard a word. He may be dead for all I know."

"I may run across him in Paris. Would you like me to let you know about him?"

She hesitated a minute.

"If he's in any real want I'm prepared to help him a little. I'd send you a certain sum of money, and you could give it him gradually, as he needed it."

"That's very good of you," I said.

But I knew it was not kindness that prompted the offer. It is not true that suffering ennobles the character; happiness does that sometimes, but suffering, for the most part, makes men petty and vindictive.

18

In point of fact, I met Strickland before I had been a fortnight in Paris.

I quickly found myself a tiny apartment on the fifth floor
of a house in the Rue des Dames, and for a couple of hundred francs bought at a second-hand dealer's enough furniture to make it habitable. I arranged with the concierge to
make my coffee in the morning and to keep the place clean.
Then I went to see my friend Dirk Stroeve.

Dirk Stroeve was one of those persons whom, according to
your character, you cannot think of without derisive laughter
or an embarrassed shrug of the shoulders. Nature had made
him a buffoon. He was a painter, but a very bad one, whom
I had met in Rome, and I still remembered his pictures. He
had a genuine enthusiasm for the commonplace. His soul
palpitating with love of art, he painted the models who hung
about the stairway of Bernini in the Piazza de Spagna,
undaunted by their obvious picturesqueness; and his studio
was full of canvases on which were portrayed moustachioed,
large-eyed peasants in peaked hats, urchins in becoming
rags, and women in bright petticoats. Sometimes they
lounged at the steps of a church, and sometimes dallied
among cypresses against a cloudless sky; sometimes they
made love by a Renaissance well-head, and sometimes they
wandered through the Campagna by the side of an ox-wag-
gon. They were carefully drawn and carefully painted. A
photograph could not have been more exact. One of the
painters at the Villa Medici had called him *Le Maître de la
Boîte à Chocolats*. To look at his pictures you would have

thought that Monet, Manet, and the rest of the Impressionists had never been.

"I don't pretend to be a great painter," he said. "I'm
not a Michael Angelo, no, but I have something. I sell. I
bring romance into the homes of all sorts of people. Do you
know, they buy my pictures not only in Holland, but in
Norway and Sweden and Denmark? It's mostly merchants
who buy them, and rich tradesmen. You can't imagine what
the winters are like in those countries, so long and dark and
cold. They like to think that Italy is like my pictures. That's
what they expect. That's what I expected Italy to be before
I came here."

And I think that was the vision that had remained with
him always, dazzling his eyes so that he could not see the
truth; and notwithstanding the brutality of fact, he continued to see with the eyes of the spirit an Italy of romantic
brigands and picturesque ruins. It was an ideal that he
painted—a poor one, common and shop-soiled, but still it
was an ideal; and it gave his character a peculiar charm.

It was because I felt this that Dirk Stroeve was not to me,
as to others, merely an object of ridicule. His fellow-painters
made no secret of their contempt for his work, but he
earned a fair amount of money, and they did not hesitate
to make free use of his purse. He was generous, and the
needy, laughing at him because he believed so naively their
stories of distress, borrowed from him with effrontery. He
was very emotional, yet his feeling, so easily aroused, had
in it something absurd, so that you accepted his kindness,
but felt no gratitude. To take money from him was like
robbing a child, and you despised him because he was so
foolish. I imagine that a pickpocket, proud of his light fingers, must feel a sort of indignation with the careless
woman who leaves in a cab a vanity-bag with all her jewels

in it. Nature had made him a butt, but had denied him insen-
sibility. He writhed under the jokes, practical and otherwise, which were perpetually made at his expense, and yet
never ceased, it seemed wilfully, to expose himself to them.
He was constantly wounded, and yet his good-nature was
such that he could not bear malice: the viper might sting
him, but he never learned by experience, and had no sooner
recovered from his pain than he tenderly placed it once
more in his bosom. His life was a tragedy written in the
terms of knockabout farce. Because I did not laugh at him
he was grateful to me, and he used to pour into my sympathetic ear the long list of his troubles. The saddest thing
about them was that they were grotesque, and the more
pathetic they were, the more you wanted to laugh.

But though so bad a painter, he had a very delicate feeling for art, and to go with him to picture-galleries was a
rare treat. His enthusiasm was sincere and his criticism
acute. He was catholic. He had not only a true appreciation
of the old masters, but sympathy with the moderns. He was
quick to discover talent, and his praise was generous. I think
I have never known a man whose judgment was surer. And
he was better educated than most painters. He was not, like
most of them, ignorant of kindred arts, and his taste for
music and literature gave depth and variety to his comprehension of painting. To a young man like myself his advice
and guidance were of incomparable value.

When I left Rome I corresponded with him, and about
once in two months received from him long letters in queer
English, which brought before me vividly his spluttering,
enthusiastic, gesticulating conversation. Some time before
I went to Paris he had married an Englishwoman, and was
now settled in a studio in Montmartre. I had not seen him
for four years, and had never met his wife.

I had not announced my arrival to Stroeve, and when I rang the bell of his studio, on opening the door himself, for a moment he did not know me. Then he gave a cry of delighted surprise and drew me in. It was charming to be welcomed with so much eagerness. His wife was seated near the stove at her sewing, and she rose as I came in. He introduced me.

"Don't you remember?" he said to her. "I've talked to you about him often." And then to me: "But why didn't you let me know you were coming? How long have you been here? How long are you going to stay? Why didn't you come an hour earlier, and we would have dined together?"

He bombarded me with questions. He sat me down in a chair, patting me as though I were a cushion, pressed cigars upon me, cakes, wine. He could not let me alone. He was heart-broken because he had no whisky, wanted to make coffee for me, racked his brain for something he could possibly do for me, and beamed and laughed, and in the exuberance of his delight sweated at every pore.

"You haven't changed," I said, smiling, as I looked at him.

He had the same absurd appearance that I remembered. He was a fat little man, with short legs, young still—he could not have been more than thirty—but prematurely bald. His face was perfectly round, and he had a very high colour, a white skin, red cheeks, and red lips. His eyes were blue and round too, he wore large gold-rimmed spectacles, and his eyebrows were so fair that you could not see them. He reminded you of those jolly, fat merchants that Rubens painted.

When I told him that I meant to live in Paris for a while, and had taken an apartment, he reproached me bitterly for not having let him know. He would have found me an apartment himself, and lent me furniture—did I really mean that I had gone to the expense of buying it?—and he would have helped me to move in. He really looked upon it as unfriendly that I had not given him the opportunity of making himself useful to me. Meanwhile, Mrs. Stroeve sat quietly mending her stockings, without talking, and she listened to all he said with a quiet smile on her lips.

"So, you see, I'm married," he said suddenly; "what do you think of my wife?"

He beamed at her, and settled his spectacles on the bridge of his nose. The sweat made them constantly slip down.

"What on earth do you expect me to say to that?" I laughed.

"Really, Dirk," put in Mrs. Stroeve, smiling.

"But isn't she wonderful? I tell you, my boy, lose no time; get married as soon as ever you can. I'm the happiest man alive. Look at her sitting there. Doesn't she make a picture? Chardin, eh? I've seen all the most beautiful women in the world; I've never seen anyone more beautiful than Madame Dirk Stroeve."

"If you don't be quiet, Dirk, I shall go away."

"*Mon petit choux,*" he said.

She flushed a little, embarrassed by the passion in his tone. His letters had told me that he was very much in love with his wife, and I saw that he could hardly take his eyes off her. I could not tell if she loved him. Poor pantaloon, he was not an object to excite love, but the smile in her eyes was affectionate, and it was possible that her reserve concealed a very deep feeling. She was not the ravishing creature that his love-sick fancy saw, but she had a grave comeliness. She was rather tall, and her gray dress, simple and quite well-cut, did not hide the fact that her figure was beautiful. It was a figure that might have appealed more to the sculptor than to the costumier. Her hair, brown and abundant, was plainly done, her face was very pale, and her features were good without being distinguished. She

"I wondered why she had married Dirk Stroeve"

had quiet gray eyes. She just missed being beautiful, and in missing it was not even pretty. But when Stroeve spoke of Chardin it was not without reason, and she reminded me curiously of that pleasant housewife in her mob-cap and apron whom the great painter has immortalised. I could imagine her sedately busy among her pots and pans, making a ritual of her household duties, so that they acquired a moral significance; I did not suppose that she was clever or could ever be amusing, but there was something in her grave intentness which excited my interest. Her reserve was not without mystery. I wondered why she had married Dirk Stroeve. Though she was English, I could not exactly place her, and it was not obvious from what rank in society she sprang, what had been her upbringing, or how she had lived before her marriage. She was very silent, but when she spoke it was with a pleasant voice, and her manners were natural.

I asked Stroeve if he was working.

"Working? I'm painting better than I've ever painted before."

We sat in the studio, and he waved his hand to an unfinished picture on an easel. I gave a little start. He was painting a group of Italian peasants, in the costume of the Campagna, lounging on the steps of a Roman church.

"Is that what you're doing now?" I asked.

"Yes. I can get my models here just as well as in Rome."

"Don't you think it's very beautiful?" said Mrs. Stroeve.

"This foolish wife of mine thinks I'm a great artist," said he.

His apologetic laugh did not disguise the pleasure that he felt. His eyes lingered on his picture. It was strange that his critical sense, so accurate and unconventional when he dealt with the work of others, should be satisfied in himself with what was hackneyed and vulgar beyond belief.

"Show him some more of your pictures," she said.

"Shall I?"

Though he had suffered so much from the ridicule of his friends, Dirk Stroeve, eager for praise and naively self-satisfied, could never resist displaying his work. He brought out a picture of two curly-headed Italian urchins playing marbles.

"Aren't they sweet?" said Mrs. Stroeve.

And then he showed me more. I discovered that in Paris he had been painting just the same stale, obviously pictur-esque things that he had painted for years in Rome. It was all false, insincere, shoddy; and yet no one was more honest, sincere, and frank than Dirk Stroeve. Who could resolve the contradiction?

I do not know what put it into my head to ask:

"I say, have you by any chance run across a painter called Charles Strickland?"

"You don't mean to say you know him?" cried Stroeve.

"Beast," said his wife.

Stroeve laughed.

"*Ma pauvre chèrie.*" He went over to her and kissed both her hands. "She doesn't like him. How strange that you should know Strickland!"

"I don't like bad manners," said Mrs. Stroeve.

Dirk, laughing still, turned to me to explain.

"You see, I asked him to come here one day and look at my pictures. Well, he came, and I showed him everything I had." Stroeve hesitated a moment with embarrassment. I do not know why he had begun the story against himself; he felt an awkwardness at finishing it. "He looked at—at my pictures, and he didn't say anything. I thought he was reserving his judgment till the end. And at last I said:

'There, that's the lot!' He said: 'I came to ask you to lend me twenty francs.' ''

"And Dirk actually gave it him," said his wife indignantly.

"I was so taken aback. I didn't like to refuse. He put the money in his pocket, just nodded, said 'Thanks,' and walked out."

Dirk Stroeve, telling the story, had such a look of blank astonishment on his round, foolish face that it was almost impossible not to laugh.

"I shouldn't have minded if he'd said my pictures were bad, but he said nothing—nothing."

"And you *will* tell the story, Dirk," said his wife.

It was lamentable that one was more amused by the ridiculous figure cut by the Dutchman than outraged by Strickland's brutal treatment of him.

"I hope I shall never see him again," said Mrs. Stroeve.

Stroeve smiled and shrugged his shoulders. He had already recovered his good-humour.

"The fact remains that he's a great artist, a very great artist."

"Strickland?" I exclaimed. "It can't be the same man."

"A big fellow with a red beard. Charles Strickland. An Englishman."

"He had no beard when I knew him, but if he had grown one it might well be red. The man I'm thinking of only began painting five years ago."

"That's it. He's a great artist."

"Impossible."

"Have I ever been mistaken?" Dirk asked me. "I tell you he has genius. I'm convinced of it. In a hundred years, if you and I are remembered at all, it will be because we knew Charles Strickland."

I was astonished, and at the same time I was very much excited. I remembered suddenly my last talk with him.

"Where can one see his work?" I asked. "Is he having any success? Where is he living?"

"No; he has no success. I don't think he's ever sold a picture. When you speak to men about him they only laugh. But I *know* he's a great artist. After all, they laughed at Manet. Corot never sold a picture. I don't know where he lives, but I can take you to see him. He goes to a café in the Avenue de Clichy at seven o'clock every evening. If you like we'll go there to-morrow."

"I'm not sure if he'll wish to see me. I think I may remind him of a time he prefers to forget. But I'll come all the same. Is there any chance of seeing any of his pictures?"

"Not from him. He won't show you a thing. There's a little dealer I know who has two or three. But you mustn't go without me; you wouldn't understand. I must show them to you myself."

"Dirk, you make me impatient," said Mrs. Stroeve. "How can you talk like that about his pictures when he treated you as he did?" She turned to me. "Do you know, when some Dutch people came here to buy Dirk's pictures he tried to persuade them to buy Strickland's? He insisted on bringing them here to show."

"What did *you* think of them?" I asked her, smiling.

"They were awful."

"Ah, sweetheart, you don't understand."

"Well, your Dutch people were furious with you. They thought you were having a joke with them."

Dirk Stroeve took off his spectacles and wiped them. His flushed face was shining with excitement.

"Why should you think that beauty, which is the most precious thing in the world, lies like a stone on the beach for the careless passer-by to pick up idly? Beauty is something wonderful and strange that the artist fashions out of the chaos of the world in the torment of his soul. And when he has made it, it is not given to all to know it. To recognise it you must repeat the adventure of the artist. It is a melody that he sings to you, and to hear it again in your own heart you want knowledge and sensitiveness and imagination.''

''Why did I always think your pictures beautiful, Dirk? I admired them the very first time I saw them.''

Stroeve's lips trembled a little.

''Go to bed, my precious. I will walk a few steps with our friend, and then I will come back.''

Dirk Stroeve agreed to fetch me on the following evening and take me to the café at which Strickland was most likely to be found. I was interested to learn that it was the same as that at which Strickland and I had drunk absinthe when I had gone over to Paris to see him. The fact that he had never changed suggested a sluggishness of habit which seemed to me characteristic.

''There he is,'' said Stroeve, as we reached the café.

Though it was October, the evening was warm, and the tables on the pavement were crowded. I ran my eyes over them, but did not see Strickland.

''Look. Over there, in the corner. He's playing chess.''

I noticed a man bending over a chess-board, but could see only a large felt hat and a red beard. We threaded our way among the tables till we came to him.

*"We threaded our way among the
tables until we came to him"*

"Strickland."

He looked up.

"Hulloa, fatty. What do you want?"

"I've brought an old friend to see you."

Strickland gave me a glance, and evidently did not recognise me. He resumed his scrutiny of the chess-board.

"Sit down, and don't make a noise," he said.

He moved a piece and straightway became absorbed in
the game. Poor Stroeve gave me a troubled look, but I was

not disconcerted by so little. I ordered something to drink, and waited quietly till Strickland had finished. I welcomed the opportunity to examine him at my ease. I certainly should never have known him. In the first place his red beard, ragged and untrimmed, hid much of his face, and his hair was long; but the most surprising change in him was his extreme thinness. It made his great nose protrude more arrogantly; it emphasized his cheekbones; it made his eyes seem larger. There were deep hollows at his temples. His body was cadaverous. He wore the same suit that I had seen him in five years before; it was torn and stained, threadbare, and it hung upon him loosely, as though it had been made for someone else. I noticed his hands, dirty, with long nails; they were merely bone and sinew, large and strong; but I had forgotten that they were so shapely. He gave me an extraordinary impression as he sat there, his attention riveted on his game—an impression of great strength; and I could not understand why it was that his emaciation somehow made it more striking.

Presently, after moving, he leaned back and gazed with a curious abstraction at his antagonist. This was a fat, bearded Frenchman. The Frenchman considered the position, then broke suddenly into jovial expletives, and with an impatient gesture, gathered up the pieces, flung them into their box. He cursed Strickland freely, then, calling for the waiter, paid for the drinks, and left. Stroeve drew his chair closer to the table.

"Now I suppose we can talk," he said.

Strickland's eyes rested on him, and there was in them a malicious expression. I felt sure he was seeking for some gibe, could think of none, and so was forced to silence.

"I've brought an old friend to see you," repeated Stroeve, beaming cheerfully.

Strickland looked at me thoughtfully for nearly a minute. I did not speak.

"I've never seen him in my life," he said.

I do not know why he said this, for I felt certain I had caught a gleam of recognition in his eyes. I was not so easily abashed as I had been some years earlier.

"I saw your wife the other day," I said. "I felt sure you'd like to have the latest news of her."

He gave a short laugh. His eyes twinkled.

"We had a jolly evening together," he said. "How long ago is it?"

"Five years."

He called for another absinthe. Stroeve, with voluble tongue, explained how he and I had met, and by what an accident we discovered that we both knew Strickland. I do not know if Strickland listened. He glanced at me once or twice reflectively, but for the most part seemed occupied with his own thoughts; and certainly without Stroeve's babble the conversation would have been difficult. In half an hour the Dutchman, looking at his watch, announced that he must go. He asked whether I would come too. I thought, alone, I might get something out of Strickland, and so answered that I would stay.

When the fat man had left I said:

"Dirk Stroeve thinks you're a great artist."

"What the hell do you suppose I care?"

"Will you let me see your pictures?"

"Why should I?"

"I might feel inclined to buy one."

"I might not feel inclined to sell one."

"Are you making a good living?" I asked, smiling.

He chuckled.

"Do I look it?"

"You look half starved."

"I am half starved."

"Then come and let's have a bit of dinner."

"Why do you ask me?"

"Not out of charity," I answered coolly. "I don't really care a twopenny damn if you starve or not."

His eyes lit up again.

"Come on, then," he said, getting up. "I'd like a decent meal."

I let him take me to a restaurant of his choice, but on the way I bought a paper. When we had ordered our dinner, I propped it against a bottle of St. Galmier and began to read. We ate in silence. I felt him looking at me now and again, but I took no notice. I meant to force him to conversation.

"Is there anything in the paper?" he said, as we approached the end of our silent meal.

I fancied there was in his tone a slight note of exasperation.

"I always like to read the *feuilleton* on the drama," I said.

I folded the paper and put it down beside me.

"I've enjoyed my dinner," he remarked.

"I think we might have our coffee here, don't you?"

"Yes."

We lit our cigars. I smoked in silence. I noticed that now and then his eyes rested on me with a faint smile of amusement. I waited patiently until he might be ready to speak.

"What have you been up to since I saw you last?" he asked at length.

I had not very much to say. It was a record of hard work and of little adventure; of experiments in this direction and in that; of the gradual acquisition of the knowledge of books and of men. I took care to ask Strickland nothing about his own doings. I showed not the least interest in him, and at last I was rewarded. He began to talk of himself. But with his poor gift of expression he gave but indications of what he had gone through, and I had to fill up the gaps with my own imagination. It was tantalising to get no more than hints into a character that interested me so much. It was like making one's way through a mutilated manuscript. I received the impression of a life which was a bitter struggle against every sort of difficulty; but I realised that much which would have seemed horrible to most people did not in the least affect him. Strickland was distinguished from most Englishmen by his perfect indifference to comfort; it did not irk him to live always in one shabby room; he had no need to be surrounded by beautiful things. I do not suppose he had ever noticed how dingy was the paper on the wall of the room in which on my first visit I found him. He did not want arm-chairs to sit in; he really felt more at his ease on a kitchen chair. He ate with appetite, but was indifferent to what he ate; to him it was only food that he devoured to still the pangs of hunger; and when no food was to be had he seemed capable of doing without. I learned that for six months he had lived on a loaf of bread and a bottle of milk a day. He was a sensual man, and yet was indifferent to sensual things. He looked upon privation as no hardship. There was something impressive in the manner in which he lived a life wholly of the spirit.

When the small sum of money which he brought with him from London came to an end he suffered from no dismay. He sold no pictures; I think he made little attempt to sell any; he set about finding some way to make a bit of money. He told me with grim humour of the time he had spent acting as guide to Cockneys who wanted to see the night side of life in Paris; it was an occupation that appealed to his sardonic temper and somehow or other he had acquired a wide acquaintance with the more disreputable quarters of the city. He told me of the long hours he spent walking about the Boulevard de la Madeleine on the lookout for Englishmen, preferably the worse for liquor, who desired to see things which the law forbade. When in luck he was able to make a tidy sum; but the shabbiness of his clothes at last frightened the sight-seers, and he could not find people adventurous enough to trust themselves to him. Then he happened on a job to translate the advertisements of patent medicines which were sent broadcast to the medical profession in England. During a strike he had been employed as a house-painter.

Meanwhile he had never ceased to work at his art; but had soon tired of the studios, entirely by himself. He had never been so poor that he could not buy canvas and paint, and really he needed nothing else. So far as I could make out, he painted with great difficulty, and in his unwillingness to accept help from anyone lost much time in finding out for himself the solution of technical problems which preceding generations had already worked out one by one. He was aiming at something, I knew not what, and perhaps he hardly knew himself; and I got again more strongly the impression of a man possessed. He did not seem quite sane. It seemed to me that he would not show his pictures because he was really not interested in them. He lived in a dream,

and the reality meant nothing to him. I had the feeling
that he worked on a canvas with all the force of his violent
personality, oblivious of everything in his effort to get what
he saw with the mind's eye; and then, having finished, not
the picture perhaps, for I had an idea that he seldom
brought anything to completion, but the passion that fired
him, he lost all care for it. He was never satisfied with what
he had done; it seemed to him of no consequence compared
with the vision that obsessed his mind.

"Why don't you ever send your work to exhibitions?"
I asked. "I should have thought you'd like to know what
people thought about it."

"Would you?"

I cannot describe the unmeasurable contempt he put into
the two words.

"Don't you want fame? It's something that most artists
haven't been indifferent to."

"Children. How can you care for the opinion of the
crowd, when you don't care twopence for the opinion of the
individual?"

"We're not all reasonable beings," I laughed.

"Who makes fame? Critics, writers, stockbrokers,
women."

"Wouldn't it give you a rather pleasing sensation to
think of people you didn't know and had never seen receiv-
ing emotions, subtle and passionate, from the work of your
hands? Everyone likes power. I can't imagine a more wonderful exercise of it than to move the souls of men to pity
or terror."

"Melodrama."

"Why do you mind if you paint well or badly?"

"I don't. I only want to paint what I see."

"I wonder if I could write on a desert island, with the

certainty that no eyes but mine would ever see what I had written.''

Strickland did not speak for a long time, but his eyes shone strangely, as though he saw something that kindled his soul to ecstasy.

''Sometimes I've thought of an island lost in a boundless sea, where I could live in some hidden valley, among strange trees, in silence. There I think I could find what I want.''

He did not express himself quite like this. He used gestures instead of adjectives, and he halted. I have put into my own words what I think he wanted to say.

''Looking back on the last five years, do you think it was worth it?'' I asked.

He looked at me, and I saw that he did not know what I meant. I explained.

''You gave up a comfortable home and a life as happy as the average. You were fairly prosperous. You seem to have had a rotten time in Paris. If you had your time over again would you do what you did?''

''Rather.''

''Do you know that you haven't asked anything about your wife and children? Do you never think of them?''

''No.''

''I wish you weren't so damned monosyllabic. Have you never had a moment's regret for all the unhappiness you caused them?''

His lips broke into a smile, and he shook his head.

''I should have thought sometimes you couldn't help thinking of the past. I don't mean the past of seven or eight years ago, but further back still, when you first met your wife, and loved her, and married her. Don't you remember the joy with which you first took her in your arms?''

"I don't think of the past. The only thing that matters is the everlasting present."

I thought for a moment over this reply. It was obscure, perhaps, but I thought that I saw dimly his meaning.

"Are you happy?" I asked.

"Yes."

I was silent. I looked at him reflectively. He held my stare, and presently a sardonic twinkle lit up his eyes.

"I'm afraid you disapprove of me?"

"Nonsense," I answered promptly; "I don't disapprove of the boa-constrictor; on the contrary, I'm interested in his mental processes."

"It's a purely professional interest you take in me?"

"Purely."

"It's only right that you shouldn't disapprove of me. You have a despicable character."

"Perhaps that's why you feel at home with me," I retorted.

He smiled dryly, but said nothing. I wish I knew how to describe his smile. I do not know that it was attractive, but it lit up his face, changing the expression, which was generally sombre, and gave it a look of not ill-natured malice. It was a slow smile, starting and sometimes ending in the eyes; it was very sensual, neither cruel nor kindly, but suggested rather the inhuman glee of the satyr. It was his smile that made me ask him:

"Haven't you been in love since you came to Paris?"

"I haven't got time for that sort of nonsense. Life isn't long enough for love and art."

"Your appearance doesn't suggest the anchorite."

"All that business fills me with disgust."

"Human nature is a nuisance, isn't it?" I said.

"Why are you sniggering at me?"

"Because I don't believe you."

"Then you're a damned fool."

I paused, and I looked at him searchingly.

"What's the good of trying to humbug me?" I said.

"I don't know what you mean."

I smiled.

"Let me tell you. I imagine that for months the matter never comes into your head, and you're able to persuade yourself that you've finished with it for good and all. You rejoice in your freedom, and you feel that at last you can call your soul your own. You seem to walk with your head among the stars. And then, all of a sudden you can't stand it any more, and you notice that all the time your feet have been walking in the mud. And you want to roll yourself in it. And you find some woman, coarse and low and vulgar, some beastly creature in whom all the horror of sex is blatant, and you fall upon her like a wild animal. You drink till you're blind with rage."

He stared at me without the slightest movement. I held his eyes with mine. I spoke very slowly.

"I'll tell you what must seem strange, that when it's over you feel so extraordinarily pure. You feel like a disembodied spirit, immaterial; and you seem to be able to touch beauty as though it were a palpable thing; and you feel an intimate communion with the breeze, and with the trees breaking into leaf, and with the iridescence of the river. You feel like God. Can you explain that to me?"

He kept his eyes fixed on mine till I had finished, and then he turned away. There was on his face a strange look, and I thought that so might a man look when he had died under the torture. He was silent. I knew that our conversation was ended.

I settled down in Paris and began to write a play. I led a very regular life, working in the morning, and in the afternoon lounging about the gardens of the Luxembourg or sauntering through the streets. I spent long hours in the Louvre, the most friendly of all galleries and the most convenient for meditation; or idled on the quays, fingering second-hand books that I never meant to buy. I read a page here and there, and made acquaintance with a great many authors whom I was content to know thus desultorily. In the evenings I went to see my friends. I looked in often on the Stroeves, and sometimes shared their modest fare. Dirk Stroeve flattered himself on his skill in cooking Italian dishes, and I confess that his *spaghetti* were very much better than his pictures. It was a dinner for a King when he brought in a huge dish of it, succulent with tomatoes, and we ate it together with the good household bread and a bottle of red wine. I grew more intimate with Blanche Stroeve, and I think, because I was English and she knew few English people, she was glad to see me. She was pleasant and simple, but she remained always rather silent, and I knew not why, gave me the impression that she was concealing something. But I thought that was perhaps no more than a natural reserve accentuated by the verbose frankness of her husband. Dirk never concealed anything. He discussed the most intimate matters with a complete lack of self-consciousness. Sometimes he embarrassed his wife, and the only time I saw her put out of countenance was when he insisted on telling me that he had taken a purge, and went into somewhat realistic details on the subject. The

"I looked in often on the Stroeves"

perfect seriousness with which he narrated his misfortunes convulsed me with laughter, and this added to Mrs. Stroeve's irritation.

"You seem to like making a fool of yourself," she said.

His round eyes grew rounder still, and his brow puckered in dismay as he saw that she was angry.

"Sweetheart, have I vexed you? I'll never take another. It was only because I was bilious. I lead a sedentary life. I don't take enough exercise. For three days I hadn't . . ."

"For goodness sake, hold your tongue," she interrupted, tears of annoyance in her eyes.

His face fell, and he pouted his lips like a scolded child. He gave me a look of appeal, so that I might put things right, but, unable to control myself, I shook with helpless laughter.

We went one day to the picture-dealer in whose shop Stroeve thought he could show me at least two or three of Strickland's pictures, but when we arrived were told that Strickland himself had taken them away. The dealer did not know why.

"But don't imagine to yourself that I make myself bad blood on that account. I took them to oblige Monsieur Stroeve, and I said I would sell them if I could. But really——" He shrugged his shoulders. "I'm interested in the young men, but *voyons,* you yourself, Monsieur Stroeve, you don't think there's any talent there."

"I give you my word of honour, there's no one painting to-day in whose talent I am more convinced. Take my word for it, you are missing a good affair. Some day those pictures will be worth more than all you have in your shop. Remember Monet, who could not get anyone to buy his pictures for a hundred francs. What are they worth now?"

"True. But there were a hundred as good painters as Monet who couldn't sell their pictures at that time, and their pictures are worth nothing still. How can one tell? Is merit enough to bring success? Don't believe it. *Du reste,* it has still to be proved that this friend of yours has merit. No one claims it for him but Monsieur Stroeve."

"And how, then, will you recognise merit?" asked Dirk,

red in the face with an anger he could not possibly conceal.

"There is only one way—by success."

"Philistine," cried Dirk.

"But think of the great artists of the past—Raphael, Michael Angelo, Ingres, Delacroix—they were all successful."

"Let us go," said Stroeve to me, "or I shall kill this man."

I saw Strickland not infrequently, and now and then played chess with him. He was of uncertain temper. Sometimes he would sit silent and abstracted, taking no notice of anyone; and at others when he was in a good humour, he would talk in his own halting way. He never said a clever thing, but he had a vein of brutal sarcasm which was not ineffective, and he always said exactly what he thought. He was indifferent to the susceptibilities of others, and when he wounded them was amused. He was constantly offending Dirk Stroeve so bitterly that he flung away, vowing he would never speak to him again; but there was a solid force in Strickland that attracted the fat Dutchman against his will, so that he came back, fawning like a clumsy dog, though he knew that his only greeting would be the blow he dreaded.

I do not know why Strickland put up with me. Our relations were peculiar. One day he asked me to lend him fifty francs.

"I wouldn't dream of it," I replied.

"Why not?"

"It wouldn't amuse me."

"I'm frightfully hard up, you know."

"I don't care."

"You don't care if I starve?"

"Why on earth should I?" I asked in my turn.

He looked at me for a minute or two, pulling his untidy beard. I smiled at him.

"What are you amused at?" he said, with a gleam of anger in his eyes.

"You're so simple. You recognise no obligations. No one is under any obligation to you."

"Wouldn't it make you uncomfortable if I went and hanged myself because I'd been turned out of my room as I couldn't pay the rent?"

"Not a bit."

He chuckled.

"You're bragging. If I really did you'd be overwhelmed with remorse."

"Try it, and we'll see," I retorted.

A smile flickered in his eyes, and he stirred his absinthe in silence.

"Would you like to play chess?" I asked.

"I don't mind."

We set up the pieces, and when the board was ready he considered it with a comfortable eye. There is a sense of satisfaction in looking at your men all ready for the fray.

"Did you really think I'd lend you money?" I asked.

"I didn't see why you shouldn't."

"You surprise me."

"Why?"

"It's disappointing to find that at heart you are sentimental. I should have liked you better if you hadn't made that ingenuous appeal so directly to my sympathies."

"I should have despised you if you'd been moved by it," he answered.

"That's better," I laughed.

We began to play. We were both absorbed in the game. When it was finished I said to him:

"Look here, if you're hard up, let me see your pictures. If there's anything I like I'll buy it."

"Go to hell," he answered.

He got up and was about to go away. I stopped him.

"You haven't paid for your absinthe," I said, smiling.

He cursed me, flung down the money and left.

I did not see him for several days after that, but one evening, when I was sitting in the café, reading a paper, he came up and sat beside me.

"You haven't hanged yourself after all," I remarked.

"No. I've got a commission. I'm painting the portrait of a retired plumber for two hundred francs."*

"How did you manage that?"

"The woman where I get my bread recommended me. He'd told her he was looking out for someone to paint him. I've got to give her twenty francs."

"What's he like?"

"Splendid. He's got a great red face like a leg of mutton, and on his right cheek there's an enormous mole with long hairs growing out of it."

Strickland was in a good humour, and when Dirk Stroeve came up and sat down with us he attacked him with ferocious banter. He showed a skill I should never have credited him with in finding the places where the unhappy Dutchman

---

* This picture, formerly in the possession of a wealthy manufacturer at Lille, who fled from that city on the approach of the Germans, is now in the National Gallery at Stockholm. The Swede is adept at the gentle pastime of fishing in troubled waters.

was most sensitive. Strickland employed not the rapier of
sarcasm but the bludgeon of invective. The attack was so
unprovoked that Stroeve, taken unawares, was defenceless.
He reminded you of a frightened sheep running aimlessly
hither and thither. He was startled and amazed. At last the
tears ran from his eyes. And the worst of it was that,
though you hated Strickland, and the exhibition was horrible, it was impossible not to laugh. Dirk Stroeve was one
of those unlucky persons whose most sincere emotions are
ridiculous.

But after all when I look back upon that winter in Paris,
my pleasantest recollection is of Dirk Stroeve. There was
something very charming in his little household. He and
his wife made a picture which the imagination gratefully
dwelt upon, and the simplicity of his love for her had a
deliberate grace. He remained absurd, but the sincerity of
his passion excited one's sympathy. I could understand
how his wife must feel for him, and I was glad that her
affection was so tender. If she had any sense of humour,
it must amuse her that he should place her on a pedestal
and worship her with such an honest idolatry, but even
while she laughed she must have been pleased and touched.
He was the constant lover, and though she grew old, losing
her rounded lines and her fair comeliness, to him she would
certainly never alter. To him she would always be the love-
liest woman in the world. There was a pleasing grace in
the orderliness of their lives. They had but the studio, a
bedroom, and a tiny kitchen. Mrs. Stroeve did all the house-
work herself; and while Dirk painted bad pictures, she
went marketing, cooked the luncheon, sewed, occupied herself like a busy ant all the day; and in the evening sat in
the studio, sewing again, while Dirk played music which I
am sure was far beyond her comprehension. He played with

taste, but with more feeling than was always justified, and into his music poured all his honest, sentimental, exuberant soul.

Their life in its own way was an idyl, and it managed to achieve a singular beauty. The absurdity that clung to everything connected with Dirk Stroeve gave it a curious note, like an unresolved discord, but made it somehow more modern, more human; like a rough joke thrown into a serious scene, it heightened the poignancy which all beauty has.

Shortly before Christmas Dirk Stroeve came to ask me to spend the holiday with him. He had a characteristic sentimentality about the day and wanted to pass it among his friends with suitable ceremonies. Neither of us had seen Strickland for two or three weeks—I because I had been busy with friends who were spending a little while in Paris, and Stroeve because, having quarrelled with him more violently than usual, he had made up his mind to have nothing more to do with him. Strickland was impossible, and he swore never to speak to him again. But the season touched him with gentle feeling, and he hated the thought of Strickland spending Christmas Day by himself; he ascribed his own emotions to him, and could not bear that on an occasion given up to good-fellowship the lonely painter should be abandoned to his own melancholy. Stroeve had set up a Christmas-tree in his studio, and I suspected that we should both find absurd little presents hanging on its festive branches; but he was shy about seeing Strickland again;

it was a little humiliating to forgive so easily insults so outrageous, and he wished me to be present at the reconcilia-
tion on which he was determined.

We walked together down the Avenue de Clichy, but
Strickland was not in the café. It was too cold to sit outside,
and we took our places on leather benches within. It was hot
and stuffy, and the air was gray with smoke. Strickland did
not come, but presently we saw the French painter who
occasionally played chess with him. I had formed a casual
acquaintance with him, and he sat down at our table.
Stroeve asked him if he had seen Strickland.

"He's ill," he said. "Didn't you know?"

"Seriously?"

"Very, I understand."

Stroeve's face grew white.

"Why didn't he write and tell me? How stupid of me to
quarrel with him. We must go to him at once. He can have
no one to look after him. Where does he live?"

"I have no idea," said the Frenchman.

We discovered that none of us knew how to find him.
Stroeve grew more and more distressed.

"He might die, and not a soul would know anything about
it. It's dreadful. I can't bear the thought. We must find him
at once."

I tried to make Stroeve understand that it was absurd
to hunt vaguely about Paris. We must first think of some
plan.

"Yes; but all this time he may be dying, and when we
get there it may be too late to do anything."

"Sit still and let us think," I said impatiently.

The only address I knew was the Hôtel des Belges, but
Strickland had long left that, and they would have no recollection of him. With that queer idea of his to keep his where-

abouts secret, it was unlikely that, on leaving, he had said where he was going. Besides, it was more than five years ago. I felt pretty sure that he had not moved far. If he continued to frequent the same café as when he had stayed at the hotel, it was probably because it was the most convenient. Suddenly I remembered that he had got his commission to paint a portrait through the baker from whom he bought his bread, and it struck me that there one might find his address. I called for a directory and looked out the bakers. There were five in the immediate neighbourhood, and the only thing was to go to all of them. Stroeve accompanied me unwillingly. His own plan was to run up and down the streets that led out of the Avenue de Clichy and ask at every house if Strickland lived there. My commonplace scheme, was after all, effective, for in the second shop we asked at the woman behind the counter acknowledged that she knew him. She was not certain where he lived, but it was in one of the three houses opposite. Luck favoured us, and in the first we tried the concierge told us that we should find him on the top floor.

"It appears that he's ill," said Stroeve.

"It may be," answered the concierge indifferently. *"En effet,* I have not seem him for several days."

Stroeve ran up the stairs ahead of me, and when I reached the top floor I found him talking to a workman in his shirt-sleeves who had opened a door at which Stroeve had knocked. He pointed to another door. He believed that the person who lived there was a painter. He had not seen him for a week. Stroeve made as though he were about to knock, and then turned to me with a gesture of helplessness. I saw that he was panic-stricken.

"Supposing he's dead?"

"Not he," I said.

I knocked. There was no answer. I tried the handle, and found the door unlocked. I walked in, and Stroeve followed me. The room was in darkness. I could only see that it was an attic, with a sloping roof; and a faint glimmer, no more than a less profound obscurity, came from a skylight.

"Strickland," I called.

"For a moment I hesitated to strike a light"

There was no answer. It was really rather mysterious, and it seemed to me that Stroeve, standing just behind, was trembling in his shoes. For a moment I hesitated to strike a light. I dimly perceived a bed in the corner, and I wondered whether the light would disclose lying on it a dead body.

"Haven't you got a match, you fool?"

Strickland's voice, coming out of the darkness, harshly, made me start.

Stroeve cried out.

"Oh, my God, I thought you were dead."

I struck a match, and looked about for a candle. I had a rapid glimpse of a tiny apartment, half room, half studio, in which was nothing but a bed, canvases with their faces to the wall, an easel, a table, and a chair. There was no carpet on the floor. There was no fire-place. On the table, crowded with paints, palette-knives, and litter of all kinds, was the end of a candle. I lit it. Strickland was lying in the bed, uncomfortably because it was too small for him, and he had put all his clothes over him for warmth. It was obvious at a glance that he was in a high fever. Stroeve, his voice cracking with emotion, went up to him.

"Oh, my poor friend, what is the matter with you? I had no idea you were ill. Why didn't you let me know? You must know I'd have done anything in the world for you. Were you thinking of what I said? I didn't mean it. I was wrong. It was stupid of me to take offence."

"Go to hell," said Strickland.

"Now, be reasonable. Let me make you comfortable. Haven't you anyone to look after you?"

He looked round the squalid attic in dismay. He tried to arrange the bed-clothes. Strickland, breathing laboriously, kept an angry silence. He gave me a resentful glance. I stood quite quietly, looking at him.

"If you want to do something for me, you can get me some milk," he said at last. "I haven't been able to get out for two days."

There was an empty bottle by the side of the bed, which had contained milk, and in a piece of newspaper a few crumbs.

"What have you been having?" I asked.

"Nothing."

"For how long?" cried Stroeve. "Do you mean to say you've had nothing to eat or drink for two days? It's horrible."

"I've had water."

His eyes dwelt for a moment on a large can within reach of an outstretched arm.

"I'll go immediately," said Stroeve. "Is there anything you fancy?"

I suggested that he should get a thermometer, and a few grapes, and some bread. Stroeve, glad to make himself useful, clattered down the stairs.

"Damned fool," muttered Strickland.

I felt his pulse. It was beating quickly and feebly. I asked him one or two questions, but he would not answer, and when I pressed him he turned his face irritably to the wall. The only thing was to wait in silence. In ten minutes Stroeve, panting, came back. Besides what I had suggested, he brought candles, and meat-juice, and a spirit-lamp. He was a practical little fellow, and without delay set about making bread-and-milk. I took Strickland's temperature. It was a hundred and four. He was obviously very ill.

Presently we left him. Dirk was going home to dinner, and I proposed to find a doctor and bring him to see Strickland; but when we got down into the street, fresh after the stuffy attic, the Dutchman begged me to go immediately to his studio. He had something in mind which he would not tell me, but he insisted that it was very necessary for me to accompany him. Since I did not think a doctor could at the moment do any more than we had done, I consented. We found Blanche Stroeve laying the table for dinner. Dirk went up to her, and took both her hands.

"Dear one, I want you to do something for me," he said.

She looked at him with the grave cheerfulness which was one of her charms. His red face was shining with sweat, and he had a look of comic agitation, but there was in his round, surprised eyes an eager light.

"Strickland is very ill. He may be dying. He is alone in a filthy attic, and there is not a soul to look after him. I want you to let me bring him here."

She withdrew her hands quickly, I had never seen her make so rapid a movement, and her cheeks flushed.

"Oh no."

"Oh, my dear one, don't refuse. I couldn't bear to leave him where he is. I shouldn't sleep a wink for thinking of him."

"I have no objection to your nursing him."

Her voice was cold and distant.

"But he'll die."

"Let him."

Stroeve gave a little gasp. He wiped his face. He turned
to me for support, but I did not know what to say.

"He's a great artist."

"What do I care? I hate him."

"Oh, my love, my precious, you don't mean that. I beseech you to let me bring him here. We can make him comfortable. Perhaps we can save him. He shall be no trouble
to you. I will do everything. We'll make him up a bed in
the studio. We can't let him die like a dog. It would be inhuman."

"Why can't he go to a hospital?"

"A hospital! He needs the care of loving hands. He must
be treated with infinite tact."

I was surprised to see how moved she was. She went on
laying the table, but her hands trembled.

"I have no patience with you. Do you think if you were
ill he would stir a finger to help you?"

"But what does that matter? I should have you to nurse
me. It wouldn't be necessary. And besides, I'm different;
I'm not of any importance."

"You have no more spirit than a mongrel cur. You lie
down on the ground and ask people to trample on you."

Stroeve gave a little laugh. He thought he understood
the reason of his wife's attitude.

"Oh, my poor dear, you're thinking of that day he came
here to look at my pictures. What does it matter if he
didn't think them any good? It was stupid of me to show
them to him. I dare say they're not very good."

He looked round the studio ruefully. On the easel was
a half-finished picture of a smiling Italian peasant, holding
a bunch of grapes over the head of a dark-eyed girl.

"Even if he didn't like them he should have been civil.
He needn't have insulted you. He showed that he despised

you, and you lick his hand. Oh, I hate him.''

''Dear child, he has genius. You don't think I believe that I have it. I wish I had; but I know it when I see it, and I honour it with all my heart. It's the most wonderful thing in the world. It's a great burden to its possessors. We should be very tolerant with them, and very patient.''

I stood apart, somewhat embarrassed by the domestic scene, and wondered why Stroeve had insisted on my coming with him. I saw that his wife was on the verge of tears.

''But it's not only because he's a genius that I ask you to let me bring him here; it's because he's a human being, and he is ill and poor.''

''I will never have him in my house—never.''

Stroeve turned to me.

''Tell her that it's a matter of life and death. It's impossible to leave him in that wretched hole.''

''It's quite obvious that it would be much easier to nurse him here,'' I said, ''but of course it would be very inconvenient. I have an idea that someone will have to be with him day and night.''

''My love, it's not you who would shirk a little trouble.''

''If he comes here, I shall go,'' said Mrs. Stroeve violently.

''I don't recognise you. You're so good and kind.''

''Oh, for goodness sake, let me be. You drive me to distraction.''

Then at last the tears came. She sank into a chair, and buried her face in her hands. Her shoulders shook convulsively. In a moment Dirk was on his knees beside her, with his arms round her, kissing her, calling her all sorts of pet names, and the facile tears ran down his own cheeks. Presently she released herself and dried her eyes.

''Leave me alone,'' she said, not unkindly; and then to

me, trying to smile: "What must you think of me?"

Stroeve, looking at her with perplexity, hesitated. His forehead was all puckered, and his red mouth set in a pout. He reminded me oddly of an agitated guinea-pig.

"Then it's No, darling?" he said at last.

She gave a gesture of lassitude. She was exhausted.

"The studio is yours. Everything belongs to you. If you want to bring him here, how can I prevent you?"

A sudden smile flashed across his round face.

"Then you consent? I knew you would. Oh, my precious."

Suddenly she pulled herself together. She looked at him with haggard eyes. She clasped her hands over her heart as though its beating were intolerable.

"Oh, Dirk, I've never since we met asked you to do anything for me."

"You know there's nothing in the world that I wouldn't do for you."

"I beg you not to let Strickland come here. Anyone else you like. Bring a thief, a drunkard, any outcast off the streets, and I promise you I'll do everything I can for them gladly. But I beseech you not to bring Strickland here."

"But why?"

"I'm frightened of him. I don't know why, but there's something in him that terrifies me. He'll do us some great harm. I know it. I feel it. If you bring him here it can only end badly."

"But how unreasonable!"

"No, no. I know I'm right. Something terrible will happen to us."

"Because we do a good action?"

She was panting now, and in her face was a terror which was inexplicable. I do not know what she thought. I felt that she was possessed by some shapeless dread which robbed her of all self-control. As a rule she was so calm; her agitation now was amazing. Stroeve looked at her for a while with puzzled consternation.

"You are my wife; you are dearer to me than anyone in the world. No one shall come here without your entire consent."

She closed her eyes for a moment, and I thought she was going to faint. I was a little impatient with her! I had not suspected that she was so neurotic a woman. Then I heard Stroeve's voice again. It seemed to break oddly on the silence.

"Haven't you been in bitter distress once when a helping hand was held out to you? You know how much it means. Wouldn't you like to do someone a good turn when you have the chance?"

The words were ordinary enough, and to my mind there was in them something so hortatory that I almost smiled. I was astonished at the effect they had on Blanche Stroeve. She started a little, and gave her husband a long look. His eyes were fixed on the ground. I did not know why he seemed embarrassed. A faint colour came into her cheeks, and then her face became white—more than white, ghastly; you felt that the blood had shrunk away from the whole surface of her body; and even her hands were pale. A shiver passed through her. The silence of the studio seemed to gather body, so that it became an almost palpable presence. I was bewildered.

"Bring Strickland here, Dirk. I'll do my best for him."

"My precious," he smiled.

He wanted to take her in his arms, but she avoided him.

"Don't be affectionate before strangers, Dirk," she said. "It makes me feel such a fool."

Her manner was quite normal again, and no one could

have told that so shortly before she had been shaken by such a great emotion.

Next day we moved Strickland. It needed a good deal of firmness and still more patience to induce him to come, but he was really too ill to offer any effective resistance to Stroeve's entreaties and to my determination. We dressed him, while he feebly cursed us, got him downstairs into a cab, and eventually to Stroeve's studio. He was so exhausted by the time we arrived that he allowed us to put him to bed without a word. He was ill for six weeks. At one time it looked as though he could not live more than a few hours, and I am convinced that it was only through the Dutchman's doggedness that he pulled through. I have never known a more difficult patient. It was not that he was exacting and querulous; on the contrary, he never complained, he asked for nothing, he was perfectly silent; but he seemed to resent the care that was taken of him; he received all inquiries about his feelings or his needs with a jibe, a sneer, or an oath. I found him detestable, and as soon as he was out of danger I had no hesitation in telling him so.

"Go to hell," he answered briefly.

Dirk Stroeve, giving up his work entirely, nursed Strickland with tenderness and sympathy. He was dexterous to make him comfortable, and he exercised a cunning of which I should never have thought him capable to induce him to take the medicines prescribed by the doctor. Nothing was too much trouble for him. Though his means were adequate to the needs of himself and his wife, he certainly had no money to waste; but now he was wantonly extravagant in the purchase of delicacies, out of season and dear, which might tempt Strickland's capricious appetite. I shall never forget the tactful patience with which he persuaded him to take nourishment. He was never put out by Strickland's rudeness; if it was merely sullen, he appeared not to notice it; if it was aggressive, he only chuckled. When Strickland, recovering somewhat, was in a good humour and amused himself by laughing at him, he deliberately did absurd things to excite his ridicule. Then he would give me little happy glances, so that I might notice in how much better form the patient was. Stroeve was sublime.

But it was Blanche who most surprised me. She proved herself not only a capable, but a devoted nurse. There was nothing in her to remind you that she had so vehemently struggled against her husband's wish to bring Strickland to the studio. She insisted on doing her share of the offices needful to the sick. She arranged his bed so that it was possible to change the sheet without disturbing him. She washed him. When I remarked on her competence, she told me with that pleasant little smile of hers that for a while she had worked in a hospital. She gave no sign that she hated Strickland so desperately. She did not speak to him much, but she was quick to forestall his wants. For a fortnight it was necessary that someone should stay with him all night, and she took turns at watching with her husband. I wondered what she thought during the long darkness as she sat by the bedside. Strickland was a weird figure as he lay there, thinner than ever, with his ragged red beard

"She insisted on doing her share"

and his eyes staring feverishly into vacancy; his illness seemed to have made them larger, and they had an unnatural brightness.

"Does he ever talk to you in the night?" I asked her once.

"Never."

"Do you dislike him as much as you did?"

"More, if anything."

She looked at me with her calm gray eyes. Her expression was so placid, it was hard to believe that she was capable of the violent emotion I had witnessed.

"Has he ever thanked you for what you do for him?"

"No," she smiled.

"He's inhuman."

"He's abominable."

Stroeve was, of course, delighted with her. He could not do enough to show his gratitude for the whole-hearted de-

votion with which she had accepted the burden he laid
on her. But he was a little puzzled by the behaviour of
Blanche and Strickland towards one another.

"Do you know, I've seen them sit there for hours together without saying a word?"

On one occasion, when Strickland was so much better
that in a day or two he was to get up, I sat with them in the
studio. Dirk and I were talking. Mrs. Stroeve sewed, and
I thought I recognised the shirt she was mending as Strickland's. He lay on his back; he did not speak. Once I saw
that his eyes were fixed on Blanche Stroeve, and there was
in them a curious irony. Feeling their gaze, she raised her
own, and for a moment they stared at one another. I could
not quite understand her expression. Her eyes had in them
a strange perplexity, and perhaps—but why?—alarm. In a
moment Strickland looked away and idly surveyed the
ceiling, but she continued to stare at him, and now her look
was quite inexplicable.

In a few days Strickland began to get up. He was nothing
but skin and bone. His clothes hung upon him like rags on
a scarecrow. With his untidy beard and long hair, his features, always a little larger than life, now emphasised by
illness, he had an extraordinary aspect; but it was so odd
that it was not quite ugly. There was something monu-
mental in his ungainliness. I do not know how to express
precisely the impression he made upon me. It was not exactly spirituality that was obvious, though the screen of
the flesh seemed almost transparent, because there was in
his face an outrageous sensuality; but, though it sounds
nonsense, it seemed as though his sensuality were curiously
spiritual. There was in him something primitive. He seemed
to partake of those obscure forces of nature which the

Greeks personified in shapes part human and part beast, the satyr and the faun. I thought of Marsyas, whom the god flayed because he had dared to rival him in song. Strickland seemed to bear in his heart strange harmonies and unadventured patterns, and I foresaw for him an end of torture and despair. I had again the feeling that he was possessed of a devil; but you could not say that it was a devil of evil, for it was a primitive force that existed before good and ill.

He was still too weak to paint, and he sat in the studio, silent, occupied with God knows what dreams, or reading. The books he liked were queer; sometimes I would find him poring over the poems of Mallarmé, and he read them as a child reads, forming the words with his lips, and I wondered what strange emotion he got from those subtle cadences and obscure phrases; and again I found him absorbed in the detective novels of Gaboriau. I amused myself by thinking that in his choice of books he showed pleasantly the irreconcilable sides of his fantastic nature. It was singular to notice that even in the weak state of his body he had no thought for its comfort. Stroeve liked his ease, and in his studio were a couple of heavily upholstered arm-chairs and a large divan. Strickland would not go near them, not from any affectation of stoicism, for I found him seated on a three-legged stool when I went into the studio one day and he was alone, but because he did not like them. For choice he sat on a kitchen chair without arms. It often exasperated me to see him. I never knew a man so entirely indifferent to his surroundings.

Two or three weeks passed. One morning, having come to a pause in my work, I thought I would give myself a holiday, and I went to the Louvre. I wandered about looking at the pictures I knew so well, and let my fancy play idly with the emotions they suggested. I sauntered into the long gallery, and there suddenly saw Stroeve. I smiled, for his appearance, so rotund and yet so startled, could never fail to excite a smile, and then as I came nearer I noticed that he seemed singularly disconsolate. He looked woebegone and yet ridiculous, like a man who has fallen into the water with all his clothes on, and, being rescued from death, frightened still, feels that he only looks a fool. Turning round, he stared at me, but I perceived that he did not see me. His round blue eyes looked harassed behind his glasses.

"Stroeve," I said.

He gave a little start, and then smiled, but his smile was rueful.

"Why are you idling in this disgraceful fashion?" I asked gaily.

"It's a long time since I was at the Louvre. I thought I'd come and see if they had anything new."

"But you told me you had to get a picture finished this week."

"Strickland's painting in my studio."

"Well?"

"I suggested it myself. He's not strong enough to go back to his own place yet. I thought we could both paint there. Lots of fellows in the Quarter share a studio. I thought it would be **fun.** I've always thought it would be jolly to have someone to talk to when one was tired of work."

He said all this slowly, detaching statement from statement with a little awkward silence, and he kept his kind, foolish eyes fixed on mine. They were full of tears.

"I don't think I understand," I said.

"Strickland can't work with anyone else in the studio."

"Damn it all, it's your studio. That's his lookout."

He looked at me pitifully. His lips were trembling.

"What happened?" I asked, rather sharply.

He hesitated and flushed. He glanced unhappily at one of the pictures on the wall.

"He wouldn't let me go on painting. He told me to get out."

"But why didn't you tell him to go to hell?"

"He turned me out. I couldn't very well struggle with him. He threw my hat after me, and locked the door."

I was furious with Strickland, and was indignant with myself, because Dirk Stroeve cut such an absurd figure that I felt inclined to laugh.

"But what did your wife say?"

"She'd gone out to do the marketing."

"Is he going to let her in?"

"I don't know."

I gazed at Stroeve with perplexity. He stood like a school-boy with whom a master is finding fault.

"Shall I get rid of Strickland for you?" I asked.

He gave a little start, and his shining face grew very red.

"No. You'd better not do anything."

He nodded to me and walked away. It was clear that for some reason he did not want to discuss the matter. I did not understand.

The explanation came a week later. It was about ten o'clock
at night; I had been dining by myself at a restaurant, and
having returned to my small apartment, was sitting in my
parlour, reading. I heard the cracked tinkling of the bell,
and, going into the corridor, opened the door. Stroeve stood
before me.

"Can I come in?" he asked.

In the dimness of the landing I could not see him very
well, but there was something in his voice that surprised
me. I knew he was of abstemious habit or I should have
thought he had been drinking. I led the way into my sitting
room and asked him to sit down.

"Thank God I've found you," he said.

"What's the matter?" I asked in astonishment at his
vehemence.

I was able now to see him well. As a rule he was neat in
his person, but now his clothes were in disorder. He looked
suddenly bedraggled. I was convinced he had been drinking, and I smiled. I was on the point of chaffing him on his
state.

"I didn't know where to go," he burst out. "I came here
earlier, but you weren't in."

"I dined late," I said.

I changed my mind: it was not liquor that had driven
him to this obvious desperation. His face, usually so rosy,
was now strangely mottled. His hands trembled.

"Has anything happened?" I asked.

"My wife has left me."

He could hardly get the words out. He gave a little gasp,

and the tears began to trickle down his round cheeks. I did not know what to say. My first thought was that she had come to the end of her forbearance with his infatuation for Strickland, and, goaded by the latter's cynical behaviour, had insisted that he should be turned out. I knew her capable of temper, for all the calmness of her manner; and if Stroeve still refused, she might easily have flung out of the studio with vows never to return. But the little man was so distressed that I could not smile.

"My dear fellow, don't be unhappy. She'll come back. You mustn't take very seriously what women say when they're in a passion."

"You don't understand. She's in love with Strickland."

"What!" I was startled at this, but the idea had no sooner taken possession of me than I saw it was absurd. "How can you be so silly? You don't mean to say you're jealous of Strickland?" I almost laughed. "You know very well that she can't bear the sight of him."

"You don't understand," he moaned.

"You're an hysterical ass," I said a little impatiently. "Let me give you a whisky-and-soda, and you'll feel better."

I supposed that for some reason or other—and Heaven knows what ingenuity men exercise to torment themselves —Dirk had got it into his head that his wife cared for Strickland, and with his genius for blundering he might quite well have offended her so that, to anger him, perhaps, she had taken pains to foster his suspicion.

"Look here," I said, "let's go back to your studio. If you've made a fool of yourself you must eat humble pie. Your wife doesn't strike me as the sort of woman to bear malice."

"How can I go back to the studio?" he said wearily. "They're there. I've left it to them."

"Then it's not your wife who's left you; it's you who've left your wife."

"For God's sake don't talk to me like that."

Still I could not take him seriously. I did not for a moment believe what he had told me. But he was in very real distress.

"Well, you've come here to talk to me about it. You'd better tell me the whole story."

"This afternoon I couldn't stand it any more. I went to Strickland and told him I thought he was quite well enough to go back to his own place. I wanted the studio myself."

"No one but Strickland would have needed telling," I said. "What did he say?"

"He laughed a little; you know how he laughs, not as though he were amused, but as though you were a damned fool, and said he'd go at once. He began to put his things together. You remember I fetched from his room what I thought he needed, and he asked Blanche for a piece of paper and some string to make a parcel."

Stroeve stopped, gasping, and I thought he was going to faint. This was not at all the story I had expected him to tell me.

"She was very pale, but she brought the paper and the string. He didn't say anything. He made the parcel and he whistled a tune. He took no notice of either of us. His eyes had an ironic smile in them. My heart was like lead. I was afraid something was going to happen, and I wished I hadn't spoken. He looked round for his hat. Then she spoke:

" 'I'm going with Strickland, Dirk,' she said. 'I can't live with you any more.'

"I tried to speak, but the words wouldn't come. Strickland didn't say anything. He went on whistling as though it had nothing to do with him."

Stroeve stopped again and mopped his face. I kept quite still. I believed him now, and I was astounded. But all the same I could not understand.

Then he told me, in a trembling voice, with the tears pouring down his cheeks, how he had gone up to her, trying to take her in his arms, but she had drawn away and begged him not to touch her. He implored her not to leave him. He told her how passionately he loved her, and reminded her of all the devotion he had lavished upon her. He spoke to her of the happiness of their life. He was not angry with her. He did not reproach her.

"Please let me go quietly, Dirk," she said at last. "Don't you understand that I love Strickland? Where he goes I shall go."

"But you must know that he'll never make you happy. For your own sake don't go. You don't know what you've got to look forward to."

"It's your fault. You insisted on his coming here."

He turned to Strickland.

"Have mercy on her," he implored him. "You can't let her do anything so mad."

"She can do as she chooses," said Strickland. "She's not forced to come."

"My choice is made," she said, in a dull voice.

Strickland's injurious calm robbed Stroeve of the rest of his self-control. Blind rage seized him, and without knowing what he was doing he flung himself on Strickland. Strickland was taken by surprise and he staggered, but he was very strong, even after his illness, and in a moment, he did not exactly know how, Stroeve found himself on the floor.

"You funny little man," said Strickland.

Stroeve picked himself up. He noticed that his wife had remained perfectly still, and to be made ridiculous before her increased his humiliation. His spectacles had tumbled off in the struggle, and he could not immediately see them. She picked them up and silently handed them to him. He seemed suddenly to realise his unhappiness, and though he knew he was making himself still more absurd, he began to cry. He hid his face in his hands. The others watched him without a word. They did not move from where they stood.

"Oh, my dear," he groaned at last, "how can you be so cruel?"

"I can't help myself, Dirk," she answered.

"I've worshipped you as no woman was ever worshipped before. If in anything I did I displeased you, why didn't you tell me, and I'd have changed. I've done everything I could for you."

She did not answer. Her face was set, and he saw that he was only boring her. She put on a coat and her hat. She moved towards the door, and he saw that in a moment she would be gone. He went up to her quickly and fell on his knees before her, seizing her hands: he abandoned all self-respect.

"Oh, don't go, my darling. I can't live without you; I shall kill myself. If I've done anything to offend you I beg you to forgive me. Give me another chance. I'll try harder still to make you happy."

"Get up, Dirk. You're making yourself a perfect fool."

He staggered to his feet, but still he would not let her go.

*"Oh, don't go, my darling,
I can't live without you"*

"Where are you going?" he said hastily. "You don't know what Strickland's place is like. You can't live there. It would be awful."

"If I don't care, I don't see why you should."

"Stay a minute longer. I must speak. After all, you can't grudge me that."

"What is the good? I've made up my mind. Nothing that you can say will make me alter it."

He gulped, and put his hand to his heart to ease its painful beating.

"I'm not going to ask you to change your mind, but I want you to listen to me for a minute. It's the last thing I shall ever ask you. Don't refuse me that."

She paused, looking at him with those reflective eyes of hers, which now were so different to him. She came back into the studio and leaned against the table.

"Well?"

Stroeve made a great effort to collect himself.

"You must be a little reasonable. You can't live on air, you know. Strickland hasn't got a penny."

"I know."

"You'll suffer the most awful privations. You know why he took so long to get well. He was half starved."

"I can earn money for him."

"How?"

"I don't know. I shall find a way."

A horrible thought passed through the Dutchman's mind, and he shuddered.

"I think you must be mad. I don't know what has come over you."

She shrugged her shoulders.

"Now may I go?"

"Wait one second longer."

He looked round his studio wearily; he had loved it because her presence had made it gay and homelike; he shut his eyes for an instant; then he gave her a long look as though to impress on his mind the picture of her. He got up and took his hat.

"No; I'll go."

"You?"

She was startled. She did not know what he meant.

"I can't bear to think of you living in that horrible, filthy attic. After all, this is your home just as much as mine. You'll be comfortable here. You'll be spared at least the worst privations."

He went to the drawer in which he kept his money and took out several bank-notes.

"I would like to give you half what I've got here."

He put them on the table. Neither Strickland nor his wife spoke.

Then he recollected something else.

"Will you pack up my clothes and leave them with the concierge? I'll come and fetch them to-morrow." He tried to smile. "Good-bye, my dear. I'm grateful for all the happiness you gave me in the past."

He walked out and closed the door behind him. With my mind's eye I saw Strickland throw his hat on a table, and, sitting down, begin to smoke a cigarette.

I kept silence for a little while, thinking of what Stroeve had told me. I could not stomach his weakness, and he saw my disapproval.

"You know as well as I do how Strickland lived," he said tremulously. "I couldn't let her live in those circumstances—I simply couldn't."

"That's your business," I answered.

"What would *you* have done?" he asked.

"She went with her eyes open. If she had to put up with certain inconveniences it was her own lookout."

"Yes; but, you see, you don't love her."

"Do you love her still?"

"Oh, more than ever. Strickland isn't the man to make a woman happy. It can't last. I want her to know that I shall never fail her."

"Does that mean that you're prepared to take her back?"

"I shouldn't hesitate. Why, she'll want me more than ever then. When she's alone and humiliated and broken it would be dreadful if she had nowhere to go."

He seemed to bear no resentment. I suppose it was commonplace in me that I felt slightly outraged at his lack of spirit. Perhaps he guessed what was in my mind, for he said:

"I couldn't expect her to love me as I loved her. I'm a buffoon. I'm not the sort of man that women love. I've always known that. I can't blame her if she's fallen in love with Strickland."

"You certainly have less vanity than any man I've ever known," I said.

"I love her so much better than myself. It seems to me that when vanity comes into love it can only be because really you love yourself best. After all, it constantly happens that a man when he's married falls in love with somebody else; when he gets over it he returns to his wife, and she takes him back, and everyone thinks it very natural. Why should it be different with women?"

"I dare say that's logical," I smiled, "but most men are made differently, and they can't."

But while I talked to Stroeve I was puzzling over the suddenness of the whole affair. I could not imagine that he had had no warning. I remembered the curious look I had seen in Blanche Stroeve's eyes; perhaps its explanation was that she was growing dimly conscious of a feeling in her heart that must have surprised and alarmed her.

"Did you have no suspicion before to-day that there was anything between them?" I asked.

He did not answer for a while. There was a pencil on the table, and unconsciously he drew a head on the blotting-paper.

"Please say so, if you hate my asking you questions," I said.

"It eases me to talk. Oh, if you knew the frightful anguish in my heart." He threw the pencil down. "Yes, I've known it for a fortnight. I knew it before she did."

"Why on earth didn't you send Strickland packing?"

"I couldn't believe it. It seemed so improbable. She couldn't bear the sight of him. It was more than improbable; it was incredible. I thought it was merely jealousy. You see, I've always been jealous, but I trained myself never to show it; I was jealous of every man she knew; I was jealous of you. I knew she didn't love me as I loved her. That was only natural, wasn't it? But she allowed me to love her, and that was enough to make me happy. I forced myself to go out for hours together in order to leave them by themselves; I wanted to punish myself for suspicions which were unworthy of me; and when I came back I found they didn't want me—not Strickland, he didn't care if I was there or not, but Blanche. She shuddered when I went to kiss her. When at last I was certain I didn't know what to do; I knew they'd only laugh at me if I made a scene. I thought if I held my tongue and pretended not to see, everything would come right. I made up my mind to get him away quietly, without quarrelling. Oh, if you only knew what I've suffered!"

Then he told me again of his asking Strickland to go. He

chose his moment carefully, and tried to make his request sound casual; but he could not master the trembling of his voice; and he felt himself that into words that he wished to seem jovial and friendly there crept the bitterness of his jealousy. He had not expected Strickland to take him up on the spot and make his preparations to go there and then; above all, he had not expected his wife's decision to go with him. I saw that now he wished with all his heart that he had held his tongue. He preferred the anguish of jealousy to the anguish of separation.

" I wanted to kill him, and I only made a fool of myself."

He was silent for a long time, and then he said what I knew was in his mind.

"If I'd only waited, perhaps it would have gone all right. I shouldn't have been so impatient. Oh, poor child, what have I driven her to?"

I shrugged my shoulders, but did not speak. I had no sympathy for Blanche Stroeve, but knew that it would only pain poor Dirk if I told him exactly what I thought of her.

He had reached that stage of exhaustion when he could not stop talking. He went over again every word of the scene. Now something occurred to him that he had not told me before; now he discussed what he ought to have said instead of what he did say; then he lamented his blindness. He regretted that he had done this, and blamed himself that he had omitted the other. It grew later and later, and at last I was as tired as he.

"What are you going to do now?" I said finally.

"What can I do? I shall wait till she sends for me."

"Why don't you go away for a bit?"

"No, no; I must be at hand when she wants me."

For the present he seemed quite lost. He had made no

plans. When I suggested that he should go to bed he said
he could not sleep; he wanted to go out and walk about the
streets till day. He was evidently in no state to be left
alone. I persuaded him to stay the night with me, and I
put him into my own bed. I had a divan in my sitting-room,
and could very well sleep on that. He was by now so worn
out that he could not resist my firmness. I gave him a suf-
ficient dose of veronal to insure his unconsciousness for
several hours. I thought that was the best service I could
render him.

But the bed I made up for myself was sufficiently uncomfortable to give me a wakeful night, and I thought a good
deal of what the unlucky Dutchman had told me. I was not
so much puzzled by Blanche Stroeve's action, for I saw in
that merely the result of a physical appeal. I do not suppose she had ever really cared for her husband, and what I
had taken for love was no more than the feminine response
to caresses and comfort which in the minds of most women
passes for it. It is a passive feeling capable of being roused
for any object, as the vine can grow on any tree; and the
wisdom of the world recognises its strength when it urges
a girl to marry the man who wants her with the assurance
that love will follow. It is an emotion made up of the satisfaction in security, pride of property, the pleasure of being
desired, the gratification of a household, and it is only by
an amiable vanity that women ascribe to it spiritual value.

It is an emotion which is defenceless against passion. I suspected that Blanche Stroeve's violent dislike of Strickland had in it from the beginning a vague element of sexual attraction. Who am I that I should seek to unravel the mysterious intricacies of sex? Perhaps Stroeve's passion excited without satisfying that part of her nature, and she hated Strickland because she felt in him the power to give her what she needed. I think she was quite sincere when she struggled against her husband's desire to bring him into the studio; I think she was frightened of him, though she knew not why; and I remembered how she had foreseen disaster. I think in some curious way the horror which she felt for him was a transference of the horror which she felt for herself because he so strangely troubled her. His appearance was wild and uncouth; there was aloofness in his eyes and sensuality in his mouth; he was big and strong; he gave the impression of untamed passion; and perhaps she felt in him, too, that sinister element which had made me think of those wild beings of the world's early history when matter, retaining its early connection with the earth, seemed to possess yet a spirit of its own. If he affected her at all, it was inevitable that she should love or hate him. She hated him.

And then I fancy that the daily intimacy with the sick man moved her strangely. She raised his head to give him food, and it was heavy against her hand; when she had fed him she wiped his sensual mouth and his red beard. She washed his limbs; they were covered with thick hair; and when she dried his hands, even in his weakness they were strong and sinewy. His fingers were long; they were the capable, fashioning fingers of the artist; and I know not what troubling thoughts they excited in her. He slept very

quietly, without a movement, so that he might have been
dead, and he was like some wild creature of the woods,
resting after a long chase; and she wondered what fancies
passed through his dreams. Did he dream of the nymph
flying through the woods of Greece with the satyr in hot
pursuit? She fled, swift of foot and desperate, but he gained
on her step by step, till she felt his hot breath on her neck;
and still she fled silently, and silently he pursued, and when
at last he seized her was it terror that thrilled her heart or
was it ecstasy?

Blanche Stroeve was in the cruel grip of appetite. Perhaps she hated Strickland still, but she hungered for him,
and everything that had made up her life till then became
of no account. She ceased to be a woman, complex, kind and
petulant, considerate and thoughtless; she was a Mænad.
She was desire.

But perhaps this is very fanciful; and it may be that she
was merely bored with her husband and went to Strickland
out of a callous curiosity. She may have had no particular
feeling for him, but succumbed to his wish from propinquity
or idleness, to find then that she was powerless in a snare of
her own contriving. How did I know what were the thoughts
and emotions behind that placid brow and those cool gray
eyes?

But if one could be certain of nothing in dealing with
creatures so incalculable as human beings, there were ex-
planations of Blanche Stroeve's behaviour which were at
all events plausible. On the other hand, I did not understand
Strickland at all. I racked my brain, but could in no way
account for an action so contrary to my conception of him.
It was not strange that he should so heartlessly have betrayed his friend's confidence, nor that he hesitated not at

all to gratify a whim at the cost of another's misery. That
was in his character. He was a man without any conception
of gratitude. He had no compassion. The emotions common
to most of us simply did not exist in him, and it was as absurd to blame him for not feeling them as for blaming the
tiger because he is fierce and cruel. But it was the whim I
could not understand.

I could not believe that Strickland had fallen in love with
Blanche Stroeve. I did not believe him capable of love.
That is an emotion in which tenderness is an essential part,
but Strickland had no tenderness either for himself or for
others; there is in love a sense of weakness, a desire to
protect, an eagerness to do good and to give pleasure—if
not unselfishness, at all events a selfishness which marvel-
lously conceals itself; it has in it a certain diffidence. These
were not traits which I could imagine in Strickland. Love
is absorbing; it takes the lover out of himself; the most
clear-sighted, though he may know, cannot realise that his
love will cease; it gives body to what he knows is illusion,
and, knowing it is nothing else, he loves it better than reality. It makes a man a little more than himself, and at the
same time a little less. He ceases to be himself. He is no
longer an individual, but a thing, an instrument to some
purpose foreign to his ego. Love is never quite devoid of
sentimentality, and Strickland was the least inclined to
that infirmity of any man I have known. I could not believe
that he would ever suffer that possession of himself which
love is; he could never endure a foreign yoke. I believed
him capable of uprooting from his heart, though it might
be with agony, so that he was left battered and ensan-
guined, anything that came between himself and that un-
comprehended craving that urged him constantly to he

knew not what. If I have succeeded at all in giving the
complicated impression that Strickland made on me, it will
not seem outrageous to say that I felt he was at once too
great and too small for love.

But I suppose that everyone's conception of the passion
is formed on his own idiosyncrasies, and it is different
with every different person. A man like Strickland would
love in a manner peculiar to himself. It was vain to seek the
analysis of his emotion.

Next day, though I pressed him to remain, Stroeve left me.
I offered to fetch his things from the studio, but he insisted
on going himself; I think he hoped they had not thought of
getting them together, so that he would have an opportunity
of seeing his wife again and perhaps inducing her to come
back to him. But he found his traps waiting for him in the
porter's lodge, and the concierge told him that Blanche had
gone out. I do not think he resisted the temptation of giving her an account of his troubles. I found that he was
telling them to everyone he knew; he expected sympathy,
but only excited ridicule.

He bore himself most unbecomingly. Knowing at what
time his wife did her shopping, one day, unable any longer
to bear not seeing her, he waylaid her in the street. She
would not speak to him, but he insisted on speaking to her.
He spluttered out words of apology for any wrong he had
committed towards her; he told her he loved her devotedly

"She would not speak to him"

and begged her to return to him. She would not answer; she walked hurriedly, with averted face. I imagined him with his fat little legs trying to keep up with her. Panting a little in his haste, he told her how miserable he was; he

besought her to have mercy on him; he promised, if she
would forgive him, to do everything she wanted. He offered
to take her for a journey. He told her that Strickland would
soon tire of her. When he repeated to me the whole sordid
little scene I was outraged. He had shown neither sense nor
dignity. He had omitted nothing that could make his wife
despise him. There is no cruelty greater than a woman's
to a man who loves her and whom she does not love; she
has no kindness then, no tolerance even, she has only an
insane irritation. Blanche Stroeve stopped suddenly, and
as hard as she could slapped her husband's face. She took
advantage of his confusion to escape, and ran up the stairs
to the studio. No word had passed her lips.

When he told me this he put his hand to his cheek as
though he still felt the smart of the blow, and in his eyes
was a pain that was heartrending and an amazement that
was ludicrous. He looked like an overblown schoolboy, and
though I felt so sorry for him, I could hardly help laughing.

Then he took to walking along the street which she must
pass through to get to the shops, and he would stand at the
corner, on the other side, as she went along. He dared not
speak to her again, but sought to put into his round eyes
the appeal that was in his heart. I suppose he had some
idea that the sight of his misery would touch her. She
never made the smallest sign that she saw him. She never
even changed the hour of her errands or sought an alterna-
tive route. I have an idea that there was some cruelty in
her indifference. Perhaps she got enjoyment out of the torture she inflicted. I wondered why she hated him so much.

I begged Stroeve to behave more wisely. His want of
spirit was exasperating.

"You're doing no good at all by going on like this," I
said. "I think you'd have been wiser if you'd hit her over

the head with a stick. She wouldn't have despised you as she does now.''

I suggested that he should go home for a while. He had often spoken to me of the silent town, somewhere up in the north of Holland, where his parents still lived. They were poor people. His father was a carpenter, and they dwelt in a little old red-brick house, neat and clean, by the side of a sluggish canal. The streets were wide and empty; for two hundred years the place had been dying, but the houses had the homely stateliness of their time. Rich merchants, sending their wares to the distant Indies, had lived in them calm and prosperous lives, and in their decent decay they kept still an aroma of their splendid past. You could wander along the canal till you came to broad green fields, with windmills here and there, in which cattle, black and white, grazed lazily. I thought that among those surroundings, with their recollections of his boyhood, Dirk Stroeve would forget his unhappiness. But he would not go.

''I must be here when she needs me,'' he repeated. ''It would be dreadful if something terrible happened and I were not at hand.''

''What do you think is going to happen?'' I asked.

''I don't know. But I'm afraid.''

I shrugged my shoulders.

For all his pain, Dirk Stroeve remained a ridiculous object. He might have excited sympathy if he had grown worn and thin. He did nothing of the kind. He remained fat, and his round, red cheeks shone like ripe apples. He had great neatness of person, and he continued to wear his spruce black coat and his bowler hat, always a little too small for him, in a dapper, jaunty manner. He was getting something of a paunch, and sorrow had no effect on it. He looked more than ever like a prosperous bagman. It is hard that

a man's exterior should tally so little sometimes with his
soul. Dirk Stroeve had the passion of Romeo in the body
of Sir Toby Belch. He had a sweet and generous nature,
and yet was always blundering; a real feeling for what
was beautiful and the capacity to create only what was commonplace; a peculiar delicacy of sentiment and gross manners. He could exercise tact when dealing with the affairs
of others, but none when dealing with his own. What a cruel
practical joke old Nature played when she flung so many
contradictory elements together, and left the man face to
face with the perplexing callousness of the universe.

I did not see Strickland for several weeks. I was disgusted
with him, and if I had had an opportunity should have been
glad to tell him so, but I saw no object in seeking him out
for the purpose. I am a little shy of any assumption of
moral indignation; there is always in it an element of
self-satisfaction which makes it awkward to anyone who
has a sense of humour. It requires a very lively passion to
steel me to my own ridicule. There was a sardonic sincerity
in Strickland which made me sensitive to anything that
might suggest a pose.

But one evening when I was passing along the Avenue de
Clichy in front of the café which Strickland frequented and
which I now avoided, I ran straight into him. He was accompanied by Blanche Stroeve, and they were just going
to Strickland's favourite corner.

"Where the devil have you been all this time?" said he.

"I thought you must be away."

His cordiality was proof that he knew I had no wish to speak to him. He was not a man with whom it was worth while wasting politeness.

"No," I said; "I haven't been away."

"Why haven't you been here?"

"There are more cafés in Paris than one, at which to trifle away an idle hour."

Blanche then held out her hand and bade me good-evening. I do not know why I had expected her to be somehow changed; she wore the same gray dress that she wore so often, neat and becoming, and her brow was as candid, her eyes as untroubled, as when I had been used to see her occupied with her household duties in the studio.

"Come and have a game of chess," said Strickland.

I do not know why at the moment I could think of no excuse. I followed them rather sulkily to the table at which Strickland always sat, and he called for the board and the chessmen. They both took the situation so much as a matter of course that I felt it absurd to do otherwise. Mrs. Stroeve watched the game with inscrutable face. She was silent, but she had always been silent. I looked at her mouth for an expression that could give me a clue to what she felt; I watched her eyes for some tell-tale flash, some hint of dismay or bitterness; I scanned her brows for any passing line that might indicate a settling emotion. Her face was a mask that told nothing. Her hands lay on her lap motionless, one in the other loosely clasped. I knew from what I had heard that she was a woman of violent passions; and that injurious blow that she had given Dirk, the man who had loved her so devotedly, betrayed a sudden temper and a horrid cruelty. She had abandoned the safe shelter of her husband's protection and the comfortable ease of a

well-provided establishment for what she could not but
see was an extreme hazard. It showed an eagerness for
adventure, a readiness for the hand-to-mouth, which the
care she took of her home and her love of good housewifery
made not a little remarkable. She must be a woman of complicated character, and there was something dramatic in
the contrast of that with her demure appearance.

*"Mrs. Stroeve watched the
game with inscrutable face"*

I was excited by the encounter, and my fancy worked
busily while I sought to concentrate myself on the game I
was playing. I always tried my best to beat Strickland, because he was a player who despised the opponent he van-
quished; his exultation in victory made defeat more difficult
to bear. On the other hand, if he was beaten he took it with

complete good-humour. He was a bad winner and a good loser. Those who think that a man betrays his character nowhere more clearly than when he is playing a game might on this draw subtle inferences.

When he had finished I called the waiter to pay for the drinks, and left them. The meeting had been devoid of incident. No word had been said to give me anything to think about, and any surmises I might make were unwarranted. I was intrigued. I could not tell how they were getting on. I would have given much to be a disembodied spirit so that I could see them in the privacy of the studio and hear what they talked about. I had not the smallest indication on which to let my imagination work.

Two or three days later Dirk Stroeve called on me.

"I hear you've seen Blanche," he said.

"How on earth did you find out?"

"I was told by someone who saw you sitting with them. Why didn't you tell me?"

"I thought it would only pain you."

"What do I care if it does? You must know that I want to hear the smallest thing about her."

I waited for him to ask me questions.

"What does she look like?" he said.

"Absolutely unchanged."

"Does she seem happy?"

I shrugged my shoulders.

"How can I tell? We were in a café; we were playing

chess; I had no opportunity to speak to her.''

"Oh, but couldn't you tell by her face?''

I shook my head. I could only repeat that by no word, by no hinted gesture, had she given an indication of her feelings. He must know better than I how great were her powers of self-control. He clasped his hands emotionally.

"Oh, I'm so frightened. I know something is going to happen, something terrible, and I can do nothing to stop it.''

"What sort of thing?'' I asked.

"Oh, I don't know,'' he moaned, seizing his head with his hands. "I foresee some terrible catastrophe.''

Stroeve had always been excitable, but now he was beside himself; there was no reasoning with him. I thought it probable enough that Blanche Stroeve would not continue to find life with Strickland tolerable, but one of the falsest of proverbs is that you must lie on the bed that you have made. The experience of life shows that people are constantly doing things which must lead to disaster, and yet by some chance manage to evade the result of their folly. When Blanche quarrelled with Strickland she had only to leave him, and her husband was waiting humbly to forgive and forget. I was not prepared to feel any great sympathy for her.

"You see, you don't love her,'' said Stroeve.

"After all, there's nothing to prove that she is unhappy. For all we know they may have settled down into a most domestic couple.''

Stroeve gave me a look with his woeful eyes.

"Of course it doesn't much matter to you, but to me it's so serious, so intensely serious.''

I was sorry if I had seemed impatient or flippant.

"Will you do something for me?'' asked Stroeve.

"Willingly.''

"Will you write to Blanche for me?"

"Why can't you write yourself?"

"I've written over and over again. I didn't expect her to answer. I don't think she reads the letters."

"You make no account of feminine curiosity. Do you think she could resist?"

"She could—mine."

I looked at him quickly. He lowered his eyes. That answer of his seemed to me strangely humiliating. He was conscious that she regarded him with an indifference so profound that the sight of his handwriting would have not the slightest effect on her.

"Do you really believe that she'll ever come back to you?" I asked.

"I want her to know that if the worst comes to the worst she can count on me. That's what I want you to tell her."

I took a sheet of paper.

"What is it exactly you wish me to say?"

This is what I wrote:

Dear Mrs. Stroeve,

Dirk wishes me to tell you that if at any time you want him he will be grateful for the opportunity of being of service to you. He has no ill-feeling towards you on account of anything that has happened. His love for you is unaltered. You will always find him at the following address:

But though I was no less convinced than Stroeve that the connection between Strickland and Blanche would end disastrously, I did not expect the issue to take the tragic form it did. The summer came, breathless and sultry, and even at night there was no coolness to rest one's jaded nerves. The sun-baked streets seemed to give back the heat that had beat down on them during the day, and the passers-by dragged their feet along them wearily. I had not seen Strickland for weeks. Occupied with other things, I had ceased to think of him and his affairs. Dirk, with his vain lamentations, had begun to bore me, and I avoided his society. It was a sordid business, and I was not inclined to trouble myself with it further.

One morning I was working. I sat in my pyjamas. My thoughts wandered, and I thought of the sunny beaches of Brittany and the freshness of the sea. By my side was the empty bowl in which the concierge had brought me my *café au lait* and the fragment of *croissant* which I had not had appetite enough to eat. I heard the concierge in the next room emptying my bath. There was a tinkle at my bell, and I left her to open the door. In a moment I heard Stroeve's voice asking if I was in. Without moving, I shouted to him to come. He entered the room quickly, and came up to the table at which I sat.

"She's killed herself," he said hoarsely.

"What do you mean?" I cried, startled.

He made movements with his lips as though he were speaking, but no sound issued from them. He gibbered like an idiot. My heart thumped against my ribs, and, I do not know why, I flew into a temper.

"For God's sake, collect yourself, man," I said. "What on earth are you talking about?"

He made despairing gestures with his hands, but still no

"His round blue eyes were ghastly with terror"

words came from his mouth. He might have been struck dumb. I do not know what came over me; I took him by the shoulders and shook him. Looking back, I am vexed that I made such a fool of myself; I suppose the last restless nights had shaken my nerves more than I knew.

"Let me sit down," he gasped at length.

I filled a glass with St. Galmier, and gave it to him to

drink. I held it to his mouth as though he were a child. He gulped down a mouthful, and some of it was spilt on his shirt-front.

"Who's killed herself?"

I do not know why I asked, for I knew whom he meant. He made an effort to collect himself.

"They had a row last night. He went away."

"Is she dead?"

"No; they've taken her to the hospital."

"Then what are you talking about?" I cried impatiently. "Why did you say she'd killed herself?"

"Don't be cross with me. I can't tell you anything if you talk to me like that."

I clenched my hands, seeking to control my irritation. I attempted a smile.

"I'm sorry. Take your time. Don't hurry, there's a good fellow."

His round blue eyes behind the spectacles were ghastly with terror. The magnifying-glasses he wore distorted them.

"When the concierge went up this morning to take a letter she could get no answer to her ring. She heard some-one groaning. The door wasn't locked, and she went in. Blanche was lying on the bed. She'd been frightfully sick. There was a bottle of oxalic acid on the table."

Stroeve hid his face in his hands and swayed backwards and forwards, groaning.

"Was she conscious?"

"Yes. Oh, if you knew how she's suffering! I can't bear it. I can't bear it."

His voice rose to a shriek.

"Damn it all, you haven't got to bear it," I cried impatiently. "She's got to bear it."

"How can you be so cruel?"

"What have you done?"

"They sent for a doctor and for me, and they told the police. I'd given the concierge twenty francs, and told her to send for me if anything happened."

He paused a minute, and I saw that what he had to tell me was very hard to say.

"When I went she wouldn't speak to me. She told them to send me away. I swore that I forgave her everything, but she wouldn't listen. She tried to beat her head against the wall. The doctor told me that I mustn't remain with her. She kept on saying, 'Send him away!' I went, and waited in the studio. And when the ambulance came and they put her on a stretcher, they made me go in the kitchen so that she shouldn't know I was there."

While I dressed—for Stroeve wished me to go at once with him to the hospital—he told me that he had arranged for his wife to have a private room, so that she might at least be spared the sordid promiscuity of a ward. On our way he explained to me why he desired my presence; if she still refused to see him, perhaps she would see me. He begged me to repeat to her that he loved her still; he would reproach her for nothing, but desired only to help her; he made no claim on her, and on her recovery would not seek to induce her to return to him; she would be perfectly free.

But when we arrived at the hospital, a gaunt, cheerless building, the mere sight of which was enough to make one's heart sick, and after being directed from this official to that, up endless stairs and through long, bare corridors, found the doctor in charge of the case, we were told that the patient was too ill to see anyone that day. The doctor was a little bearded man in white, with an offhand manner. He evidently looked upon a case as a case, and anxious relatives as a nuisance which must be treated with firmness. Moreover, to him the affair was commonplace; it was just an hysterical woman who had quarrelled with her lover and taken poison; it was constantly happening. At first he thought that Dirk was the cause of the disaster, and he was needlessly brusque with him. When I explained that he was the husband, anxious to forgive, the doctor looked at him suddenly, with curious, searching eyes. I seemed to see in them a hint of mockery; it was true that Stroeve had the head of the husband who is deceived. The doctor faintly shrugged his shoulders.

"There is no immediate danger," he said, in answer to our questioning. "One doesn't know how much she took. It may be that she will get off with a fright. Women are constantly trying to commit suicide for love, but generally they take care not to succeed. It's generally a gesture to arouse pity or terror in their lover."

There was in his tone a frigid contempt. It was obvious that to him Blanche Stroeve was only a unit to be added to the statistical list of attempted suicides in the city of Paris during the current year. He was busy, and could waste no more time on us. He told us that if we came at a certain hour next day, should Blanche be better, it might be possible for her husband to see her.

I scarcely know how we got through that day. Stroeve could not bear to be alone, and I exhausted myself in efforts to distract him. I took him to the Louvre, and he pretended to look at pictures, but I saw that his thoughts were constantly with his wife. I forced him to eat, and after luncheon

I induced him to lie down, but he could not sleep. He accepted willingly my invitation to remain for a few days in my apartment. I gave him books to read, but after a page or two he would put the book down and stare miserably into space. During the evening we played innumerable games of piquet, and bravely, not to disappoint my efforts, he tried to appear interested. Finally I gave him a draught, and he sank into uneasy slumber.

When we went again to the hospital we saw a nursing sister. She told us that Blanche seemed a little better, and she went in to ask if she would see her husband. We heard voices in the room in which she lay, and presently the nurse returned to say that the patient refused to see anyone. We had told her that if she refused to see Dirk the nurse was to ask if she would see me, but this she refused also. Dirk's lips trembled.

"I dare not insist," said the nurse. "She is too ill. Perhaps in a day or two she may change her mind."

"Is there anyone else she wants to see?" asked Dirk, in a voice so low it was almost a whisper.

"She says she only wants to be left in peace."

Dirk's hands moved strangely, as though they had nothing to do with his body, with a movement of their own.

"Will you tell her that if there is anyone else she wishes to see I will bring him? I only want her to be happy."

The nurse looked at him with her calm, kind eyes, which had seen all the horror and pain of the world, and yet, filled with the vision of a world without sin, remained serene.

"I will tell her when she is a little calmer."

Dirk, filled with compassion, begged her to take the message at once.

"It may cure her. I beseech you to ask her now."

With a faint smile of pity, the nurse went back into the

room. We heard her low voice, and then, in a voice I did not recognise, the answer:

"No. No. No."

The nurse came out again and shook her head.

"Was that she who spoke then?" I asked. "Her voice sounded so strange."

"It appears that her vocal cords have been burnt by the acid."

Dirk gave a low cry of distress. I asked him to go on and wait for me at the entrance, for I wanted to say something to the nurse. He did not ask what it was, but went silently. He seemed to have lost all power of will; he was like an obedient child.

"Has she told you why she did it?" I asked.

"No. She won't speak. She lies on her back quite quietly. She doesn't move for hours at a time. But she cries always. Her pillow is all wet. She's too weak to use a handkerchief, and the tears just run down her face."

It gave me a sudden wrench of the heart-strings. I could have killed Strickland then, and I knew that my voice was trembling when I bade the nurse good-bye.

I found Dirk waiting for me on the steps. He seemed to see nothing, and did not notice that I had joined him till I touched him on the arm. We walked along in silence. I tried to imagine what had happened to drive the poor creature to that dreadful step. I presumed that Strickland knew what had happened, for someone must have been to see him from the police, and he must have made his statement. I did not know where he was. I supposed he had gone back to the shabby attic which served him as a studio. It was curious that she should not wish to see him. Perhaps she refused to have him sent for because she knew he would refuse to come. I wondered what an abyss of cruelty she must have looked into that in horror she refused to live.

The next week was dreadful. Stroeve went twice a day to the hospital to enquire after his wife, who still declined to see him; and came away at first relieved and hopeful because he was told that she seemed to be growing better, and then in despair because, the complication which the doctor had feared having ensued, recovery was impossible. The nurse was pitiful to his distress, but she had little to say that could console him. The poor woman lay quite still, refusing to speak, with her eyes intent, as though she watched for the coming of death. It could now be only the question of a day or two; and when, late one evening, Stroeve came to see me I knew it was to tell me she was dead. He was absolutely exhausted. His volubility had left him at last, and he sank down wearily on my sofa. I felt that no words of condolence availed, and I let him lie there quietly. I feared he would think it heartless if I read, so I sat by the window, smoking a pipe, till he felt inclined to speak.

"You've been very kind to me," he said at last. "Everyone's been very kind."

"Nonsense," I said, a little embarrassed.

"At the hospital they told me I might wait. They gave me a chair, and I sat outside the door. When she became unconscious they said I might go in. Her mouth and chin were all burnt by the acid. It was awful to see her lovely skin all wounded. She died very peacefully, so that I didn't know she was dead till the sister told me.''

He was too tired to weep. He lay on his back limply, as though all the strength had gone out of his limbs, and presently I saw that he had fallen asleep. It was the first natural sleep he had had for a week. Nature, sometimes so cruel, is sometimes merciful. I covered him and turned down the light. In the morning when I awoke he was still asleep. He had not moved. His gold-rimmed spectacles were still on his nose.

The circumstances of Blanche Stroeve's death necessitated all manner of dreadful formalities, but at last we were allowed to bury her. Dirk and I alone followed the hearse to the cemetery. We went at a foot-pace, but on the way back we trotted, and there was something to my mind singularly horrible in the way the driver of the hearse whipped up his horses. It seemed to dismiss the dead with a shrug of the shoulders. Now and then I caught sight of the swaying hearse in front of us, and our own driver urged his pair so that we might not remain behind. I felt in myself, too, the desire to get the whole thing out of my mind. I was beginning to be bored with a tragedy that did not really concern me, and pretending to myself that I spoke in order to distract Stroeve, I turned with relief to other subjects.

"Don't you think you'd better go away for a bit?" I said. "There can be no object in your staying in Paris now."

He did not answer, but I went on ruthlessly:

"Have you made any plans for the immediate future?"

"No."

"You must try and gather together the threads again. Why don't you go down to Italy and start working?"

Again he made no reply, but the driver of our carriage came to my rescue. Slackening his pace for a moment, he leaned over and spoke. I could not hear what he said, so I put my head out of the window; he wanted to know where we wished to be set down. I told him to wait a minute.

"You'd better come and have lunch with me," I said to Dirk. "I'll tell him to drop us in the Place Pigalle."

"I'd rather not. I want to go to the studio."

I hesitated a moment.

"Would you like me to come with you?" I asked then.

"No; I should prefer to be alone."

"All right."

I gave the driver the necessary direction, and in renewed silence we drove on. Dirk had not been to the studio since the wretched morning on which they had taken Blanche to the hospital. I was glad he did not want me to accompany him, and when I left him at the door I walked away with relief I took a new pleasure in the streets of Paris, and I looked with smiling eyes at the people who hurried to and fro. The day was fine and sunny, and I felt in myself a more acute delight in life. I could not help it; I put Stroeve and his sorrows out of my mind. I wanted to enjoy.

I did not see him again for nearly a week. Then he fetched me soon after seven one evening and took me out to dinner. He was dressed in the deepest mourning, and on his bowler was a broad black band. He had even a black border to his handkerchief. His garb of woe suggested that he had lost in one catastrophe every relation he had in the world, even to cousins by marriage twice removed. His plumpness and his red, fat cheeks made his mourning not a little incongruous. It was cruel that his extreme unhappiness should have in it something of buffoonery.

He told me he had made up his mind to go away, though not to Italy, as I had suggested, but to Holland.

"I'm starting to-morrow. This is perhaps the last time we shall ever meet."

I made an appropriate rejoinder, and he smiled wanly.

"I haven't been home for five years. I think I'd forgotten it all; I seemed to have come so far away from my father's house that I was shy at the idea of revisiting it; but now I feel it's my only refuge."

He was sore and bruised, and his thoughts went back to the tenderness of his mother's love. The ridicule he had endured for years seemed now to weigh him down, and the final blow of Blanche's treachery had robbed him of the resiliency which had made him take it so gaily. He could no longer laugh with those who laughed at him. He was an outcast. He told me of his childhood in the tidy brick house, and of his mother's passionate orderliness. Her kitchen was a miracle of clean brightness. Everything was always in its place, and nowhere could you see a speck of dust.

Cleanliness, indeed, was a mania with her. I saw a neat little old woman, with cheeks like apples, toiling away from morning to night, through the long years, to keep her house trim and spruce. His father was a spare old man, his hands gnarled after the work of a lifetime, silent and upright; in the evening he read the paper aloud, while his wife and daughter (now married to the captain of a fishing smack), unwilling to lose a moment, bent over their sewing. Nothing ever happened in that little town, left behind by the advance of civilisation, and one year followed the next till death came, like a friend, to give rest to those who had laboured so diligently.

"My father wished me to become a carpenter like himself. For five generations we've carried on the same trade, from father to son. Perhaps that is the wisdom of life, to tread in your father's steps, and look neither to the right nor to the left. When I was a little boy I said I would marry the daughter of the harness-maker who lived next door. She was a little girl with blue eyes and a flaxen pigtail. She would have kept my house like a new pin, and I should have had a son to carry on the business after me."

Stroeve sighed a little and was silent. His thoughts dwelt among pictures of what might have been, and the safety of the life he had refused filled him with longing.

"The world is hard and cruel. We are here none knows why, and we go none knows whither. We must be very humble. We must see the beauty of quietness. We must go through life so inconspicuously that Fate does not notice us. And let us seek the love of simple, ignorant people. Their ignorance is better than all our knowledge. Let us be silent, content in our little corner, meek and gentle like them. That is the wisdom of life."

To me it was his broken spirit that expressed itself, and I

rebelled against his renunciation. But I kept my own counsel.

"What made you think of being a painter?" I asked.

He shrugged his shoulders.

"It happened that I had a knack for drawing. I got prizes for it at school. My poor mother was very proud of my gift, and she gave me a box of water-colours as a present. She showed my sketches to the pastor and the doctor and the judge. And they sent me to Amsterdam to try for a scholarship, and I won it. Poor soul, she was so proud; and though it nearly broke her heart to part from me, she smiled, and would not show me her grief. She was pleased that her son should be an artist. They pinched and saved so that I should have enough to live on, and when my first picture was exhibited they came to Amsterdam to see it, my father and mother and my sister, and my mother cried when she looked at it." His kind eyes glistened. "And now on every wall of the old house there is one of my pictures in a beautiful gold frame."

He glowed with happy pride. I thought of those cold scenes of his, with their picturesque peasants and cypresses and olive-trees. They must look queer in their garish frames on the walls of the peasant house.

"The dear soul thought she was doing a wonderful thing for me when she made me an artist, but perhaps, after all, it would have been better for me if my father's will had prevailed and I were now but an honest carpenter."

"Now that you know what art can offer, would you change your life? Would you have missed all the delight it has given you?"

"Art is the greatest thing in the world," he answered, after a pause.

He looked at me for a minute reflectively; he seemed to

hesitate; then he said: "Did you know that I had been to see Strickland?"

"You?"

I was astonished. I should have thought he could not bear to set eyes on him. Stroeve smiled faintly.

"You know already that I have no proper pride."

"What do you mean by that?"

He told me a singular story.

When I left him, after we had buried poor Blanche, Stroeve walked into the house with a heavy heart. Something impelled him to go to the studio, some obscure desire for self-torture, and yet he dreaded the anguish that he foresaw. He dragged himself up the stairs; his feet seemed unwilling to carry him; and outside the door he lingered for a long time, trying to summon up courage to go in. He felt horribly sick. He had an impulse to run down the stairs after me and beg me to go in with him; he had a feeling that there was somebody in the studio. He remembered how often he had waited for a minute or two on the landing to get his breath after the ascent, and how absurdly his impatience to see Blanche had taken it away again. To see her was a delight that never staled, and even though he had not been out an hour he was as excited at the prospect as if they had been parted for a month. Suddenly he could not believe that she was dead. What had happened could only be a dream, a frightful dream; and when he turned the key and opened the door, he would see her bending

slightly over the table in the gracious attitude of the woman
in Chardin's *Benedicité,* which always seemed to him so
exquisite. Hurriedly he took the key out of his pocket,
opened, and walked in.

The apartment had no look of desertion. His wife's tidi-
ness was one of the traits which had so much pleased him;
his own upbringing had given him a tender sympathy for
the delight in orderliness; and when he had seen her instinctive desire to put each thing in its appointed place it had
given him a little warm feeling in his heart. The bedroom
looked as though she had just left it: the brushes were
neatly placed on the toilet-table, one on each side of the
comb; someone had smoothed down the bed on which she
had spent her last night in the studio; and her nightdress in
a little case lay on the pillow. It was impossible to believe
that she would never come into that room again.

But he felt thirsty, and went into the kitchen to get himself some water. Here, too, was order. On a rack were the
plates that she had used for dinner on the night of her quarrel with Strickland, and they had been carefully washed.
The knives and forks were put away in a drawer. Under a
cover were the remains of a piece of cheese, and in a tin box
was a crust of bread. She had done her marketing from day
to day, buying only what was strictly needful, so that nothing was left over from one day to the next. Stroeve knew
from the enquiries made by the police that Strickland had
walked out of the house immediately after dinner, and the
fact that Blanche had washed up the things as usual gave
him a little thrill of horror. Her methodicalness made her
suicide more deliberate. Her self-possession was frighten-
ing. A sudden pang seized him, and his knees felt so weak
that he almost fell. He went back into the bedroom and
threw himself on the bed. He cried out her name.

"Blanche. Blanche."

The thought of her suffering was intolerable. He had a sudden vision of her standing in the kitchen—it was hardly larger than a cupboard—washing the plates and glasses, the forks and spoons, giving the knives a rapid polish on the knife-board; and then putting everything away, giving the sink a scrub, and hanging the dish-cloth up to dry—it was there still, a gray torn rag; then looking round to see that everything was clean and nice. He saw her roll down her sleeves and remove her apron—the apron hung on a peg behind the door—and take the bottle of oxalic acid and go with it into the bedroom.

The agony of it drove him up from the bed and out of the room. He went into the studio. It was dark, for the curtains had been drawn over the great window, and he pulled them quickly back; but a sob broke from him as with a rapid glance he took in the place where he had been so happy. Nothing was changed here, either. Strickland was indifferent to his surroundings, and he had lived in the other's studio without thinking of altering a thing. It was deliberately artistic. It represented Stroeve's idea of the proper environment for an artist. There were bits of old brocade on the walls, and the piano was covered with a piece of silk, beautiful and tarnished; in one corner was a copy of the Venus of Milo, and in another of the Venus of the Medici. Here and there was an Italian cabinet surmounted with Delft, and here and there a bas-relief. In a handsome gold frame was a copy of Velasquez' Innocent X., that Stroeve had made in Rome, and placed so as to make the most of their decorative effect were a number of Stroeve's pictures, all in splendid frames. Stroeve had always been very proud of his taste. He had never lost his appreciation for the romantic atmosphere of a studio, and though now the sight

of it was like a stab in his heart, without thinking what he
was at, he changed slightly the position of a Louis XV.
table which was one of his treasures. Suddenly he caught
sight of a canvas with its face to the wall. It was a much
larger one than he himself was in the habit of using, and
he wondered what it did there. He went over to it and leaned
it towards him so that he could see the painting. It was a
nude. His heart began to beat quickly, for he guessed at
once that it was one of Strickland's pictures. He flung it
back against the wall angrily—what did he mean by leaving it there?—but his movement caused it to fall face down-
wards, on the ground. No matter whose the picture, he could
not leave it there in the dust and he raised it; but then
curiosity got the better of him. He thought he would like to
have a proper look at it, so he brought it along and set it on
the easel. Then he stood back in order to see it at his ease.

He gave a gasp. It was the picture of a woman lying on
a sofa, with one arm beneath her head and the other along
her body; one knee was raised, and the other leg was
stretched out. The pose was classic. Stroeve's head swam.
It was Blanche. Grief and jealousy and rage seized him, and
he cried out hoarsely; he was inarticulate; he clenched his
fists and raised them threateningly at an invisible enemy.
He screamed at the top of his voice. He was beside himself.
He could not bear it. That was too much. He looked round
wildly for some instrument; he wanted to hack the picture
to pieces; it should not exist another minute. He could see
nothing that would serve his purpose; he rummaged about
his painting things; somehow he could not find a thing; he
was frantic. At last he came upon what he sought, a large
scraper, and he pounced on it with a cry of triumph. He
seized it as though it were a dagger, and ran to the picture.

As Stroeve told me this he became as excited as when the

incident occurred, and he took hold of a dinner-knife on the table between us, and brandished it. He lifted his arm as though to strike, and then, opening his hand, let it fall with a clatter to the ground. He looked at me with a tremulous smile. He did not speak.

"Fire away," I said.

"I don't know what happened to me. I was just going to make a great hole in the picture, I had my arm all ready for the blow, when suddenly I seemed to see it."

"See what?"

"The picture. It was a work of art. I couldn't touch it. I was afraid."

Stroeve was silent again, and he stared at me with his mouth open and his round blue eyes starting out of his head.

"It was a great, a wonderful picture. I was seized with awe. I had nearly committed a dreadful crime. I moved a little to see it better, and my foot knocked against the scraper. I shuddered."

I really felt something of the emotion that had caught him. I was strangely impressed. It was as though I were suddenly transported into a world in which the values were changed. I stood by, at a loss, like a stranger in a land where the reactions of man to familiar things are all different from those he has known. Stroeve tried to talk to me about the picture, but he was incoherent, and I had to guess at what he meant. Strickland had burst the bonds that hitherto had held him. He had found, not himself, as the phrase goes, but a new soul with unsuspected powers. It was not only the bold simplification of the drawing which showed so rich and so singular a personality; it was not only the painting, though the flesh was painted with a passionate sensuality which had in it something miraculous; it was not only the solidity, so that you felt extraordinarily the weight of the body; there was also a spirituality, troubling and new, which led the imagination along unsuspected ways, and suggested dim empty spaces, lit only by the eternal stars, where the soul, all naked, adventured fearful to the discovery of new mysteries.

If I am rhetorical it is because Stroeve was rhetorical. (Do we not know that man in moments of emotion expresses himself naturally in the terms of a novelette?) Stroeve was trying to express a feeling which he had never known before, and he did not know how to put it into common terms. He was like the mystic seeking to describe the ineffable. But one fact he made clear to me; people talk of beauty lightly, and having no feeling for words, they use that one carelessly, so that it loses its force; and the thing it stands for, sharing its name with a hundred trivial objects, is deprived of dignity. They call beautiful a dress, a dog, a sermon; and when they are face to face with Beauty cannot recognise it. The false emphasis with which they try to deck their worthless thoughts blunts their susceptibilities. Like the charlatan who counterfeits a spiritual force he has sometimes felt, they lose the power they have abused. But Stroeve, the unconquerable buffoon, had a love and an understanding of beauty which were as honest and sincere as was his own sincere and honest soul. It meant to him what God means to the believer, and when he saw it he was afraid.

"What did you say to Strickland when you saw him?"

"I asked him to come with me to Holland."

I was dumbfounded. I could only look at Stroeve in stupid amazement.

"We both loved Blanche. There would have been room for him in my mother's house. I think the company of poor, simple people would have done his soul a great good. I think he might have learnt from them something that would be very useful to him.''

''What did he say?''

''He smiled a little. I suppose he thought me very silly. He said he had other fish to fry.''

I could have wished that Strickland had used some other phrase to indicate his refusal.

''He gave me the picture of Blanche.''

I wondered why Strickland had done that. But I made no remark, and for some time we kept silence.

''What have you done with all your things?'' I said at last.

''I got a Jew in, and he gave me a round sum for the lot. I'm taking my pictures home with me. Besides them I own nothing in the world now but a box of clothes and a few books.''

''I'm glad you're going home,'' I said.

I felt that his chance was to put all the past behind him. I hoped that the grief which now seemed intolerable would be softened by the lapse of time, and a merciful forgetfulness would help him to take up once more the burden of life. He was young still, and in a few years he would look back on all his misery with a sadness in which there would be something not unpleasurable. Sooner or later he would marry some honest soul in Holland, and I felt sure he would be happy. I smiled at the thought of the vast number of bad pictures he would paint before he died.

Next day I saw him off for Amsterdam.

40

For the next month, occupied with my own affairs, I saw no one connected with this lamentable business, and my mind ceased to be occupied with it. But one day, when I was walking along, bent on some errand, I passed Charles Strickland. The sight of him brought back to me all the horror which I was not unwilling to forget, and I felt in me a sudden repulsion for the cause of it. Nodding, for it would have been childish to cut him, I walked on quickly; but in a minute I felt a hand on my shoulder.

"You're in a great hurry," he said cordially.

It was characteristic of him to display geniality with any-one who showed a disinclination to meet him, and the cool-ness of my greeting can have left him in little doubt of that.

"I am," I answered briefly.

"I'll walk along with you," he said.

"Why?" I asked.

"For the pleasure of your society."

I did not answer, and he walked by my side silently. We continued thus for perhaps a quarter of a mile. I began to feel a little ridiculous. As last we passed a stationer's, and it occurred to me that I might as well buy some paper. It would be an excuse to be rid of him.

"I'm going in here," I said. "Good-bye."

"I'll wait for you."

I shrugged my shoulders, and went into the shop. I reflected that French paper was bad, and that, foiled of my purpose, I need not burden myself with a purchase that I did not need. I asked for something I knew could not be pro-vided, and in a minute came out into the street.

"Did you get what you wanted?" he asked.

"No."

We walked on in silence, and then came to a place where several streets met. I stopped at the curb.

"Which way do you go?" I enquired.

"Your way," he smiled.

"I'm going home."

"I'll come along with you and smoke a pipe."

"You might wait for an invitation," I retorted frigidly.

"I would if I thought there was any chance of getting one."

"Do you see that wall in front of you?" I said, pointing.

"Yes."

"In that case I should have thought you could see also that I don't want your company."

"I vaguely suspected it, I confess."

I could not help a chuckle. It is one of the defects of my character that I cannot altogether dislike anyone who makes me laugh. But I pulled myself together.

"I think you're detestable. You're the most loathsome beast that it's ever been my misfortune to meet. Why do you seek the society of someone who hates and despises you?"

"My dear fellow, what the hell do you suppose I care what you think of me?"

"Damn it all," I said, more violently because I had an inkling my motive was none too creditable, "I don't want to know you."

"Are you afraid I shall corrupt you?"

His tone made me feel not a little ridiculous. I knew that he was looking at me sideways, with a sardonic smile.

"I suppose you are hard up," I remarked insolently.

"I should be a damned fool if I thought I had any chance of borrowing money from you."

"You've come down in the world if you can bring yourself to flatter."

He grinned.

"You'll never really dislike me so long as I give you the
opportunity to get off a good thing now and then."

I had to bite my lip to prevent myself from laughing.
What he said had a hateful truth in it, and another defect
of my character is that I enjoy the company of those, however depraved, who can give me a Roland for my Oliver. I
began to feel that my abhorrence for Strickland could only
be sustained by an effort on my part. I recognised my moral
weakness, but saw that my disapprobation had in it already
something of a pose; and I knew that if I felt it, his own
keen instinct had discovered it, too. He was certainly laughing at me up his sleeve. I left him the last word, and sought
refuge in a shrug of the shoulders and taciturnity.

 41

We arrived at the house in which I lived. I would not ask
him to come in with me, but walked up the stairs without a
word. He followed me, and entered the apartment on my
heels. He had not been in it before, but he never gave a
glance at the room I had been at pains to make pleasing to
the eye. There was a tin of tobacco on the table, and, taking
out his pipe, he filled it. He sat down on the only chair that
had no arms and tilted himself on the back legs.

"If you're going to make yourself at home, why don't you
sit in an arm-chair?" I asked irritably.

"Why are you concerned about my comfort?"

"I'm not," I retorted, "but only about my own. It makes me uncomfortable to see someone sit on an uncomfortable chair."

He chuckled, but did not move. He smoked on in silence, taking no further notice of me, and apparently was absorbed in thought. I wondered why he had come.

Until long habit has blunted the sensibility, there is something disconcerting to the writer in the instinct which causes him to take an interest in the singularities of human nature so absorbing that his moral sense is powerless against it. He recognises in himself an artistic satisfaction in the contemplation of evil which a little startles him; but sincerity forces him to confess that the disapproval he feels for certain actions is not nearly so strong as his curiosity in their reasons. The character of a scoundrel, logical and complete, has a fascination for his creator which is an outrage to law and order. I expect that Shakespeare devised Iago with a gusto which he never knew when, weaving moonbeams with his fancy, he imagined Desdemona. It may be that in his rogues the writer gratifies instincts deep-rooted in him, which the manners and customs of a civilised world have forced back to the mysterious recesses of the subconscious. In giving to the character of his invention flesh and bones he is giving life to that part of himself which finds no other means of expression. His satisfaction is a sense of liberation.

The writer is more concerned to know than to judge.

There was in my soul a perfectly genuine horror of Strickland, and side by side with it a cold curiosity to discover his motives. I was puzzled by him, and I was eager to see how he regarded the tragedy he had caused in the lives of people who had used him with so much kindness. I applied the scalpel boldly.

"Stroeve told me that picture you painted of his wife was the best thing you've ever done."

Strickland took his pipe out of his mouth, and a smile lit up his eyes.

"It was great fun to do."

"Why did you give it him?"

"I'd finished it. It wasn't any good to me."

"Do you know that Stroeve nearly destroyed it?"

"It wasn't altogether satisfactory."

He was quiet for a moment or two, then he took his pipe out of his mouth again, and chuckled.

"Do you know that the little man came to see me?"

"Weren't you rather touched by what he had to say?"

"No; I thought it damned silly and sentimental."

"I suppose it escaped your memory that you'd ruined his life?" I remarked.

He rubbed his bearded chin reflectively.

"He's a very bad painter."

"But a very good man."

"And an excellent cook," Strickland added derisively.

His callousness was inhuman, and in my indignation I was not inclined to mince my words.

"As a mere matter of curiosity I wish you'd tell me, have you felt the smallest twinge of remorse for Blanche Stroeve's death?"

I watched his face for some change of expression, but it remained impassive.

"Why should I?" he asked.

"Let me put the facts before you. You were dying, and Dirk Stroeve took you into his own house. He nursed you like a mother. He sacrificed his time and his comfort and his money for you. He snatched you from the jaws of death."

Strickland shrugged his shoulders.

"The absurd little man enjoys doing things for other people. That's his life."

"Granting that you owed him no gratitude, were you obliged to go out of your way to take his wife from him? Until you came on the scene they were happy. Why couldn't you leave them alone?"

"What makes you think they were happy?"

"It was evident."

"You are a discerning fellow. Do you think she could ever have forgiven him for what he did for her?"

"What do you mean by that?"

"Don't you know why he married her?"

I shook my head.

"She was a governess in the family of some Roman prince, and the son of the house seduced her. She thought he was going to marry her. They turned her out into the street neck and crop. She was going to have a baby, and she tried to commit suicide. Stroeve found her and married her."

"It was just like him. I never knew anyone with so compassionate a heart."

I had often wondered why that ill-assorted pair had married, but just that explanation had never occurred to me. That was perhaps the cause of the peculiar quality of Dirk's love for his wife. I had noticed in it something more than passion. I remembered also how I had always fancied that her reserve concealed I knew not what; but now I saw in it more than the desire to hide a shameful secret. Her tranquillity was like the sullen calm that broods over an island which has been swept by a hurricane. Her cheerfulness was the cheerfulness of despair. Strickland interrupted my reflections with an observation the profound cynicism of which startled me.

"A woman can forgive a man for the harm he does her," he said, "but she can never forgive him for the sacrifices he makes on her account."

"It must be reassuring to you to know that you certainly run no risk of incurring the resentment of the women you come in contact with," I retorted.

A slight smile broke on his lips.

"You are always prepared to sacrifice your principles for a repartee," he answered.

"What happened to the child?"

"Oh, it was still-born, three or four months after they were married."

Then I came to the question which had seemed to me most puzzling.

"Will you tell me why you bothered about Blanche Stroeve at all?"

He did not answer for so long that I nearly repeated it.

"How do I know?" he said at last. "She couldn't bear the sight of me. It amused me."

"I see."

He gave a sudden flash of anger.

"Damn it all, I wanted her."

But he recovered his temper immediately, and looked at me with a smile.

"At first she was horrified."

"Did you tell her?"

"There wasn't any need. She knew. I never said a word. She was frightened. At last I took her."

I do not know what there was in the way he told me this that extraordinarily suggested the violence of his desire.

It was disconcerting and rather horrible. His life was strangely divorced from material things, and it was as though his body at times wreaked a fearful revenge on his spirit. The satyr in him suddenly took possession, and he was powerless in the grip of an instinct which had all the strength of the primitive forces of nature. It was an obsession so complete that there was no room in his soul for prudence or gratitude.

"But why did you want to take her away with you?" I asked.

"I didn't," he answered, frowning. "When she said she was coming I was nearly as surprised as Stroeve. I told her that when I'd had enough of her she'd have to go, and she said she'd risk that." He paused a little. "She had a wonderful body, and I wanted to paint a nude. When I'd finished my picture I took no more interest in her."

"And she loved you with all her heart."

He sprang to his feet and walked up and down the small room.

"I don't want love. I haven't time for it. It's weakness. I am a man, and sometimes I want a woman. When I've satisfied my passion I'm ready for other things. I can't overcome my desire, but I hate it; it imprisons my spirit; I look forward to the time when I shall be free from all desire and can give myself without hindrance to my work. Because women can do nothing except love, they've given it a ridiculous importance. They want to persuade us that it's the whole of life. It's an insignificant part. I know lust. That's normal and healthy. Love is a disease. Women are the instruments of my pleasure; I have no patience with their claim to be helpmates, partners, companions."

I had never heard Strickland speak so much at one time.

He spoke with a passion of indignation. But neither here nor elsewhere do I pretend to give his exact words; his vocabulary was small, and he had no gift for framing sentences, so that one had to piece his meaning together out of interjections, the expression of his face, gestures and hackneyed phrases.

"You should have lived at a time when women were chattels and men the masters of slaves," I said.

"It just happens that I am a completely normal man."

I could not help laughing at this remark, made in all seriousness; but he went on, walking up and down the room like a caged beast, intent on expressing what he felt, but found such difficulty in putting coherently.

"When a woman loves you she's not satisfied until she possesses your soul. Because she's weak, she has a rage for domination, and nothing less will satisfy her. She has a small mind, and she resents the abstract which she is unable to grasp. She is occupied with material things, and she is jealous of the ideal. The soul of man wanders through the uttermost regions of the universe, and she seeks to imprison it in the circle of her account-book. Do you remember my wife? I saw Blanche little by little trying all her tricks. With infinite patience she prepared to snare me and bind me. She wanted to bring me down to her level; she cared nothing for me, she only wanted me to be hers. She was willing to do everything in the world for me except the one thing I wanted: to leave me alone."

I was silent for a while.

"What did you expect her to do when you left her?"

"She could have gone back to Stroeve," he said irritably. "He was ready to take her."

"You're inhuman," I answered. "It's as useless to talk

to you about these things as to describe colours to a man who was born blind.''

He stopped in front of my chair, and stood looking down at me with an expression in which I read a contemptuous amazement.

''Do you really care a twopenny damn if Blanche Stroeve is alive or dead?''

I thought over his question, for I wanted to answer it truthfully, at all events to my soul.

''It may be a lack of sympathy in myself if it does not make any great difference to me that she is dead. Life had a great deal to offer her. I think it's terrible that she should have been deprived of it in that cruel way, and I am ashamed because I do not really care.''

''You have not the courage of your convictions. Life has no value. Blanche Stroeve didn't commit suicide because I left her, but because she was a foolish and unbalanced woman. But we've talked about her quite enough; she was an entirely unimportant person. Come, and I'll show you my pictures.''

He spoke as though I were a child that needed to be distracted. I was sore, but not with him so much as with myself. I thought of the happy life that pair had led in the cosy studio in Montmartre, Stroeve and his wife, their simplicity, kindness, and hospitality; it seemed to me cruel that it should have been broken to pieces by a ruthless chance; but the cruellest thing of all was that in fact it made no great difference. The world went on, and no one was a penny the worse for all that wretchedness. I had an idea that Dirk, a man of greater emotional reactions than depth of feeling, would soon forget; and Blanche's life, begun with who knows what bright hopes and what dreams, might just as well have never been lived. It all seemed useless and inane.

Strickland had found his hat, and stood looking at me.

"Are you coming?"

"Why do you seek my acquaintance?" I asked him. "You know that I hate and despise you."

He chuckled good-humouredly.

"Your only quarrel with me really is that I don't care a twopenny damn what you think about me."

I felt my cheeks grow red with sudden anger. It was impossible to make him understand that one might be outraged by his callous selfishness. I longed to pierce his armour of complete indifference. I knew also that in the end there was truth in what he said. Unconsciously, perhaps, we treasure the power we have over people by their regard for our opinion of them, and we hate those upon whom we have no such influence. I suppose it is the bitterest wound to human pride. But I would not let him see that I was put out.

"Is it possible for any man to disregard others entirely?" I said, though more to myself than to him. "You're dependent on others for everything in existence. It's a preposterous attempt to try to live only for yourself and by yourself. Sooner or later you'll be ill and tired and old, and then you'll crawl back into the herd. Won't you be ashamed when you feel in your heart the desire for comfort and sympathy? You're trying an impossible thing. Sooner or later the human being in you will yearn for the common bonds of humanity."

"Come and look at my pictures."

"Have you ever thought of death?"

"Why should I? It doesn't matter."

I stared at him. He stood before me, motionless, with a

mocking smile in his eyes; but for all that, for a moment I had an inkling of a fiery, tortured spirit, aiming at something greater than could be conceived by anything that was bound up with the flesh. I had a fleeting glimpse of a pursuit of the ineffable. I looked at the man before me in his shabby clothes, with his great nose and shining eyes, his red beard and untidy hair; and I had a strange sensation that it was only an envelope, and I was in the presence of a disembodied spirit.

"Let us go and look at your pictures," I said.

The Moon
AND Sixpence

II

42

I did not know why Strickland had suddenly offered to show
them to me. I welcomed the opportunity. A man's work re-
veals him. In social intercourse he gives you the surface that
he wishes the world to accept, and you can only gain a true
knowledge of him by inferences from little actions, of which
he is unconscious, and from fleeting expressions, which cross
his face unknown to him. Sometimes people carry to such
perfection the mask they have assumed that in due course
they actually become the person they seem. But in his book or
his picture the real man delivers himself defenceless. His pretentiousness will only expose his vacuity. The lathe painted to
look like iron is seen to be but a lathe. No affectation of peculiarity can conceal a commonplace mind. To the acute observer
no one can produce the most casual work without disclosing
the innermost secrets of his soul.

As I walked up the endless stairs of the house in which
Strickland lived, I confess that I was a little excited. It seemed
to me that I was on the threshold of a surprising adventure.
I looked about the room with curiosity. It was even smaller
and more bare than I remembered it. I wondered what those
friends of mine would say who demanded vast studios, and
vowed they could not work unless all the conditions were to
their liking.

"You'd better stand there," he said, pointing to a spot from
which, presumably, he fancied I could see to best advantage
what he had to show me.

"You don't want me to talk, I suppose," I said.

"No, blast you; I want you to hold your tongue."

He placed a picture on the easel, and let me look at it for a

*"He showed me
about thirty
canvases"*

minute or two; then took it down and put another in its place.
I think he showed me about thirty canvases. It was the result
of the six years during which he had been painting. He had
never sold a picture. The canvases were of different sizes. The
smaller were pictures of still-life and the largest were landscapes. There were about half a dozen portraits.

"That is the lot," he said at last.

I wish I could say that I recognised at once their beauty and their great originality. Now that I have seen many of them again and the rest are familiar to me in reproductions, I am astonished that at first sight I was bitterly disappointed. I felt nothing of the peculiar thrill which it is the property of art to give. The impression that Strickland's pictures gave me was disconcerting; and the fact remains, always to reproach me, that I never even thought of buying any. I missed a wonderful chance. Most of them have found their way into museums, and the rest are the treasured possessions of wealthy amateurs. I try to find excuses for myself. I think that my taste is good, but I am conscious that it has no originality. I know very little about painting, and I wander along trails that others have blazed for me. At that time I had the greatest admiration for the Impressionists. I longed to possess a Sisley and a Degas, and I worshipped Manet. His *Olympia* seemed to me the greatest picture of modern times, and *Le Déjeuner sur l'Herbe* moved me profoundly. These works seemed to me the last word in painting.

I will not describe the pictures that Strickland showed me. Descriptions of pictures are always dull, and these, besides, are familiar to all who take an interest in such things. Now that his influence has so enormously affected modern painting, now that others have charted the country which he was among the first to explore, Strickland's pictures, seen for the first time, would find the mind more prepared for them; but it must be remembered that I had never seen anything of the sort. First of all I was taken aback by what seemed to me the clumsiness of his technique. Accustomed to the drawing of the old masters, and convinced that Ingres was the greatest draughtsman of recent times, I thought that Strickland drew very badly. I knew nothing of the simplification at which he aimed. I remember a still-life of oranges on a plate, and I was bothered because the plate was not round and the oranges were lop-sided. The portraits were a little larger than life-size, and this gave them an ungainly look. To my eyes the faces looked like caricatures. They were painted in a way that was entirely new to me. The landscapes puzzled me even more. There were two or three pictures of the forest at Fontainebleau and several of streets in Paris: my first feeling was that they might have been painted by a drunken cab driver. I was perfectly bewildered. The colour seemed to me extraordinarily crude. It passed through my mind that the whole thing was a stupendous, incomprehensible farce. Now that I look back I am more than ever impressed by Stroeve's acuteness. He saw from the first that here was a revolution in art, and he recognised in its beginnings the genius which now all the world allows.

But if I was puzzled and disconcerted, I was not unimpressed. Even I, in my colossal ignorance, could not but feel that here, trying to express itself, was real power. I was excited and interested. I felt that these pictures had something to say to me that was very important for me to know, but I could not tell what it was. They seemed to me ugly, but they suggested without disclosing a secret of momentous significance. They were strangely tantalising. They gave me an emotion that I could not analyse. They said something that words were powerless to utter. I fancy that Strickland saw vaguely some spiritual meaning in material things that was so strange that he could only suggest it with halting symbols. It was as though he found in the chaos of the universe a new pattern, and were attempting clumsily, with anguish of soul, to set it down. I saw a tormented spirit striving for the release of expression.

I turned to him.

"I wonder if you haven't mistaken your medium," I said.

"What the hell do you mean?"

"I think you're trying to say something, I don't quite know what it is, but I'm not sure that the best way of saying it is by means of painting."

When I imagined that on seeing his pictures I should get a clue to the understanding of his strange character I was mistaken. They merely increased the astonishment with which he filled me. I was more at sea than ever. The only thing that seemed clear to me—and perhaps even this was fanciful—was that he was passionately striving for liberation from some power that held him. But what the power was and what line the liberation would take remained obscure. Each one of us is alone in the world. He is shut in a tower of brass, and can communicate with his fellows only by signs, and the signs have no common value, so that their sense is vague and uncertain. We seek pitifully to convey to others the treasures of our heart, but they have not the power to accept them, and so we go lonely, side by side but not together, unable to know our fellows and unknown by them. We are like people living in a country whose language they know so little that, with all manner of beautiful and profound things to say, they are condemned to the banalities of the conversation manual. Their brain is seething with ideas, and they can only tell you that the umbrella of the gardener's aunt is in the house.

The final impression I received was of a prodigious effort to express some state of the soul, and in this effort, I fancied, must be sought the explanation of what so utterly perplexed me. It was evident that colours and forms had a significance for Strickland that was peculiar to himself. He was under an intolerable necessity to convey something that he felt, and he created them with that intention alone. He did not hesitate to simplify or to distort if he could get nearer to that unknown thing he sought. Facts were nothing to him, for beneath the mass of irrelevant incidents he looked for something significant to himself. It was as though he had become aware of the soul of the universe and were compelled to express it. Though these pictures confused and puzzled me, I could not be unmoved by the emotion that was patent in them; and, I knew not why, I felt in myself a feeling that with regard to Strickland was the last I had ever expected to experience. I felt an overwhelming compassion.

"I think I know now why you surrendered to your feeling for Blanche Stroeve," I said to him.

"Why?"

"I think your courage failed. The weakness of your body communicated itself to your soul. I do not know what infinite yearning possesses you, so that you are driven to a perilous, lonely search for some goal where you expect to find a final release from the spirit that torments you. I see you as the eternal pilgrim to some shrine that perhaps does not exist. I do not know to what inscrutable Nirvana you aim. Do you know yourself? Perhaps it is Truth and Freedom that you seek, and for a moment you thought that you might find release in Love. I think your tired soul sought rest in a woman's arms, and when you found no rest there you hated her. You had no pity for her, because you have no pity for yourself. And you killed her out of fear, because you trembled still at the danger you had barely escaped."

He smiled dryly and pulled his beard.

"You are a dreadful sentimentalist, my poor friend."

A week later I heard by chance that Strickland had gone to Marseilles. I never saw him again.

43

Looking back, I realise that what I have written about Charles Strickland must seem very unsatisfactory. I have given incidents that came to my knowledge, but they remain obscure because I do not know the reasons that led to them. The strangest, Strickland's determination to become a painter, seems to be arbitrary; and though it must have had causes in the circumstances of his life, I am ignorant of them. From his own conversation I was able to glean nothing. If I were writing a novel, rather than narrating such facts as I know of a curious personality, I should have invented much to account for this change of heart. I think I should have shown a strong vocation in boyhood, crushed by the will of his father or sacrificed to the necessity of earning a living; I should have pictured him impatient of the restraints of life; and in the struggle between his passion for art and the duties of his station I could have aroused sympathy for him. I should so have made him a more imposing figure. Perhaps it would have been possible to see in him a new Prometheus. There was here, maybe, the opportunity for a modern version of the hero who for the good of mankind exposes himself to the agonies of the damned. It is always a moving subject.

On the other hand, I might have found his motives in the influence of the married relation. There are a dozen ways in which this might be managed. A latent gift might reveal itself on acquaintance with the painters and writers whose society his wife sought; or domestic incompatibility might turn him upon himself; a love affair might fan into bright flame a fire which I could have shown smouldering dimly in his heart. I think then I should have drawn Mrs. Strickland quite differently. I should have abandoned the facts and made her a nagging, tiresome woman, or else a bigoted one with no sympathy for the claims of the spirit. I should have made Strickland's marriage a long torment from which escape was the only possible issue. I think I should have emphasised his patience with the unsuitable mate, and the compassion which made him unwilling to throw off the yoke that oppressed him. I should certainly have eliminated the children.

An effective story might also have been made by bringing him into contact with some old painter whom the pressure of want or the desire for commercial success had made false to the genius of his youth, and who, seeing in Strickland the possibilities which himself had wasted, influenced him to forsake all and follow the divine tyranny of art. I think there would have been something ironic in the picture of the successful old man, rich and honoured, living in another the life which he, though knowing it was the better part, had not had the strength to pursue.

The facts are much duller. Strickland, a boy fresh from school, went into a broker's office without any feeling of distaste. Until he married he led the ordinary life of his fellows, gambling mildly on the Exchange, interested to the extent of a sovereign or two on the result of the Derby or the Oxford and Cambridge Race. I think he boxed a little in his spare time. On his chimney-piece he had photographs of Mrs. Langtry and Mary Anderson. He read *Punch* and the *Sporting Times*. He went to dances in Hampstead.

It matters less that for so long I should have lost sight of him. The years during which he was struggling to acquire proficiency in a difficult art were monotonous, and I do not know that there was anything significant in the shifts to which he was put to earn enough money to keep him. An ac-

count of them would be an account of the things he had seen
happen to other people. I do not think they had any effect on
his own character. He must have acquired experiences which
would form abundant material for a picaresque novel of modern Paris, but he remained aloof, and judging from his conversation there was nothing in those years that had made a
particular impression on him. Perhaps when he went to Paris
he was too old to fall a victim to the glamour of his environment. Strange as it may seem, he always appeared to me not
only practical, but immensely matter-of-fact. I suppose his
life during this period was romantic, but he certainly saw no
romance in it. It may be that in order to realise the romance
of life you must have something of the actor in you; and,
capable of standing outside yourself, you must be able to
watch your actions with an interest at once detached and absorbed. But no one was more single-minded than Strickland.
I never knew anyone who was less self-conscious. But it is un-
fortunate that I can give no description of the arduous steps
by which he reached such mastery over his art as he ever
acquired; for if I could show him undaunted by failure, by an
unceasing effort of courage holding despair at bay, doggedly
persistent in the face of self-doubt, which is the artist's bitterest enemy, I might excite some sympathy for a personality which, I am all too conscious, must appear singularly
devoid of charm. But I have nothing to go on. I never once
saw Strickland at work, nor do I know that anyone else did.
He kept the secret of his struggles to himself. If in the loneliness of his studio he wrestled desperately with the Angel of
the Lord he never allowed a soul to divine his anguish.

When I come to his connection with Blanche Stroeve I am
exasperated by the fragmentariness of the facts at my dis-
posal. To give my story coherence I should describe the prog-
ress of their tragic union, but I know nothing of the three

months during which they lived together. I do not know how they got on or what they talked about. After all, there are twenty-four hours in the day, and the summits of emotion can only be reached at rare intervals. I can only imagine how they passed the rest of the time. While the light lasted and so long as Blanche's strength endured, I suppose that Strickland painted, and it must have irritated her when she saw him absorbed in his work. As a mistress she did not then exist for him, but only as a model; and then there were long hours in which they lived side by side in silence. It must have frightened her. When Strickland suggested that in her surrender to him there was a sense of triumph over Dirk Stroeve, because he had come to her help in her extremity, he opened the door to many a dark conjecture. I hope it was not true. It seems to me rather horrible. But who can fathom the subtleties of the human heart? Certainly not those who expect from it only decorous sentiments and normal emotions. When Blanche saw that, notwithstanding his moments of passion, Strickland remained aloof, she must have been filled with dismay, and even in those moments I surmise that she realised that to him she was not an individual, but an instrument of pleasure; he was a stranger still, and she tried to bind him to herself with pathetic arts. She strove to ensnare him with comfort and would not see that comfort meant nothing to him. She was at pains to get him the things to eat that he liked, and would not see that he was indifferent to food. She was afraid to leave him alone. She pursued him with attentions, and when his passion was dormant sought to excite it, for then at least she had the illusion of holding him. Perhaps she knew with her intelligence that the chains she forged only aroused his instinct of destruction, as the plate-glass window makes your fingers itch for half a brick; but her heart, incapable of reason, made her continue on a course she knew was fatal. She must have been very unhappy. But the blindness of love led her to believe what she wanted to be true, and her love was so great that it seemed impossible to her that it should not in return awake an equal love.

But my study of Strickland's character suffers from a greater defect than my ignorance of many facts. Because they were obvious and striking, I have written of his relations to women; and yet they were but an insignificant part of his life. It is an irony that they should so tragically have affected others. His real life consisted of dreams and of tremendously hard work.

Here lies the unreality of fiction. For in men, as a rule, love is but an episode which takes its place among the other affairs of the day, and the emphasis laid on it in novels gives it an importance which is untrue to life. There are few men to whom it is the most important thing in the world, and they are not very interesting ones; even women, with whom the subject is of paramount interest, have a contempt for them. They are flattered and excited by them, but have an uneasy feeling that they are poor creatures. But even during the brief intervals in which they are in love, men do other things which distract their mind; the trades by which they earn their living engage their attention; they are absorbed in sport; they can interest themselves in art. For the most part, they keep their various activities in various compartments, and they can pursue one to the temporary exclusion of the other. They have a faculty of concentration on that which occupies them at the moment, and it irks them if one encroaches on the other. As lovers, the difference between men and women is that women can love all day long, but men only at times.

With Strickland the sexual appetite took a very small place. It was unimportant. It was irksome. His soul aimed elsewhither. He had violent passions, and on occasion desire seized his body so that he was driven to an orgy of lust, but

he hated the instincts that robbed him of his self-possession.
I think, even, he hated the inevitable partner in his de-
bauchery. When he had regained command over himself, he
shuddered at the sight of the woman he had enjoyed. His
thoughts floated then serenely in the empyrean, and he felt
towards her the horror that perhaps the painted butterfly,
hovering about the flowers, feels to the filthy chrysalis from
which it has triumphantly emerged. I suppose that art is a
manifestation of the sexual instinct. It is the same emotion
which is excited in the human heart by the sight of a lovely
woman, the Bay of Naples under the yellow moon, and the
Entombment of Titian. It is possible that Strickland hated the
normal release of sex because it seemed to him brutal by comparison with the satisfaction of artistic creation. It seems
strange even to myself, when I have described a man who was
cruel, selfish, brutal and sensual, to say that he was a great
idealist. The fact remains.

He lived more poorly than an artisan. He worked harder.
He cared nothing for those things which with most people
make life gracious and beautiful. He was indifferent to money.
He cared nothing about fame. You cannot praise him because
he resisted the temptation to make any of those compromises
with the world which most of us yield to. He had no such
temptation. It never entered his head that compromise was
possible. He lived in Paris more lonely than an anchorite in
the deserts of Thebes. He asked nothing from his fellows except that they should leave him alone. He was single-hearted
in his aim, and to pursue it he was willing to sacrifice not
only himself—many can do that—but others. He had a vision.

Strickland was an odious man, but I still think he was a
great one.

44

A certain importance attaches to the views on art of painters, and this is the natural place for me to set down what I know of Strickland's opinions of the great artists of the past. I am afraid I have very little worth noting. Strickland was not a conversationalist, and he had no gift for putting what he had to say in the striking phrase that the listener remembers. He had no wit. His humour, as will be seen if I have in any way succeeded in reproducing the manner of his conversation, was sardonic. His repartee was rude. He made one laugh sometimes by speaking the truth, but this is a form of humour which gains its force only by its unusualness; it would cease to amuse if it were commonly practised.

Strickland was not, I should say, a man of great intelligence, and his views on painting were by no means out of the ordinary. I never heard him speak of those whose work had a certain analogy with his own—of Cezanne, for instance, or of Van Gogh; and I doubt very much if he had ever seen their pictures. He was not greatly interested in the Impressionists. Their technique impressed him, but I fancy that he thought their attitude commonplace. When Stroeve was holding forth at length on the excellence of Monet, he said: "I prefer Winterhalter." But I dare say he said it to annoy, and if he did he certainly succeeded.

I am disappointed that I cannot report any extravagances in his opinions on the old masters. There is so much in his character which is strange that I feel it would complete the picture if his views were outrageous. I feel the need to ascribe to him fantastic theories about his predecessors, and it is with a certain sense of disillusion that I confess he thought about them pretty much as does everybody else. I do not believe he knew El Greco. He had a great but somewhat impatient admiration for Velasquez. Chardin delighted him, and Rembrandt moved him to ecstasy. He described the impression that Rembrandt made on him with a coarseness I cannot repeat. The only painter that interested him who was at all unexpected was Brueghel the Elder. I knew very little about him at that time, and Strickland had no power to explain himself. I remember what he said about him because it was so unsatisfactory.

"He's all right," said Strickland. "I bet he found it hell to paint."

When later, in Vienna, I saw several of Peter Brueghel's pictures, I thought I understood why he had attracted Strickland's attention. Here, too, was a man with a vision of the world peculiar to himself. I made somewhat copious notes at the time, intending to write something about him, but I have lost them, and have now only the recollection of an emotion. He seemed to see his fellow-creatures grotesquely, and he was angry with them because they were grotesque; life was a confusion of ridiculous, sordid happenings, a fit subject for laughter, and yet it made him sorrowful to laugh. Brueghel gave me the impression of a man striving to express in one medium feelings more appropriate to expression in another, and it may be that it was the obscure consciousness of this that excited Strickland's sympathy. Perhaps both were trying to put down in paint ideas which were more suitable to literature.

Strickland at this time must have been nearly forty-seven.

I have said already that but for the hazard of a journey to
Tahiti I should doubtless never have written this book. It is
thither that after many wanderings Charles Strickland came,
and it is there that he painted the pictures on which his fame
most securely rests. I suppose no artist achieves completely the
realisation of the dream that obsesses him, and Strickland,
harassed incessantly by his struggle with technique, managed, perhaps, less than others to express the vision that he
saw with his mind's eye; but in Tahiti the circumstances were
favourable to him; he found in his surroundings the accidents
necessary for his inspiration to become effective, and his later
pictures give at least a suggestion of what he sought. They
offer the imagination something new and strange. It is as
though in this far country his spirit, that had wandered disembodied, seeking a tenement, at last was able to clothe itself
in flesh. To use the hackneyed phrase, here he found himself.

It would seem that my visit to this remote island should
immediately revive my interest in Strickland, but the work
I was engaged in occupied my attention to the exclusion of
something that was irrelevant, and it was not till I had been
there some days that I even remembered his connection with
it. After all, I had not seen him for fifteen years, and it was
nine since he died. But I think my arrival at Tahiti would
have driven out of my head matters of much more immediate
importance to me, and even after a week I found it not easy
to order myself soberly. I remember that on my first morning I awoke early, and when I came on to the terrace of the
hotel no one was stirring. I wandered round to the kitchen,

but it was locked, and on a bench outside it a native boy was
sleeping. There seemed no chance of breakfast for some time,

"Tahiti is like a lovely woman"

so I sauntered down to the water-front. The Chinamen were already busy in their shops. The sky had still the pallor of dawn, and there was a ghostly silence on the lagoon. Ten miles away the island of Murea, like some high fastness of the Holy Grail, guarded its mystery.

I did not altogether believe my eyes. The days that had passed since I left Wellington seemed extraordinary and unusual. Wellington is trim and neat and English; it reminds you of a seaport town on the South Coast. And for three days afterwards the sea was stormy. Gray clouds chased one another across the sky. Then the wind dropped, and the sea was calm and blue. The Pacific is more desolate than other seas; its spaces seem more vast, and the most ordinary journey upon it has somehow the feeling of an adventure. The air you breathe is an elixir which prepares you for the unexpected. Nor is it vouchsafed to man in the flesh to know aught that more nearly suggests the approach to the golden realms of fancy than the approach to Tahiti. Murea, the sister isle, comes into view in rocky splendour, rising from the desert sea mysteriously, like the unsubstantial fabric of a magic wand. With its jagged outline it is like a Montserrat of the Pacific, and you may imagine that there Polynesian knights guard with strange rites mysteries unholy for men to know. The beauty of the island is unveiled as diminishing distance shows you in distincter shape its lovely peaks, but it keeps its secret as you sail by, and, darkly inviolable, seems to fold itself together in a stony, inaccessible grimness. It would not surprise you if, as you came near seeking for an opening in the reef, it vanished suddenly from your view, and nothing met your gaze but the blue loneliness of the Pacific.

Tahiti is a lofty green island, with deep folds of a darker green, in which you divine silent valleys; there is mystery in their sombre depths, down which murmur and plash cool

streams, and you feel that in those umbrageous places life
from immemorial times has been led according to immemorial ways. Even here is something sad and terrible. But the
impression is fleeting, and serves only to give a greater
acuteness to the enjoyment of the moment. It is like the sadness which you may see in the jester's eyes when a merry
company is laughing at his sallies; his lips smile and his jokes
are gayer because in the communion of laughter he finds himself more intolerably alone. For Tahiti is smiling and friendly;
it is like a lovely woman graciously prodigal of her charm
and beauty; and nothing can be more conciliatory than the
entrance into the harbour at Papeete. The schooners moored
to the quay are trim and neat, the little town along the bay is
white and urbane, and the flamboyants, scarlet against the
blue sky, flaunt their colour like a cry of passion. They are
sensual with an unashamed violence that leaves you breathless. And the crowd that throngs the wharf as the steamer
draws alongside is gay and debonair; it is a noisy, cheerful,
gesticulating crowd. It is a sea of brown faces. You have an
impression of coloured movement against the flaming blue of
the sky. Everything is done with a great deal of bustle, the
unloading of the baggage, the examination of the customs;
and everyone seems to smile at you. It is very hot. The colour
dazzles you.

I had not been in Tahiti long before I met Captain Nichols.
He came in one morning when I was having breakfast on the
terrace of the hotel and introduced himself. He had heard

that I was interested in Charles Strickland, and announced that he was come to have a talk about him. They are as fond of gossip in Tahiti as in an English village, and one or two enquiries I had made for pictures by Strickland had been quickly spread. I asked the stranger if he had breakfasted.

"Yes; I have my coffee early," he answered, "but I don't mind having a drop of whisky."

I called the Chinese boy.

"You don't think it's too early?" said the Captain.

"You and your liver must decide that between you," I replied.

"I'm practically a teetotaller," he said, as he poured himself out a good half-tumbler of Canadian Club.

When he smiled he showed broken and discoloured teeth. He was a very lean man, of no more than average height, with gray hair cut short and a stubbly gray moustache. He had not shaved for a couple of days. His face was deeply lined, burned brown by long exposure to the sun, and he had a pair of small blue eyes which were astonishingly shifty. They moved quickly, following my smallest gesture, and they gave him the look of a very thorough rogue. But at the moment he was all heartiness and good-fellowship. He was dressed in a bedraggled suit of khaki, and his hands would have been all the better for a wash.

"I knew Strickland well," he said, as he leaned back in his chair and lit the cigar I had offered him. "It's through me he came out to the islands."

"Where did you meet him?" I asked.

"In Marseilles."

"What were you doing there?"

He gave me an ingratiating smile.

"Well, I guess I was on the beach."

My friend's appearance suggested that he was now in the

same predicament, and I prepared myself to cultivate an agreeable acquaintance. The society of beach-combers always repays the small pains you need be at to enjoy it. They are easy of approach and affable in conversation. They seldom put on airs, and the offer of a drink is a sure way to their hearts. You need no laborious steps to enter upon familiarity with them, and you can earn not only their confidence, but their gratitude, by turning an attentive ear to their discourse. They look upon conversation as the great pleasure of life, thereby proving the excellence of their civilisation, and for the most part they are entertaining talkers. The extent of their experience is pleasantly balanced by the fertility of their imagination. It cannot be said that they are without guile, but they have a tolerant respect for the law, when the law is supported by strength. It is hazardous to play poker with them, but their ingenuity adds a peculiar excitement to the best game in the world. I came to know Captain Nichols very well before I left Tahiti, and I am the richer for his acquaintance. I do not consider that the cigars and whisky he consumed at my expense (he always refused cocktails, since he was practically a teetotaller), and the few dollars, borrowed with a civil air of conferring a favour upon me, that passed from my pocket to his, were in any way equivalent to the entertainment he afforded me. I remained his debtor. I should be sorry if my conscience, insisting on a rigid attention to the matter in hand, forced me to dismiss him in a couple of lines.

I do not know why Captain Nichols first left England. It was a matter upon which he was reticent, and with persons of his kidney a direct question is never very discreet. He hinted at undeserved misfortune, and there is no doubt that he looked upon himself as the victim of injustice. My fancy played with the various forms of fraud and violence, and I agreed with him sympathetically when he remarked that the authorities in the old country were so damned technical. But it was nice to see that any unpleasantness he had endured in his native land had not impaired his ardent patriotism. He frequently declared that England was the finest country in the world, sir, and he felt a lively superiority over Americans, Colonials, Dagos, Dutchmen, and Kanakas.

But I do not think he was a happy man. He suffered from dyspepsia, and he might often be seen sucking a tablet of pepsin; in the morning his appetite was poor; but this affliction alone would hardly have impaired his spirits. He had a greater cause of discontent with life than this. Eight years before he had rashly married a wife. There are men whom a merciful Providence has undoubtedly ordained to a single life, but who from wilfulness or through circumstances they could not cope with have flown in the face of its decrees. There is no object more deserving of pity than the married bachelor. Of such was Captain Nichols. I met his wife. She was a woman of twenty-eight, I should think, though of a type whose age is always doubtful; for she cannot have looked different when she was twenty, and at forty would look no older. She gave me an impression of extraordinary tightness. Her plain face with its narrow lips was tight, her skin was stretched tightly over her bones, her smile was tight, her hair was tight, her clothes were tight, and the white drill she wore had all the effect of black bombazine. I could not imagine why Captain Nichols had married her, and having married her why he had not deserted her. Perhaps he had, often, and his melancholy arose from the fact that he could never succeed. However far he went and in howsoever secret a place he hid himself, I felt sure that Mrs. Nichols, inexorable as fate and remorseless as conscience, would presently rejoin him. He could as little escape her as the cause can escape the effect.

The rogue, like the artist and perhaps the gentleman, belongs to no class. He is not embarrassed by the *sans gêne* of the hobo, nor put out of countenance by the etiquette of the prince. But Mrs. Nichols belonged to the well-defined class, of late become vocal, which is known as the lower-middle. Her father, in fact, was a policeman. I am certain that he was an efficient one. I do not know what her hold was on the Captain, but I do not think it was love. I never heard her speak, but it may be that in private she had a copious conversation. At any rate, Captain Nichols was frightened to death of her. Sometimes, sitting with me on the terrace of the hotel, he would become conscious that she was walking in the road outside. She did not call him; she gave no sign that she was aware of his existence; she merely walked up and down composedly. Then a strange uneasiness would seize the Captain; he would look at his watch and sigh.

"Well, I must be off," he said.

Neither wit nor whisky could detain him then. Yet he was a man who had faced undaunted hurricane and typhoon, and would not have hesitated to fight a dozen unarmed niggers with nothing but a revolver to help him. Sometimes Mrs. Nichols would send her daughter, a pale-faced, sullen child of seven, to the hotel.

"Mother wants you," she said, in a whining tone.

"Very well, my dear," said Captain Nichols.

He rose to his feet at once, and accompanied his daughter along the road. I suppose it was a very pretty example of the triumph of spirit over matter, and so my digression has at least the advantage of a moral.

I have tried to put some connection into the various things Captain Nichols told me about Strickland, and I here set them down in the best order I can. They made one another's acquaintance during the latter part of the winter following my last meeting with Strickland in Paris. How he had passed the intervening months I do not know, but life must have been very hard, for Captain Nichols saw him first in the Asile de Nuit. There was a strike at Marseilles at the time, and Strickland, having come to the end of his resources, had apparently found it impossible to earn the small sum he needed to keep body and soul together.

The Asile de Nuit is a large stone building where pauper and vagabond may get a bed for a week, provided their papers are in order and they can persuade the friars in charge that they are workingmen. Captain Nichols noticed Strickland for his size and his singular appearance among the crowd that waited for the doors to open; they waited listlessly, some walking to and fro, some leaning against the wall, and others seated on the curb with their feet in the gutter; and when they filed into the office he heard the monk who read his papers address him in English. But he did not have a chance to speak to him, since, as he entered the common-room, a monk came in with a huge Bible in his arms, mounted a pulpit which was at the end of the room, and began the service which the wretched outcasts had to endure as the price of their lodging. He and Strickland were assigned to different rooms, and when, thrown out of bed at five in the morning by a stalwart monk, he had made his bed and washed his face, Strick-

land had already disappeared. Captain Nichols wandered about
the streets for an hour of bitter cold, and then made his way
to the Place Victor Gélu, where the sailor-men are wont to
congregate. Dozing against the pedestal of a statue, he saw
Strickland again. He gave him a kick to awaken him.

"Come and have breakfast, mate," he said.

"Go to hell," answered Strickland.

I recognised my friend's limited vocabulary, and I prepared
to regard Captain Nichols as a trustworthy witness.

"Busted?" asked the Captain.

"Blast you," answered Strickland.

"Come along with me. I'll get you some breakfast."

After a moment's hesitation, Strickland scrambled to his
feet, and together they went to the Bouchée de Pain, where
the hungry are given a wedge of bread, which they must eat
there and then, for it is forbidden to take it away; and then
to the Cuillère de Soupe, where for a week, at eleven and
four, you may get a bowl of thin, salt soup. The two buildings
are placed far apart, so that only the starving should be
tempted to make use of them. So they had breakfast, and so
began the queer companionship of Charles Strickland and
Captain Nichols.

They must have spent something like four months at Marseilles in one another's society. Their career was devoid of
adventure, if by adventure you mean unexpected or thrilling
incident, for their days were occupied in the pursuit of enough
money to get a night's lodging and such food as would stay
the pangs of hunger. But I wish I could give here the pictures,
coloured and racy, which Captain Nichols' vivid narrative
offered to the imagination. His account of their discoveries in
the low life of a seaport town would have made a charming
book, and in the various characters that came their way the
student might easily have found matter for a very complete

dictionary of rogues. But I must content myself with a few paragraphs. I received the impression of a life intense and brutal, savage, multi-coloured, and vivacious. It made the Marseilles that I knew, gesticulating and sunny, with its comfortable hotels and its restaurants crowded with the well-to-do, tame and commonplace. I envied men who had seen with their own eyes the sights that Captain Nichols described.

When the doors of the Asile de Nuit were closed to them, Strickland and Captain Nichols sought the hospitality of Tough Bill. This was the master of a sailors' boarding-house, a huge mulatto with a heavy fist, who gave the stranded mariner food and shelter till he found him a berth. They lived with him a month, sleeping with a dozen others, Swedes, negroes, Brazilians, on the floor of the two bare rooms in his house which he assigned to his charges; and every day they went with him to the Place Victor Gélu, whither came ships' captains in search of a man. He was married to an American woman, obese and slatternly, fallen to this pass by Heaven knows what process of degradation, and every day the boarders took it in turns to help her with the housework. Captain Nichols looked upon it as a smart piece of work on Strickland's part that he had got out of this by painting a portrait of Tough Bill. Tough Bill not only paid for the canvas, colours, and brushes, but gave Strickland a pound of smuggled tobacco into the bargain. For all I know, this picture may still adorn the parlour of the tumbledown little house somewhere near the Quai de la Joliette, and I suppose it could now be sold for fifteen hundred pounds. Strickland's idea was to ship on some vessel bound for Australia or New Zealand, and from there make his way to Samoa or Tahiti. I do not know how he had come upon the notion of going to the South Seas, though I remember that his imagination had long been haunted by an island, all green and sunny, encircled by a sea more blue than is found in Northern latitudes. I suppose that he clung to Captain Nichols because he was acquainted with those parts, and it was Captain Nichols who persuaded him that he would be more comfortable in Tahiti.

"You see, Tahiti's French," he explained to me. "And the French aren't so damned technical."

I thought I saw his point.

Strickland had no papers, but that was not a matter to disconcert Tough Bill when he saw a profit (he took the first month's wages of the sailor for whom he found a berth), and he provided Strickland with those of an English stoker who had providentially died on his hands. But both Captain Nichols and Strickland were bound East, and it chanced that the only opportunities for signing on were with ships sailing West. Twice Strickland refused a berth on tramps sailing for the United States, and once on a collier going to Newcastle. Tough Bill had no patience with an obstinacy which could only result in loss to himself, and on the last occasion he flung both Strickland and Captain Nichols out of his house without more ado. They found themselves once more adrift.

Tough Bill's fare was seldom extravagant, and you rose from his table almost as hungry as you sat down, but for some days they had good reason to regret it. They learned what hunger was. The Cuillère de Soupe and the Asile de Nuit were both closed to them, and their only sustenance was the wedge of bread which the Bouchée de Pain provided. They slept where they could, sometimes in an empty truck on a siding near the station, sometimes in a cart behind a warehouse; but it was bitterly cold, and after an hour or two of uneasy dozing they would tramp the streets again. What they felt the lack of most bitterly was tobacco, and Captain Nichols, for his part, could not do without it; he took to hunting the "Can o' Beer,"

for cigarette-ends and the butt-end of cigars which the prom-
enaders of the night before had thrown away.

"I've tasted worse smoking mixtures in a pipe," he added,
with a philosophic shrug of his shoulders, as he took a couple of cigars from the case I offered him, putting one in his
mouth and the other in his pocket.

Now and then they made a bit of money. Sometimes a
mail steamer would come in, and Captain Nichols, having
scraped acquaintance with the timekeeper, would succeed in
getting the pair of them a job as stevedores. When it was an
English boat, they would dodge into the forecastle and get a
hearty breakfast from the crew. They took the risk of running against one of the ship's officers and being hustled down
the gangway with the toe of a boot to speed their going.

"There's no harm in a kick in the hindquarters when your
belly's full," said Captain Nichols, "and personally I never
take it in bad part. An officer's got to think about discipline."

I had a lively picture of Captain Nichols flying headlong
down a narrow gangway before the uplifted foot of an angry
mate, and, like a true Englishman, rejoicing in the spirit of
the Mercantile Marine.

There were often odd jobs to be got about the fish-market.
Once they each of them earned a franc by loading trucks
with innumerable boxes of oranges that had been dumped
down on the quay. One day they had a stroke of luck: one of
the boarding-masters got a contract to paint a tramp that had
come in from Madagascar round the Cape of Good Hope, and
they spent several days on a plank hanging over the side,
covering the rusty hull with paint. It was a situation that
must have appealed to Strickland's sardonic humour. I asked
Captain Nichols how he bore himself during these hardships.

"Never knew him say a cross word," answered the Captain.

"He'd be a bit surly sometimes, but when we hadn't had a bite since morning, and we hadn't even got the price of a lie down at the Chink's, he'd be as lively as a cricket."

I was not surprised at this. Strickland was just the man to rise superior to circumstances, when they were such as to occasion despondency in most; but whether this was due to equanimity of soul or to contradictoriness it is difficult to say.

The Chink's Head was a name the beach-combers gave to a wretched inn off the Rue Bouterie, kept by a one-eyed Chinaman, where for six sous you could sleep in a cot and for three on the floor. Here they made friends with others in as desperate condition as themselves, and when they were penniless and the night was bitter cold, they were glad to borrow from anyone who had earned a stray franc during the day the price of a roof over their heads. They were not niggardly, these tramps, and he who had money did not hesitate to share it among the rest. They belonged to all the countries in the world, but this was no bar to good-fellowship; for they felt themselves freemen of a country whose frontiers include them all, the great country of Cockaine.

"But I guess Strickland was an ugly customer when he was roused," said Captain Nichols, reflectively. "One day we ran into Tough Bill in the Place, and he asked Charlie for the papers he'd given him.

" 'You'd better come and take them if you want them,' says Charlie.

"He was a powerful fellow, Tough Bill, but he didn't quite like the look of Charlie, so he began cursing him. He called him pretty near every name he could lay hands on, and when Tough Bill began cursing it was worth listening to him. Well, Charlie stuck it for a bit, then he stepped forward and he just said : 'Get out, you bloody swine.' It wasn't so much what he said, but the way he said it. Tough Bill never spoke another word; you could see him go yellow, and he walked away as if he'd remembered he had a date."

Strickland, according to Captain Nichols, did not use exactly the words I have given, but since this book is meant for family reading I have thought it better, at the expense of truth, to put into his mouth expressions familiar to the domestic circle.

"In one of the bars of the Rue Bouterie"

Now, Tough Bill was not the man to put up with humiliation at the hands of a common sailor. His power depended on his prestige, and first one, then another, of the sailors who lived in his house told them that he had sworn to do Strickland in.

One night Captain Nichols and Strickland were sitting in one of the bars of the Rue Bouterie. The Rue Bouterie is a narrow street of one-storeyed houses, each house consisting of but one room; they are like the booths in a crowded fair or the cages of animals in a circus. At every door you see a woman. Some lean lazily against the side-posts, humming to themselves or calling to the passer-by in a raucous voice, and some listlessly read. They are French, Italian, Spanish, Japanese, coloured; some are fat and some are thin; and under the thick paint on their faces, the heavy smears on their eyebrows, and the scarlet of their lips, you see the lines of age and the scars of dissipation. Some wear black shifts and flesh-coloured stockings; some with curly hair, dyed yellow, are dressed like little girls in short muslin frocks. Through the open door you see a red-tiled floor, a large wooden bed, and on a deal table a ewer and a basin. A motley crowd saunters along the streets—Lascars off a P. and O., blond Northmen from a Swedish barque, Japanese from a man-of-war, English sailors, Spaniards, pleasant-looking fellows from a French cruiser, negroes off an American tramp. By day it is merely sordid, but at night, lit only by the lamps in the little huts, the street has a sinister beauty. The hideous lust that pervades the air is oppressive and horrible, and yet there is something mysterious in the sight which haunts and troubles you. You feel I know not what primitive force which repels and yet fascinates you. Here all the decencies of civilisation are swept away, and you feel that men are face to face with a sombre reality. There is an atmosphere that is at once intense and tragic.

In the bar in which Strickland and Nichols sat a mechanical piano was loudly grinding out dance music. Round the room people were sitting at table, here half a dozen sailors uproariously drunk, there a group of soldiers; and in the middle, crowded together, couples were dancing. Bearded sailors with brown faces and large horny hands clasped their partners in a tight embrace. The women wore nothing but a shift. Now and then two sailors would get up and dance together. The noise was deafening. People were singing, shouting, laughing; and when a man gave a long kiss to the girl sitting on his knees, cat-calls from the English sailors increased the din. The air was heavy with the dust beaten up by the heavy boots of the men, and gray with smoke. It was very hot. Behind the bar was seated a woman nursing her baby. The waiter, an undersized youth with a flat, spotty face, hurried to and fro carrying a tray laden with glasses of beer.

In a little while Tough Bill, accompanied by two huge negroes, came in, and it was easy to see that he was already three parts drunk. He was looking for trouble. He lurched against a table at which three soldiers were sitting and knocked over a glass of beer. There was an angry altercation, and the owner of the bar stepped forward and ordered Tough Bill to go. He was a hefty fellow, in the habit of standing no nonsense from his customers, and Tough Bill hesitated. The landlord was not a man he cared to tackle, for the police were on his side, and with an oath he turned on his heel. Suddenly he caught sight of Strickland. He rolled up to him. He did not speak. He gathered the spittle in his mouth and spat full in Strickland's face. Strickland seized his glass and flung it at him. The dancers stopped suddenly still. There was an instant of complete silence, but when Tough Bill threw himself on Strickland the lust of battle seized them all, and in a moment there was a confused scrimmage. Tables were overturned, glasses crashed to the ground. There was a hellish row. The women scattered to the door and behind the bar. Passers-by surged in from the street. You heard curses in every tongue; the sound of blows, cries; and in the middle of the room a dozen men were fighting with all their might. On a sudden the police rushed in, and everyone who could made for the door. When the bar was more or less cleared, Tough Bill was lying insensible on the floor with a great gash in his head. Captain Nichols dragged Strickland, bleeding from a wound in his arm, his clothes in rags, into the street. His own face was covered with blood from a blow on the nose.

"I guess you'd better get out of Marseilles before Tough Bill comes out of hospital," he said to Strickland, when they had got back to the Chink's Head and were cleaning themselves.

"This beats cock-fighting," said Strickland.

I could see his sardonic smile.

Captain Nichols was anxious. He knew Tough Bill's vindictiveness. Strickland had downed the mulatto twice, and the mulatto, sober, was a man to be reckoned with. He would bide his time stealthily. He would be in no hurry, but one night Strickland would get a knife-thrust in his back, and in a day or two the corpse of a nameless beach-comber would be fished out of the dirty water of the harbour. Nichols went next evening to Tough Bill's house and made enquiries. He was in hospital still, but his wife, who had been to see him, said he was swearing hard to kill Strickland when they let him out.

A week passed.

"That's what I always say," reflected Captain Nichols, "when you hurt a man, hurt him bad. It gives you a bit of time to look about and think what you'll do next."

Then Strickland had a bit of luck. A ship bound for Australia had sent to the Sailors' Home for a stoker in place of one who had thrown himself overboard off Gibraltar in an attack of delirium tremens.

"You double down to the harbour, my lad," said the Captain to Strickland, "and sign on. You've got your papers."

Strickland set off at once, and that was the last Captain

Nichols saw of him. The ship was only in port for six hours, and in the evening Captain Nichols watched the vanishing smoke from her funnels as she ploughed East through the wintry sea.

I have narrated all this as best I could, because I like the contrast of these episodes with the life that I had seen Strickland live in Ashley Gardens when he was occupied with stocks and shares; but I am aware that Captain Nichols was an outrageous liar, and I dare say there is not a word of truth in anything he told me. I should not be surprised to learn that he had never seen Strickland in his life, and owed his knowledge of Marseilles to the pages of a magazine.

It is here that I purposed to end my book. My first idea was to begin it with the account of Strickland's last years in Tahiti and with his horrible death, and then to go back and relate what I knew of his beginnings. This I meant to do, not from wilfulness, but because I wished to leave Strickland setting out with I know not what fancies in his lonely soul for the unknown islands which fired his imagination. I liked the picture of him starting at the age of forty-seven, when most men have already settled comfortably in a groove, for a new world. I saw him, the sea gray under the mistral and foam-flecked, watching the vanishing coast of France, which he was destined never to see again; and I thought there was something gallant in his bearing and dauntless in his soul. I wished so to end on a note of hope. It seemed to emphasise the unconquerable spirit of man. But I could not manage it. Somehow I could not get into my story, and after trying once or twice I had to give it up; I started from the beginning in the usual way, and made up my mind I could only tell what I knew of Strickland's life in the order in which I learnt the facts.

Those that I have now are fragmentary. I am in the position of a biologist who from a single bone must reconstruct not only the appearance of an extinct animal, but its habits. Strickland made no particular impression on the people who came in contact with him in Tahiti. To them he was no more than a beach-comber in constant need of money, remarkable only for the peculiarity that he painted pictures which seemed to them absurd; and it was not till he had been dead for some years and agents came from the dealers in Paris and Berlin to look for any pictures which might still remain on the island, that they had any idea that among them had dwelt a man of consequence. They remembered then that they could have bought for a song canvases which now were worth large sums, and they could not forgive themselves for the opportunity which had escaped them. There was a Jewish trader called Cohen, who had come by one of Strickland's pictures in a singular way. He was a little old Frenchman, with soft kind eyes and a pleasant smile, half trader and half seaman, who owned a cutter in which he wandered boldly among the Paumotus and the Marquesas, taking out trade goods and bringing back copra, shell, and pearls. I went to see him because I was told he had a large black pearl which he was willing to sell cheaply, and when I discovered that it was beyond my means I began to talk to him about Strickland. He had known him well.

"You see, I was interested in him because he was a painter," he told me. "We don't get many painters in the islands, and I was sorry for him because he was such a bad one. I gave him his first job. I had a plantation on the peninsula, and I wanted

a white overseer. You never get any work out of the natives
unless you have a white man over them. I said to him : 'You'll
have plenty of time for painting, and you can earn a bit of
money.' I knew he was starving, but I offered him good
wages."

"I was interested in him because he was a painter"

"I can't imagine that he was a very satisfactory overseer," I said, smiling.

"I made allowances. I have always had a sympathy for artists. It is in our blood, you know. But he only remained a few months. When he had enough money to buy paints and canvases he left me. The place had got hold of him by then, and he wanted to get away into the bush. But I continued to see him now and then. He would turn up in Papeete every few months and stay a little while; he'd get money out of someone or other and then disappear again. It was on one of these visits that he came to me and asked for the loan of two hundred francs. He looked as if he hadn't had a meal for a week, and I hadn't the heart to refuse him. Of course, I never expected to see my money again. Well, a year later he came to see me once more, and he brought a picture with him. He did not mention the money he owed me, but he said: 'Here is a picture of your plantation that I've painted for you.' I looked at it. I did not know what to say, but of course I thanked him, and when he had gone away I showed it to my wife."

"What was it like?" I asked.

"Do not ask me. I could not make head or tail of it. I never saw such a thing in my life. 'What shall we do with it?' I said to my wife. 'We can never hang it up,' she said. 'People would laugh at us.' So she took it into an attic and put it away with all sorts of rubbish, for my wife can never throw anything away. It is her mania. Then, imagine to yourself, just before the war my brother wrote to me from Paris, and said: 'Do you know anything about an English painter who lived in Tahiti? It appears that he was a genius, and his pictures fetch large prices. See if you can lay your hands on anything and send it to me. There's money to be made.' So I said to my wife: 'What about that picture that Strickland gave me? Is it possible that it is still in the attic?' 'Without doubt,' she answered, 'for you know that I never throw anything away. It is my mania.' We went up to the attic, and there, among I know not what rubbish that had been gathered during the thirty years we have inhabited that house, was the picture. I looked at it again, and I said: 'Who would have thought that the overseer of my plantation on the peninsula, to whom I lent two hundred francs, had genius? Do you see anything in the picture?' 'No,' she said, 'it does not resemble the plantation and I have never seen cocoa-nuts with blue leaves; but they are mad in Paris, and it may be that your brother will be able to sell it for the two hundred francs you lent Strickland.' Well, we packed it up and we sent it to my brother. And at last I received a letter from him. What do you think he said? 'I received your picture,' he said, 'and I confess I thought it was a joke that you had played on me. I would not have given the cost of postage for the picture. I was half afraid to show it to the gentleman who had spoken to me about it. Imagine my surprise when he said it was a masterpiece, and offered me thirty thousand francs. I dare say he would have paid more, but frankly I was so taken aback that I lost my head; I accepted the offer before I was able to collect myself.' "

Then Monsieur Cohen said an admirable thing.

"I wish that poor Strickland had been still alive. I wonder what he would have said when I gave him twenty-nine thousand eight hundred francs for his picture."

I lived at the Hôtel de la Fleur, and Mrs. Johnson, the proprietress, had a sad story to tell of lost opportunity. After

Strickland's death certain of his effects were sold by auction in the market-place at Papeete, and she went to it herself because there was among the truck an American stove she wanted. She paid twenty-seven francs for it.

"There were a dozen pictures," she told me, "but they were unframed, and nobody wanted them. Some of them sold for as much as ten francs, but mostly they went for five or six. Just think, if I had bought them I should be a rich woman now."

But Tiaré Johnson would never under any circumstances have been rich. She could not keep money. The daughter of a native and an English sea-captain settled in Tahiti, when I knew her she was a woman of fifty, who looked older, and of enormous proportions. Tall and extremely stout, she would have been of imposing presence if the great good-nature of her face had not made it impossible for her to express anything but kindliness. Her arms were like legs of mutton, her breasts like giant cabbages; her face, broad and fleshy, gave you an impression of almost indecent nakedness, and vast chin succeeded to vast chin. I do not know how many of them there were. They fell away voluminously into the capaciousness of her bosom. She was dressed usually in a pink Mother Hubbard, and she wore all day long a large straw hat. But when she let down her hair, which she did now and then, for she was vain of it, you saw that it was long and dark and curly; and her eyes had remained young and vivacious. Her laughter was the most catching I ever heard; it would begin, a low peal in her throat, and would grow louder and louder till her whole vast body shook. She loved three things—a joke, a glass of wine, and a handsome man. To have known her is a privilege.

She was the best cook on the island, and she adored good food. From morning till night you saw her sitting on a low chair in the kitchen, surrounded by a Chinese cook and two or three native girls, giving her orders, chatting sociably with all and sundry, and tasting the savoury messes she devised. When she wished to do honour to a friend she cooked the dinner with her own hands. Hospitality was a passion with her, and there was no one on the island who need go without a dinner when there was anything to eat at the Hôtel de la Fleur. She never turned her customers out of her house because they did not pay their bills. She always hoped they would pay when they could. There was one man there who had fallen on adversity, and to him she had given board and lodging for several months. When the Chinese laundryman refused to wash for him without payment she had sent his things to be washed with hers. She could not allow the poor fellow to go about in a dirty shirt, she said, and since he was a man, and men must smoke, she gave him a franc a day for cigarettes. She used him with the same affability as those of her clients who paid their bills once a week.

Age and obesity had made her inapt for love, but she took a keen interest in the amatory affairs of the young. She looked upon venery as the natural occupation for men and women, and was ever ready with precept and example from her own wide experience.

"I was not fifteen when my father found that I had a lover," she said. "He was third mate on the *Tropic Bird*. A good-looking boy."

She sighed a little. They say a woman always remembers her first lover with affection; but perhaps she does not always remember him.

"My father was a sensible man."

"What did he do?" I asked.

"He thrashed me within an inch of my life, and then he made me marry Captain Johnson. I did not mind. He was older, of course, but he was good-looking too."

Tiaré—her father had called her by the name of the white, scented flower which, they tell you, if you have once smelt, will always draw you back to Tahiti in the end, however far you may have roamed—Tiaré remembered Strickland very well.

"He used to come here sometimes, and I used to see him walking about Papeete. I was sorry for him, he was so thin, and he never had any money. When I heard he was in town, I used to send a boy to find him and make him come to dinner with me. I got him a job once or twice, but he couldn't stick to anything. After a little while he wanted to get back to the bush, and one morning he would be gone."

Strickland reached Tahiti about six months after he left Marseilles. He worked his passage on a sailing vessel that was making the trip from Auckland to San Francisco, and he arrived with a box of paints, an easel, and a dozen canvases. He had a few pounds in his pocket, for he had found work in Sydney, and he took a small room in a native house outside the town. I think the moment he reached Tahiti he felt himself at home. Tiaré told me that he said to her once:

"I'd been scrubbing the deck, and all at once a chap said to me: 'Why, there it is.' And I looked up and I saw the outline of the island. I knew right away that there was the place I'd been looking for all my life. Then we came near, and I seemed to recognise it. Sometimes when I walk about it all seems familiar. I could swear I've lived here before."

"Sometimes it takes them like that," said Tiaré. "I've known men come on shore for a few hours while their ship was taking in cargo, and never go back. And I've known men who came here to be in an office for a year, and they cursed the place, and when they went away they took their dying oath they'd hang themselves before they came back again, and in six months you'd see them land once more, and they'd tell you they couldn't live anywhere else."

50

I have an idea that some men are born out of their due place. Accident has cast them amid certain surroundings, but they have always a nostalgia for a home they know not. They are strangers in their birthplace, and the leafy lanes they have known from childhood or the populous streets in which they have played, remain but a place of passage. They may spend their whole lives aliens among their kindred and remain aloof among the only scenes they have ever known. Perhaps it is this sense of strangeness that sends men far and wide in the search for something permanent, to which they may attach themselves. Perhaps some deep-rooted atavism urges the wanderer back to lands which his ancestors left in the dim beginnings of history. Sometimes a man hits upon a place to which he mysteriously feels that he belongs. Here is the home he sought, and he will settle amid scenes that he has never seen before, among men he has never known, as though they were familiar to him from his birth. Here at last he finds rest.

I told Tiaré the story of a man I had known at St. Thomas's Hospital. He was a Jew named Abraham, a blond, rather stout young man, shy and very unassuming; but he had remarkable gifts. He entered the hospital with a scholarship, and during the five years of the curriculum gained every prize that was open to him. He was made house-physician and house-surgeon. His brilliance was allowed by all. Finally he was elected to a position on the staff, and his career was assured. So far as human things can be predicted, it was certain that he would rise to the greatest heights of his profession. Honours and wealth awaited him. Before he entered upon his new duties he wished to take a holiday, and, having no private means, he went as surgeon on a tramp steamer to the Levant. It did not generally carry a doctor, but one of the senior surgeons at the hospital knew a director of the line, and Abraham was taken as a favour.

In a few weeks the authorities received his resignation of the coveted position on the staff. It created profound astonishment, and wild rumours were current. Whenever a man does anything unexpected, his fellows ascribe it to the most discreditable motives. But there was a man ready to step into Abraham's shoes, and Abraham was forgotten. Nothing more was heard of him. He vanished.

It was perhaps ten years later that one morning on board ship, about to land at Alexandria, I was bidden to line up with the other passengers for the doctor's examination. The doctor was a stout man in shabby clothes, and when he took off his hat I noticed that he was very bald. I had an idea that I had seen him before. Suddenly I remembered.

"Abraham," I said.

He turned to me with a puzzled look, and then, recognising me, seized my hand. After expressions of surprise on either side, hearing that I meant to spend the night in Alexandria, he asked me to dine with him at the English Club. When we met again I declared my astonishment at finding him there. It was a very modest position that he occupied, and there was about him an air of straitened circumstance. Then he told me his story. When he set out on his holiday in the Mediterranean he had every intention of returning to London and his appointment at St. Thomas's. One morning the tramp docked at Alexandria, and from the deck he looked at the city, white in the sunlight, and the crowd on the wharf; he saw the natives in their shabby gabardines, the blacks from the Soudan, the noisy throng of Greeks and Italians, the grave Turks in tarbooshes, the sunshine and the blue sky; and something hap-

pened to him. He could not describe it. It was like a thunder-
clap, he said, and then, dissatisfied with this, he said it was
like a revelation. Something seemed to visit his heart, and
suddenly he felt an exultation, a sense of wonderful freedom.
He felt himself at home, and he made up his mind there and
then, in a minute, that he would live the rest of his life in
Alexandria. He had no great difficulty in leaving the ship,
and in twenty-four hours, with all his belongings, he was
on shore.

"The Captain must have thought you as mad as a hatter,"
I smiled.

"I didn't care what anybody thought. It wasn't I that acted,
but something stronger within me. I thought I would go to a
little Greek hotel, while I looked about, and I felt I knew
where to find one. And do you know, I walked straight there,
and when I saw it, I recognised it at once."

"Had you been to Alexandria before?"

"No; I'd never been out of England in my life."

Presently he entered the Government service, and there he
had been ever since.

"Have you never regretted it?"

"Never, not for a minute. I earn just enough to live upon,
and I'm satisfied. I asked nothing more than to remain as I
am till I die. I've had a wonderful life."

I left Alexandria next day, and I forgot about Abraham till
a little while ago, when I was dining with another old friend
in the profession, Alec Carmichael, who was in England on
short leave. I ran across him in the street and congratulated
him on the knighthood with which his eminent services during the war had been rewarded. We arranged to spend an evening together for old time's sake, and when I agreed to dine
with him, he proposed that he should ask nobody else, so that
we could chat without interruption. He had a beautiful old

house in Queen Anne Street, and being a man of taste he had furnished it admirably. On the walls of the dining-room I saw a charming Bellotto, and there was a pair of Zoffanys that I envied. When his wife, a tall, lovely creature in cloth of gold, had left us, I remarked laughingly on the change in his present circumstances from those when we had both been medical students. We had looked upon it then as an extravagance to dine in a shabby Italian restaurant in the Westminster Bridge Road. Now Alec Carmichael was on the staff of half a dozen hospitals. I should think he earned ten thousand a year, and his knighthood was but the first of the honours which must inevitably fall to his lot.

"I've done pretty well," he said, "but the strange thing is that I owe it all to one piece of luck."

"What do you mean by that?"

"Well, do you remember Abraham? He was the man who had the future. When we were students he beat me all along the line. He got the prizes and the scholarships that I went in for. I always played second fiddle to him. If he'd kept on he'd be in the position I'm in now. That man had a genius for surgery. No one had a look in with him. When he was appointed Registrar at Thomas's I hadn't a chance of getting on the staff. I should have had to become a G.P., and you know what likelihood there is for a G.P. ever to get out of the common rut. But Abraham fell out, and I got the job. That gave me my opportunity."

"I dare say that's true."

"It was just luck. I suppose there was some kink in Abraham. Poor devil, he's gone to the dogs altogether. He's got some twopenny-halfpenny job in the medical at Alexandria—sanitary officer or something like that. I'm told he lives with an ugly old Greek woman and has half a dozen scrofulous kids. The fact is, I suppose, that it's not enough to have brains.

The thing that counts is character. Abraham hadn't got character."

Character? I should have thought it needed a good deal of character to throw up a career after half an hour's meditation, because you saw in another way of living a more intense significance. And it required still more character never to regret the sudden step. But I said nothing, and Alec Carmichael proceeded reflectively:

"Of course it would be hypocritical for me to pretend that I regret what Abraham did. After all, I've scored by it." He puffed luxuriously at the long Corona he was smoking. "But if I weren't personally concerned I should be sorry at the waste. It seems a rotten thing that a man should make such a hash of life."

I wondered if Abraham really had made a hash of life. Is to do what you most want, to live under the conditions that please you, in peace with yourself, to make a hash of life; and is it success to be an eminent surgeon with ten thousand a year and a beautiful wife? I suppose it depends on what meaning you attach to life, the claim which you acknowledge to society, and the claim of the individual. But again I held my tongue, for who am I to argue with a knight?

51

Tiaré, when I told her this story, praised my prudence, and for a few minutes we worked in silence, for we were shelling peas. Then her eyes, always alert for the affairs of her kitchen, fell on some action of the Chinese cook which aroused her violent disapproval. She turned on him with a torrent of abuse. The

Chink was not backward to defend himself, and a very lively quarrel ensued. They spoke in the native language, of which I had learnt but half a dozen words, and it sounded as though the world would shortly come to an end; but presently peace was restored and Tiaré gave the cook a cigarette. They both smoked comfortably.

"Do you know, it was I who found him his wife?" said Tiaré suddenly, with a smile that spread all over her immense face.

"The cook?"

"No, Strickland."

"But he had one already."

"That is what he said, but I told him she was in England, and England is at the other end of the world."

"True," I replied.

"He would come to Papeete every two or three months, when he wanted paints or tobacco or money, and then he would wander about like a lost dog. I was sorry for him. I had a girl here then called Ata to do the rooms; she was some sort of a relation of mine, and her father and mother were dead, so I had her to live with me. Strickland used to come here now and then to have a square meal or to play chess with one of the boys. I noticed that she looked at him when he came, and I asked her if she liked him. She said she liked him well enough. You know what these girls are; they're always pleased to go with a white man."

"Was she a native?" I asked.

"Yes; she hadn't a drop of white blood in her. Well, after I'd talked to her I sent for Strickland, and I said to him: 'Strickland, it's time for you to settle down. A man of your age shouldn't go playing about with the girls down at the front. They're bad lots, and you'll come to no good with them. You've got no money, and you can never keep a job for more

than a month or two. No one will employ you now. You say
you can always live in the bush with one or other of the natives, and they're glad to have you because you're a white
man, but it's not decent for a white man. Now, listen to me,
Strickland.' "

Tiaré mingled French with English in her conversation, for
she used both languages with equal facility. She spoke them
with a singing accent which was not unpleasing. You felt that
a bird would speak in these tones if it could speak English.

" 'Now, what do you say to marrying Ata? She's a good
girl and she's only seventeen. She's never been promiscuous
like some of these girls—a captain or a first mate, yes, but
she's never been touched by a native. *Elle se respecte, vois-tu.*
The purser of the *Oahu* told me last journey that he hadn't
met a nicer girl in the islands. It's time she settled down too,
and besides, the captains and the first mates like a change now
and then. I don't keep my girls too long. She has a bit of property down by Taravao, just before you come to the peninsula,
and with copra at the price it is now you could live quite comfortably. There's a house, and you'd have all the time you
wanted for your painting. What do you say to it?' "

Tiaré paused to take breath.

"It was then he told me of his wife in England. 'My poor
Strickland,' I said to him, 'they've all got a wife somewhere;
that is generally why they come to the islands. Ata is a sensible girl, and she doesn't expect any ceremony before the
Mayor. She's a Protestant, and you know they don't look upon
these things like the Catholics.'

"Then he said: 'But what does Ata say to it?' 'It appears
that she has a *béguin* for you,' I said. 'She's willing if you are.
Shall I call her?' He chuckled in a funny, dry way he had,
and I called her. She knew what I was talking about, the
hussy, and I saw her out of the corner of my eyes listening

with all her ears, while she pretended to iron a blouse that she
had been washing for me. She came. She was laughing, but I
could see that she was a little shy, and Strickland looked at her
without speaking."

"Was she pretty?" I asked.

"Not bad. But you must have seen pictures of her. He
painted her over and over again, sometimes with a *pareo* on
and sometimes with nothing at all. Yes, she was pretty
enough. And she knew how to cook. I taught her myself. I saw
Strickland was thinking of it, so I said to him: 'I've given her
good wages and she's saved them, and the captains and the
first mates she's known have given her a little something now
and then. She's saved several hundred francs.'

"He pulled his great red beard and smiled.

"He painted her
over and over again"

" 'Well, Ata,' he said, 'do you fancy me for a husband.'

"She did not say anything, but just giggled.

" 'But I tell you, my poor Strickland, the girl has a *béguin* for you,' I said.

" 'I shall beat you,' he said, looking at her.

" 'How else should I know you loved me,' she answered."

Tiaré broke off her narrative and addressed herself to me reflectively.

"My first husband, Captain Johnson, used to thrash me regularly. He was a man. He was handsome, six foot three, and when he was drunk there was no holding him. I would be black and blue all over for days at a time. Oh, I cried when he died. I thought I should never get over it. But it wasn't till I married George Rainey that I knew what I'd lost. You can never tell what a man is like till you live with him. I've never been so deceived in a man as I was in George Rainey. He was a fine, upstanding fellow too. He was nearly as tall as Captain Johnson, and he looked strong enough. But it was all on the surface. He never drank. He never raised his hand to me. He might have been a missionary. I made love with the officers of every ship that touched the island, and George Rainey never saw anything. At last I was disgusted with him, and I got a divorce. What was the good of a husband like that? It's a terrible thing the way some men treat women."

I condoled with Tiaré, and remarked feelingly that men were deceivers ever, then asked her to go on with her story of Strickland.

" 'Well,' I said to him, 'there's no hurry about it. Take your time and think it over. Ata has a very nice room in the annexe. Live with her for a month, and see how you like her. You can have your meals here. And at the end of a month, if you decide you want to marry her, you can just go and settle down on her property.'

"Well, he agreed to that. Ata continued to do the house-work, and I gave him his meals as I said I would. I taught Ata to make one or two dishes I knew he was fond of. He did not paint much. He wandered about the hills and bathed in the stream. And he sat about the front looking at the lagoon, and at sunset he would go down and look at Murea. He used to go fishing on the reef. He loved to moon about the harbour talk-ing to the natives. He was a nice, quiet fellow. And every eve-ning after dinner he would go down to the annexe with Ata. I saw he was longing to get away to the bush, and at the end of the month I asked him what he intended to do. He said if Ata was willing to go, he was willing to go with her. So I gave them a wedding dinner. I cooked it with my own hands. I gave them a pea soup and lobster *à la portugaise*, and a curry, and a cocoa-nut salad—you've never had one of my cocoa-nut salads, have you? I must make you one before you go—and then I made them an ice. We had all the champagne we could drink and liqueurs to follow. Oh, I'd made up my mind to do things well. And afterwards we danced in the drawing-room. I was not so fat, then, and I always loved dancing."

The drawing-room at the Hôtel de la Fleur was a small room, with a cottage piano, and a suite of mahogany furni-ture, covered in stamped velvet, neatly arranged around the walls. On round tables were photograph albums, and on the walls enlarged photographs of Tiaré and her first husband, Captain Johnson. Still, though Tiaré was old and fat, on occa-sion we rolled back the Brussels carpet, brought in the maids and one or two friends of Tiaré's, and danced, though now to the wheezy music of a gramaphone. On the verandah the air was scented with the heavy perfume of the tiaré, and overhead the Southern Cross shone in a cloudless sky.

Tiaré smiled indulgently as she remembered the gaiety of a time long passed.

"We kept it up till three, and when we went to bed I don't think anyone was very sober. I had told them they could have my trap to take them as far as the road went, because after that they had a long walk. Ata's property was right away in a fold of the mountain. They started at dawn, and the boy I sent with them didn't come back till next day.

"Yes, that's how Strickland was married."

I suppose the next three years were the happiest of Strickland's life. Ata's house stood about eight kilometres from the road that runs round the island, and you went to it along a winding pathway shaded by the luxuriant trees of the tropics. It was a bungalow of unpainted wood, consisting of two small rooms, and outside was a small shed that served as a kitchen. There was no furniture except the mats they used as beds, and a rocking-chair, which stood on the verandah. Bananas with their great ragged leaves, like the tattered habiliments of an empress in adversity, grew close up to the house. There was a tree just behind which bore alligator pears, and all about were the cocoa-nuts which gave the land its revenue. Ata's father had planted crotons round his property, and they grew in coloured profusion, gay and brilliant; they fenced the land with flame. A mango grew in front of the house, and at the edge of the clearing were two flamboyants, twin trees, that challenged the gold of the cocoa-nuts with their scarlet flowers.

Here Strickland lived, coming seldom to Papeete, on the produce of the land. There was a little stream that ran not far away, in which he bathed, and down this on occasion would come a shoal of fish. Then the natives would assemble with spears, and with much shouting would transfix the great startled things as they hurried down to the sea. Sometimes Strickland would go down to the reef, and come back with a basket of small, coloured fish that Ata would fry in cocoa-nut oil, or with a lobster; and sometimes she would make a savoury dish of the great land-crabs that scuttled away under your feet. Up the mountain were wild-orange trees, and now and then Ata would go with two or three women from the village and return laden with the green, sweet, luscious fruit. Then the cocoa-nuts would be ripe for picking, and her cousins (like all the natives, Ata had a host of relatives) would swarm up the trees and throw down the big ripe nuts. They split them open and put them in the sun to dry. Then they cut out the copra and put it into sacks, and the women would carry it down to the trader at the village by the lagoon, and he would give in exchange for it rice and soap and tinned meat and a little money. Sometimes there would be a feast in the neighbourhood, and a pig would be killed. Then they would go and eat themselves sick, and dance, and sing hymns.

But the house was a long way from the village, and the Tahitians are lazy. They love to travel and they love to gossip, but they do not care to walk, and for weeks at a time Strickland and Ata lived alone. He painted and he read, and in the evening, when it was dark, they sat together on the verandah, smoking and looking at the night. Then Ata had a baby, and the old woman who came up to help her through her trouble stayed on. Presently the granddaughter of the old woman came to stay with her, and then a youth appeared—no one quite knew where from or to whom he belonged—but he settled down with them in a happy-go-lucky way, and they all lived together.

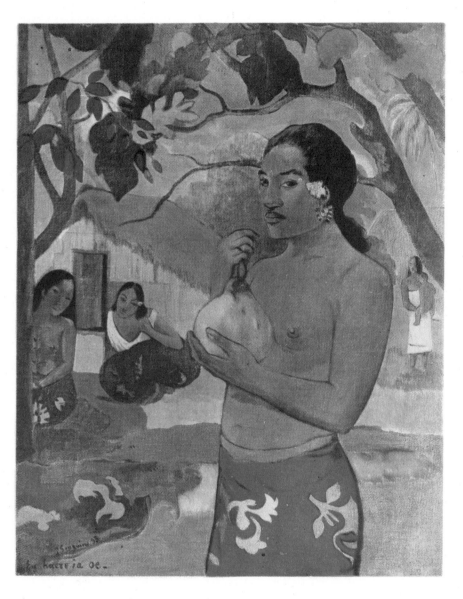

"*Then the cocoa-nuts would be ripe for picking*"

"*Tenez, voilà le Capitaine Brunot,*" said Tiaré, one day when I was fitting together what she could tell me of Strickland. "He knew Strickland well; he visited him at his house."

I saw a middle-aged Frenchman with a big black beard, streaked with gray, a sunburned face, and large, shining eyes. He was dressed in a neat suit of ducks. I had noticed him at luncheon, and Ah Lin, the Chinese boy, told me he had come from the Paumotus on the boat that had that day arrived. Tiaré introduced me to him, and he handed me his card, a large card on which was printed *René Brunot,* and underneath, *Capitaine au Long Cours.* We were sitting on a little verandah outside the kitchen, and Tiaré was cutting out a dress that she was making for one of the girls about the house. He sat down with us.

"Yes; I knew Strickland well," he said. "I am very fond of chess, and he was always glad of a game. I come to Tahiti three or four times a year for my business, and when he was at Papeete he would come here and we would play. When he married"—Captain Brunot smiled and shrugged his shoulders—"*enfin,* when he went to live with the girl that Tiaré gave him, he asked me to go and see him. I was one of the guests at the wedding feast." He looked at Tiaré, and they both laughed. "He did not come much to Papeete after that, and about a year later it chanced that I had to go to that part of the island for I forget what business, and when I had finished it I said to myself: '*Voyons,* why should I not go and see that poor Strickland?' I asked one or two natives if they knew anything about him, and I discovered that he lived not more than five kilometres from where I was. So I went.

I shall never forget the impression my visit made on me. I live on an atoll, a low island, it is a strip of land surrounding a lagoon, and its beauty is the beauty of the sea and sky and the varied colour of the lagoon, and the grace of the cocoa-nut trees; but the place where Strickland lived had the beauty of the Garden of Eden. Ah, I wish I could make you see the enchantment of that spot, a corner hidden away from all the world, with the blue sky overhead and the rich, luxuriant trees. It was a feast of colour. And it was fragrant and cool.

"I wish I could make you see the enchantment of that spot"

Words cannot describe that paradise. And here he lived, unmindful of the world and by the world forgotten. I suppose to European eyes it would have seemed astonishingly sordid. The house was dilapidated and none too clean. Three or four natives were lying on the verandah. You know how natives love to herd together. There was a young man lying full length, smoking a cigarette, and he wore nothing but a *pareo*."

The *pareo* is a long strip of trade cotton, red or blue, stamped with a white pattern. It is worn round the waist and hangs to the knees.

"A girl of fifteen, perhaps, was plaiting pandanus-leaf to make a hat, and an old woman was sitting on her haunches smoking a pipe. Then I saw Ata. She was suckling a new-born child, and another child, stark naked, was playing at her feet. When she saw me she called out to Strickland, and he came to the door. He, too, wore nothing but a *pareo*. He was an extraordinary figure, with his red beard and matted hair, and his great hairy chest. His feet were horny and scarred, so that I knew he went always bare foot. He had gone native with a vengeance. He seemed pleased to see me, and told Ata to kill a chicken for our dinner. He took me into the house to show me the picture he was at work on when I came in. In one corner of the room was the bed, and in the middle was an easel with the canvas upon it. Because I was sorry for him, I had bought a couple of his pictures for small sums, and I had sent others to friends of mine in France. And though I had bought them out of compassion, after living with them I began to like them. Indeed, I found a strange beauty in them. Everyone thought I was mad, but it turns out that I was right. I was his first admirer in the islands."

He smiled maliciously at Tiaré, and with lamentations she told us again the story of how at the sale of Strickland's effects she had neglected the pictures, but bought an American stove for twenty-seven francs.

"Have you the pictures still?" I asked.

"Yes; I am keeping them till my daughter is of marriageable age, and then I shall sell them. They will be her *dot*."

Then he went on with the account of his visit to Strick-land.

"I shall never forget the evening I spent with him. I had not intended to stay more than an hour, but he insisted that I should spend the night. I hesitated, for I confess I did not much like the look of the mats on which he proposed that I should sleep; but I shrugged my shoulders. When I was build-ing my house in the Paumotus I had slept out for weeks on a harder bed than that, with nothing to shelter me but wild shrubs; and as for vermin, my tough skin should be proof against their malice.

"We went down to the stream to bathe while Ata was pre-paring the dinner, and after we had eaten it we sat on the verandah. We smoked and chatted. The young man had a concertina, and he played the tunes popular on the music-halls a dozen years before. They sounded strangely in the tropical night thousands of miles from civilisation. I asked Strickland if it did not irk him to live in that promiscuity. No, he said; he liked to have his models under his hand. Pres-ently, after loud yawning, the natives went away to sleep, and Strickland and I were left alone. I cannot describe to you the intense silence of the night. On my island in the Paumotus there is never at night the complete stillness that there was here. There is the rustle of the myriad animals on the beach, all the little shelled things that crawl about ceaselessly, and there is the noisy scurrying of the land-crabs. Now and then in the lagoon you hear the leaping of a fish, and sometimes a hurried noisy splashing as a brown shark sends all the other fish scampering for their lives. And above all, ceaseless like time, is the dull roar of the breakers on the reef. But here there was not a sound, and the air was scented with the white flowers of the night. It was a night so beautiful that your soul seemed hardly able to bear the prison of the body. You felt that it was ready to be wafted away on the immaterial air, and death bore all the aspect of a beloved friend."

Tiaré sighed.

"Ah, I wish I were fifteen again."

Then she caught sight of a cat trying to get at a dish of prawns on the kitchen table, and with a dexterous gesture and a lively volley of abuse flung a book at its scampering tail.

"I asked him if he was happy with Ata.

" 'She leaves me alone,' he said. 'She cooks my food and looks after her babies. She does what I tell her. She gives me what I want from a woman.'

" 'And do you never regret Europe? Do you not yearn sometimes for the light of the streets in Paris or London, the companionship of your friends, and equals, *que sais-je?* for theatres and newspapers, and the rumble of omnibuses on the cobbled pavements?'

"For a long time he was silent. Then he said:

" 'I shall stay here till I die.'

" 'But are you never bored or lonely?' I asked.

"He chuckled.

" '*Mon pauvre ami,*' he said. 'It is evident that you do not know what it is to be an artist.' "

Capitaine Brunot turned to me with a gentle smile, and there was a wonderful look in his dark, kind eyes.

"He did me an injustice, for I too know what it is to have dreams. I have my visions too. In my way I also am an artist."

We were all silent for a while, and Tiaré fished out of her capacious pocket a handful of cigarettes. She handed one to each of us, and we all three smoked. At last she said:

"Since *ce monsieur* is interested in Strickland, why do you not take him to see Dr. Coutras? He can tell him something about his illness and death." "*Volontiers*," said the Captain, looking at me.

I thanked him, and he looked at his watch.

"It is past six o'clock. We should find him at home if you care to come now."

I got up without further ado, and we walked along the road that led to the doctor's house. He lived out of the town, but the Hôtel de la Fleur was on the edge of it, and we were quickly in the country. The broad road was shaded by pepper-trees, and on each side were the plantations, cocoa-nut and vanilla. The pirate birds were screeching among the leaves of the palms. We came to a stone bridge over a shallow river, and we stopped for a few minutes to see the native boys bathing. They chased one another with shrill cries and laughter, and their bodies, brown and wet, gleamed in the sunlight.

As we walked along I reflected on a circumstance which all that I had lately heard about Strickland forced on my attention. Here, on this remote island, he seemed to have aroused none of the detestation with which he was regarded at home, but compassion rather; and his vagaries were accepted with tolerance. To these people, native and European, he was a queer fish, but they were used to queer fish, and they took him for granted; the world was full of odd persons, who did odd things; and perhaps they knew that a man is not what he wants to be, but what he must be. In England and France he was the square peg in the round hole, but here the holes were any sort of shape, and no sort of peg was quite amiss. I do not think he was any gentler here, less selfish or less brutal, but the circumstances were more favourable. If he had spent his life amid these surroundings he might have passed for no worse a man than another. He received here what he neither expected nor wanted among his own people—sympathy.

I tried to tell Captain Brunot something of the astonishment with which this filled me, and for a little while he did not answer.

"It is not strange that I, at all events, should have had sympathy for him," he said at last, "for, though perhaps neither of us knew it, we were both aiming at the same thing."

"What on earth can it be that two people so dissimilar as you and Strickland could aim at?" I asked, smiling.

"Beauty."

"A large order," I murmured.

"Do you know how men can be so obsessed by love that they are deaf and blind to everything else in the world? They are as little their own masters as the slaves chained to the benches of a galley. The passion that held Strickland in bondage was no less tyrannical than love."

"How strange that you should say that!" I answered. "For long ago I had the idea that he was possessed of a devil."

"And the passion that held Strickland was a passion to create beauty. It gave him no peace. It urged him hither and thither. He was eternally a pilgrim, haunted by a divine nostalgia, and the demon within him was ruthless. There are men whose desire for truth is so great that to attain it they will shatter the very foundation of their world. Of such was Strickland, only beauty with him took the place of truth. I could only feel for him a profound compassion."

"That is strange also. A man whom he had deeply wronged told me that he felt a great pity for him." I was silent for a moment. "I wonder if there you have found the explanation of a character which has always seemed to me inexplicable. How did you hit on it?"

He turned to me with a smile.

"Did I not tell you that I, too, in my way was an artist? I realised in myself the same desire as animated him. But whereas his medium was paint, mine has been life."

Then Captain Brunot told me a story which I must repeat, since, if only by way of contrast, it adds something to my impression of Strickland. It has also to my mind a beauty of its own.

Captain Brunot was a Breton, and had been in the French Navy. He left it on his marriage, and settled down on a small property he had near Quimper to live for the rest of his days in peace; but the failure of an attorney left him suddenly penniless, and neither he nor his wife was willing to live in penury where they had enjoyed consideration. During his seafaring days he had cruised the South Seas, and he determined now to seek his fortune there. He spent some months in Papeete to make his plans and gain experience; then, on money borrowed from a friend in France, he bought an island in the Paumotus. It was a ring of land round a deep lagoon, uninhabited, and covered only with scrub and wild guava. With the intrepid woman who was his wife, and a few natives, he landed there, and set about building a house, and clearing the scrub so that he could plant cocoa-nuts. That was twenty years before, and now what had been a barren island was a garden.

"It was hard and anxious work at first, and we worked strenuously, both of us. Every day I was up at dawn, clearing, planting, working on my house, and at night when I threw myself on my bed it was to sleep like a log till morning. My wife worked as hard as I did. Then children were born to us, first a son and then a daughter. My wife and I have taught them **all they** know. We had a piano sent out from France, and she has taught them to play and to speak English, and I have taught them Latin and mathematics, and we read history together. They can sail a boat. They can swim as well as the

"Our trees have prospered, and there is shell on my reef"

natives. There is nothing about the land of which they are ignorant. Our trees have prospered, and there is shell on my reef. I have come to Tahiti now to buy a schooner. I can get enough shell to make it worth while to fish for it, and, who knows? I may find pearls. I have made something where there was nothing. I too have made beauty. Ah, you do not know what it is to look at those tall, healthy trees and think that every one I planted myself."

"Let me ask you the question that you asked Strickland. Do you never regret France and your old home in Brittany?"

"Some day, when my daughter is married and my son has a wife and is able to take my place on the island, we shall go back and finish our days in the old house in which I was born."

"You will look back on a happy life," I said.

"*Evidemment*, it is not exciting on my island, and we are very far from the world—imagine, it takes me four days to come to Tahiti—but we are happy there. It is given to few men to attempt a work and to achieve it. Our life is simple and innocent. We are untouched by ambition, and what pride we have is due only to our contemplation of the work of our hands. Malice cannot touch us, nor envy attack. Ah, *mon cher monsieur*, they talk of the blessedness of labour, and it is a meaningless phrase, but to me it has the most intense significance. I am a happy man."

"I am sure you deserve to be," I smiled.

"I wish I could think so. I do not know how I have deserved to have a wife who was the perfect friend and helpmate, the perfect mistress and the perfect mother."

I reflected for a while on the life that the Captain suggested to my imagination.

"It is obvious that to lead such an existence and make so great a success of it, you must both have needed a strong will and a determined character."

"Perhaps; but without one other factor we could have achieved nothing."

"And what was that?"

He stopped, somewhat dramatically, and stretched out his arm.

"Belief in God. Without that we should have been lost."

Then we arrived at the house of Dr. Coutras.

Mr. Coutras was an old Frenchman of great stature and exceeding bulk. His body was shaped like a huge duck's egg; and his eyes, sharp, blue, and good-natured, rested now and then with self-satisfaction on his enormous paunch. His complexion was florid and his hair white. He was a man to attract immediate sympathy. He received us in a room that might have been in a house in a provincial town in France, and the one or two Polynesian curios had an odd look. He took my hand in both of his—they were huge—and gave me a hearty look, in which, however, was great shrewdness. When he shook hands with Capitaine Brunot he enquired politely after *Madame et les enfants*. For some minutes there was an exchange of courtesies and some local gossip about the island, the prospects of copra and the vanilla crop; then we came to the object of my visit.

I shall not tell what Dr. Coutras related to me in his words, but in my own, for I cannot hope to give at second hand any impression of his vivacious delivery. He had a deep, resonant voice, fitted to his massive frame, and a keen sense of the dramatic. To listen to him was, as the phrase goes, as good as a play; and much better than most.

It appears that Dr. Coutras had gone one day to Taravao in order to see an old chiefess who was ill, and he gave a vivid picture of the obese old lady, lying in a huge bed, smoking cigarettes, and surrounded by a crowd of dark-skinned retainers. When he had seen her he was taken into another room and given dinner—raw fish, fried bananas, and chicken—*que sais-je*, the typical dinner of the *indigène*—and while he was eating it he saw a young girl being driven away from the door in tears. He thought nothing of it, but when he went out to get into his trap and drive home, he saw her again, standing a little way off; she looked at him with a woebegone air, and tears streamed down her cheeks. He asked someone what was wrong with her, and was told that she had come down from the hills to ask him to visit a white man who was sick. They had told her that the doctor could not be disturbed. He called her, and himself asked what she wanted. She told him that Ata had sent her, she who used to be at the Hôtel de la Fleur, and that the Red One was ill. She thrust into his hand a crumpled piece of newspaper, and when he opened it he found in it a hundred-franc note.

"Who is the Red One?" he asked of one of the bystanders.

He was told that that was what they called the Englishman, a painter, who lived with Ata up in the valley seven kilometres from where they were. He recognised Strickland by the description. But it was necessary to walk. It was impossible for him to go; that was why they had sent the girl away.

"I confess," said the doctor, turning to me, "that I hesitated. I did not relish fourteen kilometres over a bad pathway, and there was no chance that I could get back to Papeete that night. Besides, Strickland was not sympathetic to me. He was an idle, useless scoundrel, who preferred to live with a native woman rather than work for his living like the rest of us. *Mon Dieu*, how was I to know that one day the world would come to the conclusion that he had genius? I asked the girl if he was not well enough to have come down to see me. I asked her what she thought was the matter with him. She would not answer. I pressed her, angrily perhaps, but she looked down on the ground and began to cry. Then I shrugged my shoulders; after all, perhaps it was my duty to go, and in a very bad temper I bade her lead the way."

His temper was certainly no better when he arrived, per-
spiring freely and thirsty. Ata was on the look-out for him,
and came a little way along the path to meet him.

"Before I see anyone give me something to drink or I shall
die of thirst," he cried out. "*Pour l'amour de Dieu,* get me a
cocoa-nut."

She called out, and a boy came running along. He swarmed
up a tree, and presently threw down a ripe nut. Ata pierced a
hole in it, and the doctor took a long, refreshing draught.
Then he rolled himself a cigarette and felt in a better humour.

"Now, where is the Red One?" he asked.

"He is in the house, painting. I have not told him you were
coming. Go in and see him."

"But what does he complain of? If he is well enough to
paint, he is well enough to have come down to Taravao and
save me this confounded walk. I presume my time is no less
valuable than his."

Ata did not speak, but with the boy followed him to the
house. The girl who had brought him was by this time sitting on the verandah, and here was lying an old woman, with
her back to the wall, making native cigarettes. Ata pointed to
the door. The doctor, wondering irritably why they behaved
so strangely, entered, and there found Strickland cleaning
his palette. There was a picture on the easel. Strickland, clad
only in a *pareo,* was standing with his back to the door, but
he turned round when he heard the sound of boots. He gave
the doctor a look of vexation. He was surprised to see him, and
resented the intrusion. But the doctor gave a gasp, he was
rooted to the floor, and he stared with all his eyes. This was
not what he expected. He was seized with horror.

"You enter without ceremony," said Strickland. "What
can I do for you?"

The doctor recovered himself, but it required quite an effort for him to find his voice. All his irritation was gone, and he felt—*eh bien, oui, je ne le nie pas*—he felt an overwhelming pity.

"I am Dr. Coutras. I was down at Taravao to see the chiefess, and Ata sent for me to see you."

"She's a damned fool. I have had a few aches and pains lately and a little fever, but that's nothing; it will pass off. Next time anyone went to Papeete I was going to send for some quinine."

"Look at yourself in the glass."

Strickland gave him a glance, smiled, and went over to a cheap mirror in a little wooden frame, that hung on the wall.

"Well?"

"Do you not see a strange change in your face? Do you not see the thickening of your features and a look—how shall I describe it?—the books call it lion-faced. *Mon pauvre ami*, must I tell you that you have a terrible disease?"

"I?"

"When you look at yourself in the glass you see the typical appearance of the leper."

"You are jesting," said Strickland.

"I wish to God I were."

"Do you intend to tell me that I have leprosy?"

"Unfortunately, there can be no doubt of it."

Dr. Coutras had delivered sentence of death on many men, and he could never overcome the horror with which it filled him. He felt always the furious hatred that must seize a man condemned when he compared himself with the doctor, sane and healthy, who had the inestimable privilege of life. Strickland looked at him in silence. Nothing of emotion could be seen on his face, disfigured already by the loathsome disease.

"Do they know?" he asked at last, pointing to the persons on the verandah, now sitting in unusual, unaccountable silence.

"These natives know the signs so well," said the doctor. "They were afraid to tell you."

Strickland stepped to the door and looked out. There must have been something terrible in his face, for suddenly they all burst out into loud cries and lamentation. They lifted up their voices and they wept. Strickland did not speak. After looking at them for a moment, he came back into the room.

"How long do you think I can last?"

"Who knows? Sometimes the disease continues for twenty years. It is a mercy when it runs its course quickly."

Strickland went to his easel and looked reflectively at the picture that stood on it.

"You have had a long journey. It is fitting that the bearer of important tidings should be rewarded. Take this picture. It means nothing to you now, but it may be that one day you will be glad to have it."

Dr. Coutras protested that he needed no payment for his journey; he had already given back to Ata the hundred-franc note, but Strickland insisted that he should take the picture. Then together they went out on the verandah. The natives were sobbing violently.

"Be quiet, woman. Dry thy tears," said Strickland, addressing Ata. "There is no great harm. I shall leave thee very soon."

"They are not going to take thee away?" she cried.

At that time there was no rigid sequestration on the islands, and lepers, if they chose, were allowed to go free.

"I shall go up into the mountain," said Strickland.

Then Ata stood up and faced him.

"Ata flung herself on her knees before him"

"Let the others go if they choose, but I will not leave thee. Thou art my man and I am thy woman. If thou leavest me I shall hang myself on the tree that is behind the house. I swear it by God."

There was something immensely forcible in the way she spoke. She was no longer the meek, soft native girl, but a determined woman. She was extraordinarily transformed.

"Why shouldst thou stay with me? Thou canst go back to Papeete, and thou wilt soon find another white man. The old woman can take care of thy children, and Tiaré will be glad to have thee back."

"Thou art my man and I am thy woman. Whither thou goest I will go, too."

For a moment Strickland's fortitude was shaken, and a tear filled each of his eyes and trickled slowly down his cheeks. Then he gave the sardonic smile which was usual with him.

"Women are strange little beasts," he said to Dr. Coutras. "You can treat them like dogs, you can beat them till your arm aches, and still they love you." He shrugged his shoulders. "Of course, it is one of the most absurd illusions of Christianity that they have souls."

"What is it that thou art saying to the doctor?" asked Ata suspiciously. "Thou wilt not go?"

"If it please thee I will stay, poor child."

Ata flung herself on her knees before him, and clasped his legs with her arms and kissed them. Strickland looked at Dr. Coutras with a faint smile.

"In the end they get you, and your are helpless in their hands. White or brown, they are all the same."

Dr. Coutras felt that it was absurd to offer expressions of regret in so terrible a disaster, and he took his leave. Strickland told Tané, the boy, to lead him to the village. Dr.

Coutras paused for a moment, and then he addressed himself to me.

"I did not like him, I have told you he was not sympathetic to me, but as I walked slowly down to Taravao I could not prevent an unwilling admiration for the stoical courage which enabled him to bear perhaps the most dreadful of human afflictions. When Tané left me I told him I would send some medicine that might be of service; but my hope was small that Strickland would consent to take it, and even smaller that, if he did, it would do him good. I gave the boy a message for Ata that I would come whenever she sent for me. Life is hard, and Nature takes sometimes a terrible delight in torturing her children. It was with a heavy heart that I drove back to my comfortable home in Papeete."

For a long time none of us spoke.

"But Ata did not send for me," the doctor went on, at last, "and it chanced that I did not go to that part of the island for a long time. I had no news of Strickland. Once or twice I heard that Ata had been to Papeete to buy painting materials, but I did not happen to see her. More than two years passed before I went to Taravao again, and then it was once more to see the old chiefess. I asked them whether they had heard anything of Strickland. By now it was known everywhere that he had leprosy. First Tané, the boy, had left the house, and then, a little time afterwards, the old woman and her grandchild. Strickland and Ata were left alone with their babies. No one went near the plantation, for, as you know, the natives have a very lively horror of the disease, and in the old days when it was discovered the sufferer was killed; but sometimes, when the village boys were scrambling about the hills, they would catch sight of the white man, with his great red beard, wandering about. They fled in terror. Sometimes Ata would come down to the village at night and

arouse the trader, so that he might sell her various things of
which she stood in need. She knew that the natives looked
upon her with the same horrified aversion as they looked
upon Strickland, and she kept out of their way. Once some
women, venturing nearer than usual to the plantation, saw
her washing clothes in the brook, and they threw stones at
her. After that the trader was told to give her the message
that if she used the brook again men would come and burn
down her house."

"Brutes," I said.

"*Mais non, mon cher monsieur*, men are always the same.
Fear makes them cruel. . . . I decided to see Strickland, and
when I had finished with the chiefess asked for a boy to show

"*The natives looked upon her
with the same horrified aversion*"

me the way. But none would accompany me, and I was forced to find it alone."

When Dr. Coutras arrived at the plantation he was seized with a feeling of uneasiness. Though he was hot from walking, he shivered. There was something hostile in the air which made him hesitate, and he felt that invisible forces barred his way. Unseen hands seemed to draw him back. No one would go near now to gather the cocoa-nuts, and they lay rotting on the ground. Everywhere was desolation. The bush was encroaching, and it looked as though very soon the primeval forest would regain possession of that strip of land which had been snatched from it at the cost of so much labour. He had the sensation that here was the abode of pain. As he approached the house he was struck by the unearthly silence, and at first he thought it was deserted. Then he saw Ata. She was sitting on her haunches in the lean-to that served her as kitchen, watching some mess cooking in a pot. Near her a small boy was playing silently in the dirt. She did not smile when she saw him.

"I have come to see Strickland," he said.

"I will go and tell him."

She went to the house, ascended the few steps that led to the verandah, and entered. Dr. Coutras followed her, but waited outside in obedience to her gesture. As she opened the door he smelt the sickly sweet smell which makes the neighbourhood of the leper nauseous. He heard her speak, and then he heard Strickland's answer, but he did not recognise the voice. It had become hoarse and indistinct. Dr. Coutras raised his eyebrows. He judged that the disease had already attacked the vocal chords. Then Ata came out again.

"He will not see you. You must go away."

Dr. Coutras insisted, but she would not let him pass. Dr. Coutras shrugged his shoulders, and after a moment's reflec-

tion turned away. She walked with him. He felt that she too
wanted to be rid of him.

"Is there nothing I can do at all?" he asked.

"You can send him some paints," she said. "There is nothing else he wants."

"Can he paint still?"

"He is painting the walls of the house."

"This is a terrible life for you, my poor child."

Then at last she smiled, and there was in her eyes a look
of superhuman love. Dr. Coutras was startled by it, and
amazed. And he was awed. He found nothing to say.

"He is my man," she said.

"Where is your other child?" he asked. "When I was here
last you had two."

"Yes; it died. We buried it under the mango."

When Ata had gone with him a little way she said she
must turn back. Dr. Coutras surmised she was afraid to go
farther in case she met any of the people from the village. He
told her again that if she wanted him she had only to send
and he would come at once.

Then two years more went by, or perhaps three, for time
passes imperceptibly in Tahiti, and it is hard to keep count
of it; but at last a message was brought to Dr. Coutras that
Strickland was dying. Ata had waylaid the cart that took the
mail into Papeete, and besought the man who drove it to go
at once to the doctor. But the doctor was out when the sum-
mons came, and it was evening when he received it. It was

impossible to start at so late an hour, and so it was not till next day soon after dawn that he set out. He arrived at Taravao, and for the last time tramped the seven kilometres that led to Ata's house. The path was overgrown, and it was clear that for years now it had remained all but untrodden. It was not easy to find the way. Sometimes he had to stumble along the bed of the stream, and sometimes he had to push through shrubs, dense and thorny; often he was obliged to climb over rocks in order to avoid the hornet-nests that hung on the trees over his head. The silence was intense.

It was with a sigh of relief that at last he came upon the little unpainted house, extraordinarily bedraggled now, and unkempt; but here too was the same intolerable silence. He walked up, and a little boy, playing unconcernedly in the sunshine, started at his approach and fled quickly away: to him the stranger was the enemy. Dr. Coutras had a sense that the child was stealthily watching him from behind a tree. The door was wide open. He called out, but no one answered. He stepped in. He knocked at a door, but again there was no answer. He turned the handle and entered. The stench that assailed him turned him horribly sick. He put his handkerchief to his nose and forced himself to go in. The light was dim, and after the brilliant sunshine for a while he could see nothing. Then he gave a start. He could not make out where he was. He seemed on a sudden to have entered a magic world. He had a vague impression of a great primeval forest and of naked people walking beneath the trees. Then he saw that there were paintings on the walls.

"Mon Dieu, I hope the sun hasn't affected me," he muttered.

A slight movement attracted his attention, and he saw that Ata was lying on the floor, sobbing quietly.

"Ata," he called. "Ata."

She took no notice. Again the beastly stench almost made
him faint, and he lit a cheroot. His eyes grew accustomed
to the darkness, and now he was seized by an overwhelming
sensation as he stared at the painted walls. He knew nothing
of pictures, but there was something about these that extraordinarily affected him. From floor to ceiling the walls were
covered with a strange and elaborate composition. It was in-
describably wonderful and mysterious. It took his breath
away. It filled him with an emotion which he could not understand or analyse. He felt the awe and the delight which a
man might feel who watched the beginning of a world. It
was tremendous, sensual, passionate; and yet there was something horrible there, too, something which made him afraid.
It was the work of a man who had delved into the hidden
depths of nature and had discovered secrets which were beautiful and fearful too. It was the work of a man who knew
things which it is unholy for men to know. There was something primeval there and terrible. It was not human. It
brought to his mind vague recollections of black magic. It was
beautiful and obscene.

"*Mon Dieu*, this is genius."

The words were wrung from him, and he did not know he
had spoken.

Then his eyes fell on the bed of mats in the corner, and
he went up, and he saw the dreadful, mutilated, ghastly object
which had been Strickland. He was dead. Dr. Coutras made
an effort of will and bent over that battered horror. Then he
started violently, and terror blazed in his heart, for he felt
that someone was behind him. It was Ata. He had not heard
her get up. She was standing at his elbow, looking at what
he looked at.

"Good Heavens, my nerves are all distraught," he said.
"You nearly frightened me out of my wits."

He looked again at the poor dead thing that had been man, and then he started back in dismay.

"But he was blind."

"Yes; he had been blind for nearly a year."

At that moment we were interrupted by the appearance of Madame Coutras, who had been paying visits. She came in, like a ship in full sail, an imposing creature, tall and stout, with an ample bust and an obesity girthed in alarmingly by straight-fronted corsets. She had a bold hooked nose and three chins. She held herself upright. She had not yielded for an instant to the enervating charm of the tropics, but contrariwise was more active, more worldly, more decided than anyone in a temperate clime would have thought it possible to be. She was evidently a copious talker, and now poured forth a breathless stream of anecdote and comment. She made the conversation we had just had seem far away and unreal.

Presently Dr. Coutras turned to me.

"I still have in my *bureau* the picture that Strickland gave me," he said. "Would you like to see it?"

"Willingly."

We got up, and he led me on to the verandah which surrounded his house. We paused to look at the gay flowers that rioted in his garden.

"For a long time I could not get out of my head the recollection of the extraordinary decoration with which Strickland had covered the walls of his house," he said reflectively.

I had been thinking of it, too. It seemed to me that here

Strickland had finally put the whole expression of himself. Working silently, knowing that it was his last chance, I fancied that here he must have said all that he knew of life and all that he divined. And I fancied that perhaps here he had at last found peace. The demon which possessed him was exorcised at last, and with the completion of the work, for which all his life had been a painful preparation, rest descended on his remote and tortured soul. He was willing to die, for he had fulfilled his purpose.

"What was the subject?" I asked.

"I scarcely know. It was strange and fantastic. It was a vision of the beginnings of the world, the Garden of Eden, with Adam and Eve—*que sais-je?*—it was a hymn to the

*"They seemed to possess
something of the clay
of which they were created"*

beauty of the human form, male and female, and the praise
of Nature, sublime, indifferent, lovely, and cruel. It gave you
an awful sense of the infinity of space and of the endlessness
of time. Because he painted the trees I see about me every day,
the cocoa-nuts, the banyans, the flamboyants, the alligator-
pears, I have seen them ever since differently, as though
there were in them a spirit and a mystery which I am ever on
the point of seizing and which for ever escapes me. The colours were the colours familiar to me, and yet they were different. They had a significance which was all their own. And
those nude men and women. They were of the earth, and yet
apart from it. They seemed to possess something of the clay
of which they were created, and at the same time something
divine. You saw man in the nakedness of his primeval instincts, and you were afraid, for you saw yourself."

Dr. Coutras shrugged his shoulders and smiled.

"You will laugh at me. I am a materialist, and I am a
gross, fat man—Falstaff, eh?—the lyrical mode does not become me. I make myself ridiculous. But I have never seen
painting which made so deep an impression upon me. *Tenez,*
I had just the same feeling as when I went to the Sistine
Chapel in Rome. There too I was awed by the greatness of
the man who had painted that ceiling. It was genius, and it
was stupendous and overwhelming. I felt small and insignificant. But you are prepared for the greatness of Michael
Angelo. Nothing had prepared me for the immense surprise
of these pictures in a native hut, far away from civilisation,
in a fold of the mountain above Taravao. And Michael Angelo is sane and healthy. Those great works of his have the
calm of the sublime; but here, notwithstanding beauty, was
something troubling. I do not know what it was. It made me
uneasy. It gave me the impression you get when you are sitting next door to a room that you know is empty, but in

which, you know not why, you have a dreadful consciousness
that notwithstanding there is someone. You scold yourself;
you know it is only your nerves—and yet, and yet . . . In a
little while it is impossible to resist the terror that seizes you,
and you are helpless in the clutch of an unseen horror. Yes;
I confess I was not altogether sorry when I heard that those
strange masterpieces had been destroyed."

"Destroyed?" I cried.

"*Mais oui*; did you not know?"

"How should I know? It is true I had never heard of this
work; but I thought perhaps it had fallen into the hands of
a private owner. Even now there is no certain list of Strickland's paintings."

"When he grew blind he would sit hour after hour in those
two rooms that he had painted, looking at his works with
sightless eyes, and seeing, perhaps, more than he had ever
seen in his life before. Ata told me that he never complained
of his fate, he never lost courage. To the end his mind remained serene and undisturbed. But he made her promise
that when she had buried him—did I tell you that I dug his
grave with my own hands, for none of the natives would approach the infected house, and we buried him, she and I, sewn
up in three *pareos* joined together, under the mango-tree—he
made her promise that she would set fire to the house and not
leave it till it was burned to the ground and not a stick remained."

I did not speak for a while, for I was thinking. Then I
said:

"He remained the same to the end, then."

"Do you understand? I must tell you that I thought it my
duty to dissuade her."

"Even after what you have just said?"

"Yes; for I knew that here was a work of genius, and I did

not think we had the right to deprive the world of it. But Ata would not listen to me. She had promised. I would not stay to witness the barbarous deed, and it was only afterwards that I heard what she had done. She poured paraffin on the dry floors and on the pandanus-mats, and then she set fire. In a little while nothing remained but smouldering embers, and a great masterpiece existed no longer.

"I think Strickland knew it was a masterpiece. He had achieved what he wanted. His life was complete. He had made a world and saw that it was good. Then, in pride and contempt, he destroyed it.

"But I must show you my picture," said Dr. Coutras, moving on.

"What happened to Ata and the child?"

"They went to the Marquesas. She had relations there. I have heard that the boy works on one of Cameron's schooners. They say he is very like his father in appearance."

At the door that led from the verandah to the doctor's consulting-room, he paused and smiled.

"It is a fruit-piece. You would think it not a very suitable picture for a doctor's consulting-room, but my wife will not have it in the drawing-room. She says it is frankly obscene."

"A fruit-piece!" I exclaimed in surprise.

We entered the room, and my eyes fell at once on the picture. I looked at it for a long time.

It was a pile of mangoes, bananas, oranges, and I know not what; and at first sight it was an innocent picture enough. It would have been passed in an exhibition of the Post-Impressionists by a careless person as an excellent but not very remarkable example of the school; but perhaps afterwards it would come back to his recollection, and he would wonder why. I do not think then he could ever entirely forget it.

The colours were so strange that words can hardly tell what

a troubling emotion they gave. They were sombre blues, opaque like a delicately carved bowl in lapis lazuli, and yet with a quivering lustre that suggested the palpitation of mysterious life; there were purples, horrible like raw and putrid flesh, and yet with a glowing, sensual passion that called up vague memories of the Roman Empire of Heliogabalus; there were reds, shrill like the berries of holly—one thought of Christmas in England, and the snow, the good cheer, and the pleasure of children—and yet by some magic softened till they had the swooning tenderness of a dove's breast; there were deep yellows that died with an unnatural passion into a green as fragrant as the spring and as pure as the sparkling water of a mountain brook. Who can tell what anguished fancy made these fruits? They belonged to a Polynesian garden of the Hesperides. There was something strangely alive in them, as though they were created in a stage of the earth's dark history when things were not irrevocably fixed to their forms. They were extravagantly luxurious. They were heavy with tropical odours. They seemed to possess a sombre passion of their own. It was enchanted fruit, to taste which might open the gateway to God knows what secrets of the soul and to mysterious palaces of the imagination. They were sullen with unawaited dangers, and to eat them might turn a man to beast or god. All that was healthy and natural, all that clung to happy relationships and the simple joys of simple men, shrunk from them in dismay; and yet a fearful attraction was in them, and, like the fruit on the Tree of the Knowledge of Good and Evil they were terrible with the possibilities of the Unknown.

At last I turned away. I felt that Strickland had kept his secret to the grave.

"*Voyons, René, mon ami,*" came the loud, cheerful voice of Madame Coutras, "what are you doing all this time? Here are the *apéritifs*. Ask *Monsieur* if he will not drink a little glass of Quinquina Dubonnet."

"*Volontiers*, Madame," I said, going out on to the verandah.

The spell was broken.

The time came for my departure from Tahiti. According to the gracious custom of the island, presents were given me by the persons with whom I had been thrown in contact—baskets made of the leaves of the cocoa-nut tree, mats of pandanus, fans; and Tiaré gave me three little pearls and three jars of guava-jelly made with her own plump hands. When the mail-boat, stopping for twenty-four hours on its way from Wellington to San Francisco, blew the whistle that warned the passengers to get on board, Tiaré clasped me to her vast bosom, so that I seemed to sink into a billowy sea, and pressed her red lips to mine. Tears glistened in her eyes. And when we steamed slowly out of the lagoon, making our way gingerly through the opening in the reef, and then steered for the open sea, a certain melancholy fell upon me. The breeze was laden still with the pleasant odours of the land. Tahiti is very far away, and I knew that I should never see it again. A chapter of my life was closed, and I felt a little nearer to inevitable death.

Not much more than a month later I was in London; and after I had arranged certain matters which claimed my immediate attention, thinking Mrs. Strickland might like to hear what I knew of her husband's last years, I wrote to her. I had not seen her since long before the war, and I had to look out her address in the telephone-book. She made an appointment, and I went to the trim little house on Campden Hill which she now inhabited. She was by this time a woman of hard on sixty, but she bore her years well, and no one would have taken her for more than fifty. Her face, thin and not much lined, was of the sort that ages gracefully, so that you thought in youth she must have been a much handsomer woman than in fact she was. Her hair, not yet very gray, was becomingly arranged, and her black gown was modish. I remembered having heard that her sister, Mrs. MacAndrew, outliving her husband but a couple of years, had left money to Mrs. Strickland; and by the look of the house and the trim maid who opened the door I judged that it was a sum adequate to keep the widow in modest comfort.

When I was ushered into the drawing-room I found that Mrs. Strickland had a visitor, and when I discovered who he was, I guessed that I had been asked to come at just that time not without intention. The caller was Mr. Van Busche Taylor, an American, and Mrs. Strickland gave me particulars with a charming smile of apology to him.

"You know, we English are so dreadfully ignorant. You must forgive me if it's necessary to explain." Then she turned to me. "Mr. Van Busche Taylor is the distinguished American critic. If you haven't read his book your education has been shamefully neglected, and you must repair the omission at once. He's writing something about dear Charlie, and he's come to ask me if I can help him."

Mr. Van Busche Taylor was a very thin man with a large, bald head, bony and shining; and under the great dome of his skull his face, yellow, with deep lines in it, looked very small. He was quiet and exceedingly polite. He spoke with the accent of New England, and there was about his demeanour a bloodless frigidity which made me ask myself why on earth he was busying himself with Charles Strickland. I had been slightly tickled at the gentleness which Mrs. Strickland put into her mention of her husband's name, and while the pair conversed I took stock of the room in which we sat. Mrs. Strickland had moved with the times. Gone were the Morris papers and gone the severe cretonnes, gone were the Arundel prints that had adorned the walls of her drawing-room in Ashley Gardens; the room blazed with fantastic colour, and I wondered if she knew that those varied hues, which fashion had imposed upon her, were due to the dreams of a poor painter in a South Sea island. She gave me the answer herself.

"What wonderful cushions you have," said Mr. Van Busche Taylor.

"Do you like them?" she said, smiling. "Bakst, you know."

And yet on the walls were coloured reproductions of several of Strickland's best pictures, due to the enterprise of a publisher in Berlin.

"You're looking at my pictures," she said, following my eyes. "Of course, the originals are out of my reach, but it's a comfort to have these. The publisher sent them to me himself. They're a great consolation to me."

"They must be very pleasant to live with," said Mr. Van Busche Taylor.

"Yes; they're so essentially decorative."

"That is one of my profoundest convictions," said Mr. Van Busche Taylor. "Great art is always decorative."

Their eyes rested on a nude woman suckling a baby, while a girl was kneeling by their side holding out a flower to the indifferent child. Looking over them was a wrinkled, scraggy hag. It was Strickland's version of the Holy Family. I suspected that for the figures had sat his household above Tara-vao, and the woman and the baby were Ata and his first son. I asked myself if Mrs. Strickland had any inkling of the facts.

The conversation proceeded, and I marvelled at the tact with which Mr. Van Busche Taylor avoided all subjects that might have been in the least embarrassing, and at the in-genuity with which Mrs. Strickland, without saying a word that was untrue, insinuated that her relations with her hus-band had always been perfect. At last Mr. Van Busche Taylor rose to go. Holding his hostess' hand, he made her a graceful, though perhaps too elaborate, speech of thanks, and left us.

"I hope he didn't bore you," she said, when the door closed behind him. "Of course it's a nuisance sometimes, but I feel it's only right to give people any information I can about Charlie. There's a certain responsibility about having been the wife of a genius."

She looked at me with those pleasant eyes of hers, which had remained as candid and as sympathetic as they had been more than twenty years before. I wondered if she was making a fool of me.

"Of course you've given up your business," I said.

"Oh, yes," she answered airily. "I ran it more by way of a hobby than for any other reason, and my children persuaded me to sell it. They thought I was overtaxing my strength."

I saw that Mrs. Strickland had forgotten that she had ever done anything so disgraceful as to work for her living. She had the true instinct of the nice woman that it is only really decent for her to live on other people's money.

"They're here now," she said. "I thought they'd like to hear what you had to say about their father. You remember Robert, don't you? I'm glad to say he's been recommended for the Military Cross."

She went to the door and called them. There entered a tall

man in khaki, with the parson's collar, handsome in a somewhat heavy fashion, but with the frank eyes that I remembered in him as a boy. He was followed by his sister. She
must have been the same age as was her mother when first I
knew her, and she was very like her. She too gave one the
impression that as a girl she must have been prettier than
indeed she was.

"I suppose you don't remember them in the least," said
Mrs. Strickland, proud and smiling. "My daughter is now
Mrs. Ronaldson. Her husband's a Major in the Gunners."

"He's by way of being a pukka soldier, you know," said
Mrs. Ronaldson gaily. "That's why he's only a Major."

I remembered my anticipation long ago that she would
marry a soldier. It was inevitable. She had all the graces of
the soldier's wife. She was civil and affable, but she could
hardly conceal her intimate conviction that she was not quite
as others were. Robert was breezy.

"It's a bit of luck that I should be in London when you
turned up," he said. "I've only got three days' leave."

"He's dying to get back," said his mother.

"Well, I don't mind confessing it, I have a rattling good
time at the front. I've made a lot of good pals. It's a first-rate
life. Of course war's terrible, and all that sort of thing; but it
does bring out the best qualities in a man, there's no denying
that."

Then I told them what I had learned about Charles Strickland in Tahiti. I thought it unnecessary to say anything of
Ata and her boy, but for the rest I was as accurate as I could
be. When I had narrated his lamentable death I ceased. For a
minute or two we were all silent. Then Robert Strickland
struck a match and lit a cigarette.

"The mills of God grind slowly, but they grind exceeding
small," he said, somewhat impressively.

Mrs. Strickland and Mrs. Ronaldson looked down with a slightly pious expression which indicated, I felt sure, that they thought the quotation was from Holy Writ. Indeed, I was unconvinced that Robert Strickland did not share their illusion. I do not know why I suddenly thought of Strickland's son by Ata. They had told me he was a merry, light-hearted youth. I saw him, with my mind's eye, on the schooner on which he worked, wearing nothing but a pair of dungarees; and at night, when the boat sailed along easily before a light breeze, and the sailors were gathered on the upper deck, while the captain and the supercargo lolled in deck-chairs, smoking their pipes, I saw him dance with another lad, dance wildly, to the wheezy music of the concertina. Above was the blue sky, and the stars, and all about the desert of the Pacific Ocean.

A quotation from the Bible came to my lips, but I held my tongue, for I know that clergymen think it a little blasphemous when the laity poach upon their preserves. My Uncle Henry, for twenty-seven years Vicar of Whitstable, was on these occasions in the habit of saying that the devil could always quote scripture to his purpose. He remembered the days when you could get thirteen Royal Natives for a shilling.